THE ACCIDENT

L. H. STACEY

B
Boldwood

First published in 2017 as Tell Me No Secrets. This edition published in Great Britain in 2024 by Boldwood Books Ltd.

Copyright © L. H. Stacey, 2017

Cover Design by Head Design Ltd.

Cover Photography: iStock and Shutterstock

The moral right of L. H. Stacey to be identified as the author of this work has been asserted in accordance with the Copyright, Designs and Patents Act 1988.

All rights reserved. No part of this book may be reproduced in any form or by any electronic or mechanical means, including information storage and retrieval systems, without written permission from the author, except for the use of brief quotations in a book review.

This book is a work of fiction and, except in the case of historical fact, any resemblance to actual persons, living or dead, is purely coincidental.

Every effort has been made to obtain the necessary permissions with reference to copyright material, both illustrative and quoted. We apologise for any omissions in this respect and will be pleased to make the appropriate acknowledgements in any future edition.

A CIP catalogue record for this book is available from the British Library.

Paperback ISBN 978-1-78513-861-4

Hardback ISBN 978-1-78513-856-0

Large Print ISBN 978-1-78513-857-7

Ebook ISBN 978-1-78513-854-6

Kindle ISBN 978-1-78513-855-3

Audio CD ISBN 978-1-78513-862-1

MP3 CD ISBN 978-1-78513-859-1

Digital audio download ISBN 978-1-78513-853-9

Boldwood Books Ltd
23 Bowerdean Street
London SW6 3TN
www.boldwoodbooks.com

*For my wonderful mother, Pauline.
You were taken from us far too soon.
I wish every single day that you were still here to read my books,
and to drive everyone slightly mad, by constantly talking about
them!*

1

Kate Duggan heard the kitchen door click to a close. It was done quietly, almost secretively, but still managed to catch her attention.

She was more than aware that her boyfriend Rob was at home. But after watching him mess with his mobile phone for over an hour, she'd taken herself upstairs for a bath and was now laying on the bed, reading.

Feeling sure that he was up to no good, and with a pointed foot worthy of a prize in ballet, she slid it out from beneath the duvet. Holding her breath, she hoped that the floorboards wouldn't creak, or that the door wouldn't give her away as she crept onto the landing where she stood and listened to the whispered tones that came from the kitchen.

For a moment, she thought that someone had arrived at the house and wondered who the late-night visitor could be. But the only voice she could hear was Rob's; a clear indication that he had answered his phone and having taken the call in another room, clearly didn't want her eavesdropping.

'I'm not doing it,' she heard Rob snap. 'Stick to the damn plan.

It's under control.' In an instant, his rapidly spoken words were drowned out by the sound of the radio.

'Rob?' Kate shouted, 'Is everything okay?' She made her way down the stairs and felt the rough, cold wooden flooring beneath her feet. She glanced over her shoulder longingly towards her bedroom where her slippers were and with a sigh, she saw the amber glow spilling from her room, lighting up the shadows of the rest of the cottage. It was a warmth that always drew her in and stirred up memories that never failed to set off an ache that was deep within her. Memories of her grandmother, who had loved River Cottage but who was now sadly gone, leaving Kate alone with only the house as a small reminder that she'd ever existed at all.

'For God's sake. Stop calling...' Rob's voice temporarily rose above the sound of the radio but then diminished as he moved further away from the door. The sound of his feet against the wooden floor trudged with a monotonous echo that came and went, making Kate wonder if he were circling the island impatiently. 'Not a chance... not again.' His voice was drowned out by the noise in the room and Kate pressed her ear as close as she could to the door, in a vain attempt to hear every word that was said.

His cold words sent chills down her spine, leaving her with a deep-seated dread that Rob was involved in something bad. Something she wouldn't like. It was a thought that made her heart accelerate faster than normal and now, with a hand held to her chest, she could feel it pounding away at a dangerous and alarming rate.

What do I do? Kate began to question her actions. Doing this, skulking around and listening to private conversations, was something she shouldn't have to do. Not here, in her own home. Yet it had become normal just lately, so she could give Rob the space he apparently needed.

The Accident 3

Taking a step back, she suddenly realised just how little she knew about the man she lived with. Theirs had been a whirlwind romance that had taken her by surprise. One minute they had been going out on a first date, the next, he'd turned up on the doorstep, asking if he could stay and in a moment of madness she'd happily agreed. And now, she kicked herself for being so weak. For not making it clear that the accommodation had only been offered on a temporary basis.

She placed her fingers on the door handle, saw the way her hand was trembling with nerves and dared herself to push it wide open and burst into the room with the element of surprise. It was what she had every intention of doing, but before she could, the door was flung open and Kate found herself looking up and into Rob's dark, angry eyes.

'Kate?' Rob suddenly bellowed, 'What's your damn problem?'

In an attempt to keep her voice calm, Kate took her time and resisted the urge to yell back in response. 'What's my problem?' she asked in a confident voice, and for a split second she felt thankful for her police training, which still held one or two advantages. 'I could ask you the same thing?' She looked over his shoulder and into the small compact kitchen beyond.

'I'm not the one creeping around, am I?'

Nodding thoughtfully, she looked at him through different eyes. Rather than seeing the personal trainer she'd fallen for, the man with the perfect body, she now saw the cold glare of his eyes, the hands that were curled to form fists. A powerhouse that could easily strike out.

'Wow. Do you know what, Rob, I would apologise,' she said carefully. 'But for some reason, I thought this was my house and the last time I checked, I didn't need your damn permission to walk around it.'

'No one said you needed permission, Kate, but you should

show a little respect. Your ear was pressed to the door.' He picked up a glass, drank the dregs of his juice, then dropped it into the white sink. 'I wouldn't dream of doing that to you...'

Reeling, Kate took a step backwards. She couldn't believe he'd tried to turn this on her. She wasn't the one making secret phone calls, speaking in riddles or acting peculiar. 'Is that right?' she threw back. 'Well, for all I knew, someone was here.' She pulled at her short, satin dressing gown. 'And I'm hardly dressed for visitors, am I?'

With narrowed eyes, Rob looked her up and down and angrily ran a hand through his dark, perfectly styled hair. His other hand was pressed against his side, his phone still held tightly in his hand, the screen still lit.

'I need a drink,' she lied, and aggressively pushed her way past him. Flinging open a cupboard, she stared inside. 'So, who was on the phone?' She kept her eyes on the cupboard, gave choosing a glass far too much thought, and eventually she picked one out, held it under the tap and filled it with water.

'It's work. One of my clients. A new one.'

She nodded slowly, tried to decide which of his many clients would need a personal call so late at night. 'Rob, you're a personal trainer, not a doctor, what on earth can't wait until morning?'

'Kate,' he barked, 'this call is important.' He flicked his head to the door, a clear indication that he wanted her gone.

It was enough to make Kate take a sharp step backwards. She knew that leaving him to get on would be easier than standing there arguing. And for what felt like the hundredth time that week, she considered her options and tried to decide how she could ask him to leave, without causing a fight.

'Well, don't be long.' She couldn't resist throwing in the last word, and after giving him an unwavering glare, she spun on her heel to head for the stairs. 'I start my new job tomorrow... An early night would have been nice.' Rolling her eyes regretfully at the innuendo, she caught Rob's eye and saw the anger within. It was a look that told her to leave, that the caller was still on the phone and that whoever it was had been listening in on every word they'd said.

'Kate. I've asked nicely,' he said. 'Now, for the love of God. Go – to – bed.' Thrusting a hand towards the door and with a powerful flick of his fingers, Kate saw the door fly towards her and slam in front of her face.

Shocked, she held onto the wall. Her pride was wounded. Her temper rose. And with her mouth opening and closing, ready to shout, she slammed a hand against the door, and banged as hard as she could. 'You... you need to find somewhere else to live. Do you hear me?' She shouted angrily, then with as much control as she could find, she climbed the stairs at speed and just for good measure, she slammed the bedroom door behind her.

Sitting down on the edge of the bed, Kate reached for the glass of wine she'd poured earlier to drink in the bath and took a long, slow drink, allowing the rich, dark red liquid to coat her throat, while contemplating her future.

Placing the glass back down on the bedside table, she stared at a photograph of her and Rob with sad, wistful eyes. It had been taken on an impromptu holiday she and Rob had taken not too long after they'd met, and at a time when she'd thought they'd been happy. And without a doubt, they had been. Until Rob had become homeless and Kate had foolishly allowed him to move in with her even though it had been much too soon. But she'd hoped he was the true love she'd always been searching for; had always wanted.

'How wrong could you have been?' She spoke out loud and felt her eyes fill with tears. She looked again at the photograph and smiled at the way Rob had looped an arm tightly around her, pulling her in close, even though the temperature had been scorching. 'How could you change so much in such a short time?' she whispered to the picture, as she tried to remember the man he'd once been.

'You were kind, you were generous,' she said, 'and what's more, it was you who pursued me.' It was a thought that had crossed her mind on a regular basis. 'Why Rob? Why did you want me?' Her mind went back to the constant calls and messages Rob had left for her in those early days. Looking back, if she hadn't felt so low in herself, she'd have probably said no to his attention. The former police officer in her would have screamed cohesive control. But instead, she'd agreed to a date with Rob and had happily jumped on the rollercoaster of excitement that had come with dating him. For the first time in years, she'd felt happy and before she knew it, Rob had moved in.

'You should have known. Gorgeous men are always the same.' She recounted some of the men both she and her sister Eve had dated when they'd had their pick of the crowd. Before the accident, she'd have thought herself worthy of the attention. But not now. Now, she was a shadow of her former self. Far too thin and her long auburn hair was often scooped back unflatteringly in a ponytail. Her pale, freckled skin made her sallow looking and she hadn't thought herself as much of a catch for a while. Especially since the accident had left her with a long, puckered scar that had carved itself into her jawline, reminding her every day of what happened that night and how much her life has changed.

* * *

With the sun attempting to break through the crack in the curtains and the alarm clock bursting into life, Kate turned against her pillow. Even though she felt as though she'd barely slept a wink, she reached across the bed and slapped the alarm clock into silence.

She wanted nothing more than to go back to sleep, but couldn't. She didn't dare close her eyes, no matter how much she wanted to and instead, she slowly slid her leg across the bed, between the cold cotton sheets, and automatically sent her toes in search of Rob.

After a few moments it occurred to her that the space where he normally slept was cold and empty and through half-open eyes, she saw the perfectly straight duvet. The decorative cushion and her phone lay on top of the covers, exactly where she'd left them. A clear indication that once again, Rob had slept downstairs. Not that she cared. Not any more.

'There isn't time to think about this now.' She took in a deep breath, threw back the duvet and launched herself out of bed. As she did so, her stomach turned, and her apprehension about the day ahead began. 'Come on, you can do this.' She closed her eyes and thought back to the way her life had once been: the confidence she'd had and the way she'd have happily thrown herself into any situation, with little or zero fuss. Nowadays, she had to force herself to leave the house and more often than not, she'd have to stand for a few minutes right by the front door before finding the courage to continue.

'You're the lucky one,' her mother had told her. 'At least you walked away. Your brother didn't. And your sister, well she'll never walk again, will she?'

Tipping her face to one side, Kate stared at the long, red puckered scar that showed itself in the mirror. 'Sure. I was lucky, wasn't I?' She shook her head, took in a deep breath and looked back at the bed. 'No wonder he sneaks around. I doubt I'd want to sleep with you either.'

Flinging open the wardrobe door Kate scoured the contents, selected a neat, black pencil skirt and an ivory blouse that she'd bought especially for the occasion. Then she matched the items up with a pair of black patent leather shoes that had a heel, but importantly, were still comfortable to walk in. 'That will do,' she said with a satisfied sigh, before turning back to the mirror, 'Your face might look a mess,' she whispered, 'but your clothes don't need to, do they?'

Laying each item out on the bed, she checked them carefully, making sure that there were no creases, marks or loose, untidy seams. Appearance was everything to Kate, especially now. After scanning her perfume bottles for a good while, she picked out a deep, musky fragrance before padding down the length of the landing and into the bathroom.

The early morning sunshine flooded the room and bounced off the tiles. It caused a reflection so bright and uncomfortable that Kate felt herself squint and with no choice but to shut the sun out, she closed the venetian blinds, and blinked repeatedly until the blinding white flashes disappeared and her eyes adjusted to the light. It was only then that she noticed the splatter of toothpaste that covered the bathroom mirror like an explosion of snow. Towels had been thrown on the floor and over the edge of the bath, and a ring of dark whiskers were scattered around the sink. The mess was an everyday sign that Rob was already up and that he'd already been in the bathroom. Kate took a deep breath to control her anger at his disregard for her home... and her.

After taking a shower, Kate set to work correcting the disturbing image that stared back at her in the mirror. It was a routine she'd perfected since the accident happened: three thin coats of foundation, that were carefully placed one on top of the other; a touch of eye liner; followed by mascara, and a smudge of lip gloss that coloured both her lips and her cheeks.

'Not too much, you don't want to look like a hussy, do you?' she whispered, before twisting a towel tightly around her body and making her way back to the bedroom.

'Morning.' She heard Rob's deep husky voice before she saw him. It came from behind the open wardrobe door. He was hidden from view and for a moment Kate hesitated and tried to determine what mood he was in.

'I didn't know you were up here?' She cursed herself inwardly. Wished she hadn't said anything and moved slowly around the bed until he stepped out from behind the wardrobe door.

'Sorry, babes, you were in the shower.'

'And last night?'

'Yeah, I fell asleep. You know; football on the telly.' Noticeably, he made no reference to the argument they'd had. To him, it was as though nothing had happened and with a wide, disarming smile he walked around the bed, naked from the waist upwards. Furious, Kate didn't say a word but watched as he opened drawers without closing any of them properly and leaving more mess and untidiness in his wake.

Biting down on her lip, Kate stood back. She wasn't fond of the man that Rob had become, but she did like the way he looked and couldn't help but admire his perfect abs, or the dolphin tattoo that circumnavigated his huge bicep. For Rob's lack of effort in the home, he certainly made up for it in the gym and took pride in his appearance. That, along with the fact that he'd been dealt the Adonis card, had been one of the things that had attracted her to him: a tool Kate now realised that he'd used to his advantage.

'So, you're off to play detective today, are you?' He sat in front of the mirror, preened his hair with gel, and his beard with balm. 'What do you reckon your dad will have to say about the new job then?' He sneered while turning his face from side to side, constantly looking at and checking his appearance.

'Don't make fun, Rob. And as for my father – don't assume,' she snapped furiously. 'He's happy for me and I thought you'd be happy too.' Ever since she'd told Rob about her new career, he'd made fun about her decision and had constantly thrown sarcastic comments at her and told her about how disappointed her father would be. The problem was, deep down, Kate knew he was right.

Standing up, Rob forced his lips into an exaggerated pout – he had the look of a scolded schoolboy and with a grunt, he reached for her with strong muscular arms, pulling her towards him until her body was pressed tightly against him.

'Rob. Let go of me.' Kate struggled. She didn't appreciate his all too familiar hold. The last thing she wanted from him was intimacy. Especially today.

'Am I forgiven?' Surrounding her, Rob lowered his mouth to her shoulder, and ran a trail along her shoulder blade, until he reached the edge of her mouth, while all the time Kate struggled against him and fought to keep hold of the towel. 'Come on, Kate. You can't be mad at me forever. Can you?' His lips momentarily brushed against hers, then his fingertips travelled sensuously across the exact same route that his lips had just taken. 'Come on, baby. Forgive me. You know you want to?' With a flick of his wrist, she felt her towel drop to the floor. It landed in a heap by her feet to leave her standing naked before him.

'Bastard.' She went to grab at the towel and missed as Rob's hands caught hold of hers, and once again he pulled her firmly to him. 'Rob. I've told you to get off me.'

'Katie, Katie, Katie. You can't stay angry forever...'

His eyes searched hers and she saw the sparkle within, the deep, magical darkness that had once captivated her and for a moment, she weakened. She wanted normality, but more than anything else she wanted to be loved. But she couldn't let go of the way he'd been or how he'd treated her the night before.

'So, you want me to forgive you, do you?' Her serious expression crept into a smile. 'Which means that you must know what an asshole you were.' She pursed her lips, saw the look on his face and even though the anger still burned in her chest, she couldn't help but smile. It was hard to stay cross with him. And especially today, a day when she really didn't want to be angry. What she needed more than anything in the world was to have a day when she could concentrate on her new job. She had the opportunity to put her mind to work, something she'd desperately wanted to do, since the accident.

'But you do want to forgive me, don't you, baby?' He teased her mouth with the brushing of his lips, flicked his tongue sensuously across hers. 'Please, baby?'

Taking in a deep breath, Kate turned her face from side to side. She did all she could to avoid his lips but instead, she caught the strong scent of his aftershave – an earthy, musky smell that engulfed her senses and for a moment she found him hard to resist. She turned in towards him until their mouths hovered sensuously, just a few millimetres apart.

'Am I forgiven?' His words were little more than a whisper, and while Kate had just one eye on the clock, she decided to choose her battles more carefully and reluctantly, she nodded her forgiveness.

But just as quickly as he'd pulled her into his arms, he released his grasp. A cheeky grin tore across his face, and with lightning reactions, he grabbed at his T-shirt from the bed and threw it over his head as he headed out of the bedroom door. 'Too late, kiddo. You should've forgiven me sooner.'

Landing heavily against the bed, Kate twisted her naked body to see Rob disappearing through the door. He gave her a look over his shoulder and flashed her a wink. Only then did she notice her shoe in his hand and with a childish grin, he tossed it into the air. 'Catch!' he yelled, as he ran from the room, leaving Kate to watch her shoe fly upwards. It moved in slow motion, rebounded off the wardrobe door and shot towards the bed.

'No!' she screamed as the shoe hit the wine glass still sat on her bedside table where she left it last night. The remnants of her wine went up in the air, and with a loud and dramatic splatter, a deep red stain spread itself across her pale cream carpet.

'Damn you.' She grabbed at the fallen bath towel and dropped to her knees to begin clearing the stain. With a vibration that rattled the whole house, the back door slammed to a close and it was a clear sign that Rob was gone. And at least for today, he wasn't coming back.

Frantically, she dabbed at the carpet and did all she could to get the stain to lift. Both anger and humiliation flooded her mind, and she felt the colour rise to her cheeks in the form of a bright crimson blush. 'Why, Rob? Why the hell did you do that?' she shouted in the direction of the door. The carpet was ruined and with her blood boiling in her veins once again, certainty also formed in her mind. She wanted Rob gone.

2

With his brakes screeching to a halt, Rob skidded into the disabled parking space outside the gym. Although the space was supposed to be left vacant, he'd arrogantly designated it as being his own.

Besides, after the sleepless night he'd had tossing and turning around on the settee, he couldn't think straight. He felt the need of an energy burst and in an act of sheer frustration, he began to slam his hands against the steering wheel repeatedly and angrily. 'God damn you!' he screamed out loud. He wanted to kick himself for having been so stupid, for having been caught out on the phone and for the reckless behaviour he'd shown that morning, none of which had helped his cause.

He felt his shoulders drop as his mind exploded with uncertainty. He had no idea what was going to happen next. All he did know was that he was in too deep, that the family had a grip on him that felt like a vice and that Kate wasn't stupid and would soon see through him, if she hadn't already. He needed a plan. A backup plan, for when everything went wrong, which he knew it would. Even he wasn't blind enough to realise that drug dealing and former cops didn't mix well together, even though being with Kate had given him the perfect cover until now. No one would have suspected that 'law abiding Kate' would fall for a dealer. She was a pillar of the community, as had been her grandmother before her. Since he'd moved in, she'd provided him with everything he'd needed. But a line in the sand had been drawn, one that would always separate his world from hers.

Lifting his phone up from the passenger seat, he considered calling her in an attempt to work out what she'd overheard last night and how much she already knew. But the call would be risky. Asking Kate questions about anything would alert her senses and he wondered if it were better to cut and run, to distance himself now in the knowledge that one day he'd end up in prison with the key thrown away for a good number or years. The question was: did he bring her down with him? Ruin her life even more than he already had?

Kicking the car door open, Rob cringed as he heard the crunch of metal against brick. He saw the way the door rebounded off the wall and then back in his direction almost trapping his leg. For a moment, he stayed in his seat. Closed his eyes and took in a deep breath. But then, slowly he climbed out and assessed the damage. Another problem he would have to fix.

With his gaze rolling towards the gym he saw that the shutters were still down. Unusually, he was the first to arrive and with a slow, tentative walk, he made his way to the front of the building, where he immediately saw the newly painted graffiti. The words, 'Killer' and 'Dealer' emblazoned across the aluminium slats, then spray painted against the bright orange brick were the words, 'Anytime is heroin time'. They had clearly been left by someone with a grudge. Either way, the graffiti couldn't stay and he knew that the first hour of his day would now involve the scrubbing of walls. In his anger Rob ran to the edge of the road and searched the street, in the hope that someone was still there, spray can still in their hand. But all he saw were the fields that stood opposite, clouds that rolled in to leave the sky looking both dull and grey with no promise of sunshine.

Pulling his phone from his pocket, he flicked impatiently through his diary. He tried to work out how much time he had before his first client arrived. He recalled that it was a woman of fifty-something who'd booked in with him a few weeks before, and with a reluctant shrug, he knew that the chance of her turning up on time, or at all, was little to slim.

Kicking open the door, he immediately saw the carnage that met him inside. Weights were scattered all over the floor, water butts stood empty. Damp, used towels had been left to hang over the equipment and inside one of the changing rooms a radio crackled in and out of tune.

'Hello...' he shouted. Rob looked over his shoulder anxiously and picked up a kettlebell. 'Anyone there?' He waited. Listened. Heard nothing. Felt sure he was alone in the gym.

Slowly, he began to throw the kettlebells back where they belonged. None of them were particularly heavy, not for him. But as he threw them onto the black muti-tiered stand, he considered keeping one of them in his hand just in case. And just as he dropped the last one into place, he heard the sound of footsteps behind him.

'Roberto. Are you here alone?' Isobel Reed's sugary sweet voice filled the room, making Rob spin around on the spot to see her stepping out of the men's changing rooms. With an air of confidence, she strode towards him. It was a sight that made his heart race far more than it should have. She'd once been no more to him than his cousin's wife, now his widow, who'd indirectly inherited the Bellandini empire. But now...

'You don't mind Roberto, do you. I let myself in.' She pointed to a passage at the back of the gym, where the fire door stood. 'Might have caused a bit of damage getting in and your assistant, well... he was about to open up and wasn't very helpful. You might want to pop him to the hospital, just as soon as we're finished.' She rolled her eyes in amusement, lifted a hand to her perfectly coifed hair from which a single strand of hair had made an escape. 'Last night, Roberto, you disrespected my husband,' she said with a tut.

'Isobel, your husband is dead. Dealing got him killed. And do you know what...' he paused, took in a deep breath. 'Word's got out.' He pointed to the front door. 'Did you see my shutters. Did you see the crap that's been painted on there.' He paced back and forth, ran his hands roughly through his hair. 'I don't want to follow in his footsteps, Isobel. I don't want to be the next Bellandini shot on the doorstep.'

'You're in too deep, Roberto,' she said softly, 'Much too deep.'

'And you drove all the way here to tell me that, did you?' He tipped his head to one side. He knew he needed to get her back onside and he began to move towards her slowly and sensuously. 'I'm flattered.' Breathing in, he lifted his hand to his crotch, corrected his posture. 'But I have to say...' Walking past a bench, he pressed his hands against it, checked it for strength and knew that if he were to ever get out of the family business, he had to keep her happy. 'I've always fancied testing its rigidity.' He winked, hopefully.

'Don't be a child, Roberto. I didn't come here for you or for sex.' Isobel snapped. She took another step forward until her black Parisian jumpsuit sparkled against the lights above. The suit was embellished with sequins, all hand-stitched over lace, with a nude lining that made the whole outfit look see-through. It was an outfit more suited to night-time than first thing in a morning and suddenly Rob's mind went into overdrive and he began to not only wonder whose bed she'd just crawled out of but also who else had been listening in on what he'd stupidly said the night before.

'Really.' Rob gave her a sheepish smile and did all he could to maintain his composure. 'Then why are you here, Isobel?' He wasn't used to being turned down and with a confident stride forward, he held an arm out in the hope she'd step into it. But the smile he'd initially feigned suddenly fell from his face as he looked over Isobel's shoulder to see the two burly bodyguards emerge from the changing room. Rob watched as he saw his assistant, Ryan, dragged in behind them, his face bloodied, and bruised and he was clearly frightened.

'I came here to talk to you, Roberto. To persuade you to be a good boy, while you still have the chance.'

Taking a step hastily backwards, Rob held his hands up in the air, palms out. 'Come on Isobel, you didn't need to do that.' He pointed to Ryan. 'Now put him down and leave him alone.' He caught his employee's eye, threw him a silent apology. 'He did nothing wrong to you. Nothing.'

Striding towards him, Isobel moved slowly, and with an outstretched hand, she placed it on his shoulder and circled his body. 'Giancarlo, he thinks you need to be reminded which family you belong to.'

'Come on, Isobel.' His eyes flickered with fear, and adrenaline surged through him. 'Me and you, I thought we were friends?' Taking short intakes of breath, he began to move backwards, then felt his heart skip a beat as his foot caught against the kettlebells and they scattered around his ankles. With his arms flailing, he felt a tight, painful grip as his body was thrown mercilessly at the wall by one of Isobel's henchmen.

While Rob was held tightly against the wall, Isobel stepped forward and stared directly into Rob's eyes. 'Giancarlo thinks you're a liability, and I think he's right,' she whispered with a sadistic smile. 'You can't get anything right, can you?'

'Isobel, please...' Rob looked from one of her men to the other, and over his shoulder, towards the door. He wanted nothing more than for someone to walk in, for his fifty-something client to arrive. But with almost an hour to go that was unlikely. He stared at Ryan, caught his eye and then looked down at the kettlebell that had landed close to his feet.

'You are going to handle the goods. But to do that, Giancarlo says you need to get rid of the girl. He doesn't want her around.' Isobel lifted a hand, and patted Rob on the cheek. 'This time, you need to cause an accident that she can't escape from. Do you understand?' With that, she turned, gave the two minders a nod, then walked out of the gym and without looking over her shoulder, pulled the shutter down behind her, leaving her threat ringing in Rob's head...

3

With time now against her, Kate jumped into her bright yellow Volkswagen Beetle and with a deep breath in, she twisted her hands around the steering wheel and pressed her fingers into the leather until they turned white with the pressure.

'Come on you rusty old thing. Let's get this done.' She gave the car an anxious smile and with a deep-seated trepidation, she turned the key in the ignition and closed her eyes as the car's engine chugged into life. After the accident, she had wondered if she'd ever drive again, had found climbing into a car more than stressful and the only way she'd ever managed to force herself back into the driver's seat had been to focus on the happy memories she'd once shared with her grandmother. It had been her grandmother who had taught her to drive and had taken her over the moors, driving for miles while looking for the perfect spot to picnic. With her lip trembling with emotion at the memories, she wished that her grandmother was still alive now to offer her much-needed comfort and advice.

Reversing out of the drive, Kate kept one eye on the clock, realised that time was short, and that she had just twenty minutes to get to Bedale. She was grateful that the road that went between Caldwick and Bedale was unusually clear.

Gripping the steering wheel like a vice, the car gained momentum. It snaked easily around the long, isolated roads, and past the low stone walls where sheep happily grazed with a scattering of lambs that skipped and jumped by their side. A white swan loitered by the side of the road and Kate found herself slowing the car to a crawl, while she watched as it carefully herded its three young cygnets along the road until one after the other of her babies jumped in the river with a splash. It reminded Kate of her childhood and of her life before the accident. A time when she, James and Eve would go everywhere together and like the cygnets, if one had jumped, the other two would have followed.

Pulling into town, she looked at the church tower clock and with a satisfied nod, she saw that it still wasn't quite nine and with the wind in the right direction, she could still be on time.

Driving across the cobbles, Kate kept her eye on the pedestrians and slowed for cyclists, and smiled in the knowledge that they were all making their way to work, just like she was. When her eyes spotted a parking space, she aimed straight for it.

'No!' Hitting the brakes, she yelped out loud and narrowly missed the silver BMW that swiftly slid in front of her and into the space that should have been hers. 'That was my space, you moron!' she shouted shakily through her car's open window. With nowhere to park, arriving to work on time was now looking highly doubtful.

By the time she'd parked, it was already nine o'clock. Her breathing had accelerated and her heart was racing, but she didn't have time to stop. She couldn't think about the near miss right now but for just a few seconds she sat, and hoped that her breathing would calm.

Memories of the accident flashed into her mind. One image after the other, exploding in front of her face. The car that came from nowhere. The screech of brakes. The sound of metal upon metal. Then darkness. The screaming. The pain.

Gasping, she closed her eyes. Prayed for the flashbacks to stop. For the memories to dissipate. And for all the vivid images that were hitting her square between the eyes to fade. How she wished for it to be a part of someone else's history, rather than her own.

Climbing out of the car, Kate's mind raced. She clicked her key fob twice. Checked and double checked that the car was locked and then just to be sure, she checked it again.

'You really don't need the stress. Not today,' she declared. 'Yet here we are, stressed to the hilt.' On shaky legs, she walked unsteadily towards the address she'd been given and with her head tipped to one side, she tried to peer through the window of the building she needed to go to. The office had no signage that would help her identify it clearly. But according to her directions, she was in the right place. 'It's a grand looking building, double front and close to the church,' the woman on the telephone had told her. 'You can't miss it,' she'd said. 'There's a wine bar to one side and the most amazing bakery to the other.'

Kate noted that the bakery had no signage either. But the smell of fresh bread drifted out of the door and with her stomach growled with hunger. She'd had every intention of eating before she left home, but that was until the wine had been spilled and the clean-up mission had begun. Standing on tip toes, she made herself a silent promise that later that day she'd make her way through those doors and buy something tasty, with all the calories.

Turning back to the office, Kate felt a twinge of nervous excitement. She couldn't wait to see what lay beyond the shiny, jet-black front door. With shaking fingers, she reached for the polished brass door handle and with a last look down at her clothes, she flicked back her hair, and straightened her skirt.

'Oh, hi there. You must be Kate?' A woman, who was older than her stood up behind a reception desk. She was dressed in navy trousers, and a white organza blouse, with a blue plaid blazer that showed her off to be a woman with style. She had short, soft golden hair and immediately she reminded Kate of her grandmother, especially when she noticed her dainty pearl earrings, matching necklace and the array of gold and diamond rings that graced the third finger of her left hand. 'I'm so pleased to have another woman in the building. I've been surrounded by men, for far too long. I'm Gloria,' she said with a welcoming smile.

'Well, I'm pleased to be of service.' Kate stepped forward, watched the way Gloria fumbled with a packet of biscuits and laughed when they spilled out and onto a plate.

'Sit down, honey. I'll put the kettle on.' Gloria placed the plate of biscuits on a small mahogany table that stood to one side of the room. 'I bought the biscuits in your honour. Do you want some coffee?'

Kate nodded appreciatively. 'That'd be great. Thank you.' She went to sit down on the brown leather settee, held onto its arm and nervously perched on its edge. 'What a lovely room,' Kate admired the deep skirting boards and the ornate coving that created a backdrop to a huge mahogany reception desk.

'Mr Parker won't keep you long, he just popped into his office,' Gloria said as she poured the coffee, stirred in the milk then with a genuine smile, passed Kate the mug. 'There you go, you look like you need it.'

Taking a moment to calm herself, Kate sipped at the coffee. She heard her stomach grumble nervously and searched the walls for something to talk about. 'It's nice to have a few moments to compose myself,' she mumbled nervously. 'I've had a nightmare of a morning. First, there was an accident at home when the remnants of last night's wine ended up all over my carpet.' She held a hand up in the air, palm out. 'Don't ask. It's cream and ruined and well, it will teach me to finish my drink off in the future.' She pulled a face and grinned. 'Then, as I was just about to pull up outside, some moron stole my parking spot! I ended up having to park right down at the bottom of the high street and in these shoes, it took me forever to walk across the cobbles.'

'Ah okay, I'm sorry about that.' A deep assertive voice filled the room, as a man's broad, six-foot frame suddenly occupied the ornate doorway. 'I think the moron you're talking about, might have been me? I'm Ben Parker. Pleased to meet you.' He smiled and held out a hand to shake with hers.

It had been the last thing Kate had expected, as had the look in his eyes, filled with amusement. Internally she wanted nothing more than for the floor to open and to swallow her whole and for the life of her, she couldn't believe that in the first five minutes of being employed, she'd managed to shout at her boss, call him a moron and make herself look like a screaming banshee. And now, with her eyes averted, she couldn't decide what to say, or how to react and nervously, her hand shot upwards to protectively cover her scar. With an uneasy look over her shoulder and back at the door, she tried to work out how quickly she could reach it and whether making an exit now was preferable to being dismissed sometime later.

* * *

Ben stood for a moment without speaking; Kate seemed nice and without a doubt, he was angry with himself for having taken the space. Wished instead that he'd been the perfect gentleman. At least then, they'd have got off to a better start and the atmosphere in the room would have been a little less edgy.

Looking her up and down, Ben caught his breath. Kate was beautifully turned out. She'd obviously put some thought into her outfit and without a doubt, he liked her attention to detail. The one thing he couldn't ignore was the look of trepidation that was crossing her face. 'I'm sorry,' he whispered and smiled. Hoped she'd accept the apology and above all else he hoped she wouldn't really consider himself to be the moron she'd previously called him.

'Your coffee.' Gloria passed him a fresh mug, and glanced between him and Kate with a knowing smile. 'I brought biscuits, in Kate's honour.'

'Thanks.' He looked fondly in Gloria's direction, caught her eye and discreetly shook his head. The last thing he needed right now was for Gloria to try and fix him, or for her to play matchmaker. It was something she did and had dutifully taken on the challenge of repairing his life not too long after his wife Julia had died.

'Kate. When you're ready, maybe you'd like to follow this moron through to the office,' he said with a cheeky smile and a wink. 'Mr Parker's waiting and unless you're the prime minister, you really shouldn't keep him waiting. Not for very long. He doesn't like it.'

* * *

Kate's head spun between the door that Ben had walked through and Gloria, who had picked up another Hobnob, taken a bite and then waved it frantically around in the air, indicating to Kate that she should follow – and quickly.

'William doesn't bite, honestly. No matter what Ben says.' Gloria laughed as she stood up and pointed to the door. 'Go on. It's that way.'

'But... I thought Ben was Mr Parker,' Kate said as she jumped up from the settee, straightened her clothes and made her way to the door.

'He is dear. He's Mr Parker junior. The Mr Parker that you're about to meet, your boss, is his father.'

Kate felt the tension once again rise up in her chest. Her hands felt hot and clammy, and with her heart beating rapidly, she placed her coffee mug down on the table and stared at the exit.

Should she run now, or later?

Swallowing hard, Kate pulled open the door and found herself stood in a corridor where there were several closed doors and a staircase. 'For a Victorian terraced house, you sure have a lot of rooms,' she whispered as she studied the doors, trying to work out which one Ben would have gone through. And with the feeling of being a small, lost child, she began singing the words 'Eeny, meeny, miny, mo,' in her head as a tall, dark-haired man rushed between rooms and almost collided with her in his haste to leave the building.

'Okay. You look lost?' He stopped abruptly, pushed his glasses firmly up his nose and raised an eyebrow.

'Well, the idea of working here seemed so much more fun when the woman at the employment agency told me I had the job,' Kate said as she held out her hands. 'Where the hell did he go?'

'If you're looking for Mr Parker, he'd have gone in there.' He pointed to a door, but looked down at his watch and Kate noticed the way his smile turned worried and faded. 'Sorry, I have to go, I'm late.'

As he disappeared, Kate knocked on the door he'd pointed to and slowly pushed it open. Inside, she found a bright and airy office. One that was filled with light, and in comparison to the reception, appeared to be quite modern. The smell of fresh paint still lingered in the air and she quickly came to the conclusion that it had recently been refurbished.

'Now then, Miss Duggan, please take a seat. I'm William.' An older, more distinguished duplicate of Ben spoke. He ran a hand through dark, peppered hair and with a nervous smile, Kate glanced at where Ben had perched against a sideboard, his hands were clasped tightly together and although he smiled, his face gave nothing away.

'Thank you so much and I'm so sorry that I was late this morning,' she announced. 'And, what's more, I really didn't mean to shout at your son.' Kate was nervous and tried to cover her tracks, just in case Ben had told him about the incident. 'That's not like me at all.'

'Kate, don't ever apologise for being feisty. We like feisty women, don't we, Ben?' He grinned, stood up and walked back and forth behind the desk, until finally, he perched against the windowsill and clasped his hands tightly together. His mannerisms matched those of Ben's and they both studied her in a silence that seemed to go on for ever. 'So, you want to be a private investigator?' he finally said with words that sliced through the silence, like a newly-sharpened knife.

'Yes, sir, I'd like that very much. The agency that recommended me, well, they thought I'd be ideal for the job.' Her answer had been polite, and it occurred to her that his words could have been either a statement or a question. 'You see I've always been interested in the law.'

'So I see. You're twenty-eight, is that right?'

'Yes, sir, I am.'

'And you worked for the Metropolitan Police. As a constable?'

'I did. Yes, sir.'

'Kate, my name is William, not sir.' He walked to stand in front of the desk and gave Kate the opportunity to look him up and down. Like Ben, he was broad, handsome with tanned, weathered skin and an expensive suit. 'I see you went to law school?'

Kate nodded. 'Yes, I did. I graduated with honours.'

Ben stepped forward, a file held out in his hand. 'Father, Kate is being modest. Her report states that she was the perfect student.' He smiled and Kate saw that the mischievous sparkle had returned to his eyes. 'First Class honours.'

'So, you could have become a solicitor, after your father? Any reason why you didn't?'

Kate shrugged and closed her eyes as she thought about her answer. 'Do you want the truth?' She waited for him to nod, for the permission to continue. 'I guess I wanted to annoy him, my father that is.'

Both William and Ben looked at one another and shared a knowing look.

'Does that sound familiar, Ben?' William nodded slowly. 'My son here. He used to do everything he could to annoy me too. Must be a generational thing.' William said as he studied the file. 'The scar on your face; it happened just over a year ago, am I right?' He tapped his pen on the file. 'There was a place on the application asking about your personal life and about anything that could affect your role. Did you not think it relevant to mention the accident?'

'No, I'm sorry. I didn't think it was.' She took in a deep breath. 'It's not something I broadcast.' She looked between both William and Ben. She hadn't written anything about the accident on purpose. The last thing she'd wanted to do was explain what had happened and now, she subconsciously turned the scarred side of her face down and away. Hiding it had become a habit and in her opinion, the fewer people that saw it, the better. 'You certainly know a lot about me.'

Coughing, William drew her attention to where he now sat behind the desk. 'Kate. Don't be alarmed and don't take it personally. Ben, looked into you before you started. We make it our business to know everything about who we're employing.' He dropped the file, and gave her a warm, apologetic smile. 'So, do you want to tell me why you wanted to annoy your father?'

'Because he's a barrister,' Kate said in a matter-of-fact tone. 'He fully expected me to join the firm. Just as my brother had. Belligerently, I joined the police and went to live in London and...' she paused, thoughtfully. 'I only came back to look after my grandmother. She was sick. She needed me.'

'And after she died?' William asked.

'I was going to join the firm. It was what my father wanted and it was going to be a surprise.' She looked up, caught Ben's eye. 'But then... the accident happened and everything changed.' She bit down on her lip, took a moment before continuing. 'Taking the job at my father's firm, no longer seemed right. My brother had died and by going there, I'd have been stepping into his shoes. I couldn't do it. Then, my father sold the company because he couldn't bear it either.' With her voice drifting off, she stared at the floor. Without trying, she could still see her brother's body, and the way he'd led there, in the water, staring back at her. 'I'm sorry, you're right. I should have mentioned it on the application form,' she said, as she crossed her legs. 'It felt easier to omit the truth, than to try and explain. Yet here I am, trying to explain.'

She looked around, battled with her thoughts and felt a sense of relief when Gloria entered the room. A tray of coffee and biscuits balanced in one hand, which she carefully placed on the desk next to where William now sat.

'There you go, I brought more coffee. Just give me a shout if you need anything else.' She glanced at Kate. 'Are you okay, love?' she asked, 'I've told them to be nice to you.' She gave both Ben and William a stern but loving look, before smiling at Kate and patting her fondly on the shoulder.

'I'm always nice.' William picked up his mobile, checked the screen and then tossed it back on the desk. 'You'll be working with

Ben for the first couple of weeks. I know you did surveillance work in the force, but you need to learn our ways now. We don't break any rules. No matter how much it costs us.'

Kate looked him directly in the eye. 'Yes, sir. I really am pleased to hear that.'

'Good.' He turned to Ben. 'Take Kate out. Show her what we do.' He paused thoughtfully, 'Oh and my name, it's still William, not sir.' He gave her a warm, but determined smile. 'I'll let Ben show you to your office. And Kate,' he paused, held out a hand and with a firm grip that felt like a vice, he shook hers. 'Welcome to the firm.'

4

Kate stepped out of the bakery and into the daylight. It was uncharacteristically mild for the time of year and the heat of the sun warmed her face as she headed towards a small stone wall that stood near the church. Leaning against it, she caught her breath and with her mobile precariously balanced under her chin, she juggled her sandwich out of the paper bag, while waiting for her sister Eve to answer the phone.

'Hi there,' Kate said, as she took a small bite of the sandwich. 'How are you doing?'

'Yeah, I'm fine.' Eve's tone was warm, genuine and just for a moment, Kate closed her eyes, and tried to work out whether she was happy or sad. 'Me and Maxy, we've been out in the garden. He has a new ball to play with. Don't you, boy?'

'I'm so pleased you've got him.' Kate smiled. Getting Max had been a really good move. At least now, Eve had company during the day and being an assistance dog, Max was trained to help Eve with all the things she needed.

'You didn't come today.' Without warning, Eve's voice had gone from happy, to needy. She sounded lost and vulnerable, and Kate felt her heart leap with anxiety.

'Eve, I started my new job today.' She tried to sound excited in the hope that Eve would be excited too, even though by working full time she'd see less of her sister than she had before. A thought that neither of them had liked.

'Of course you did.' Eve sighed. 'We wondered why you didn't call in earlier, didn't we, Max?' She directed the conversation at the dog, but then sighed. 'So, how's it going?' she said to Kate.

Kate took another small bite of the sandwich; she could hear the disappointment in her sister's voice and every instinct told her to drop everything and run to Eve's side. 'Are you okay, because I could come you know, if you need me to?' She looked up at the church clock, and quickly calculated how long it would take her to get there, to nip Max out and get back again. But she knew that if she did it this once, it would become the norm and before she knew it, she'd be popping over during every lunchtime.

'I'm fine, Kate. I'm just moaning...' Her voice trailed off and Kate wondered just how fine she really was. '...We'll be fine, won't we Maxy.'

'Has Zoe been in to see you today?' Kate changed the subject. Zoe was Eve's carer who called in twice daily to ensure that Eve was washed and dressed and that Max was walked and fed.

'Of course she has. She gets paid to come here.' Eve laughed, 'Now, tell me all about the new job. How's it going?'

'Well, it's really good,' Kate began, cautiously. 'I'm loving it. The owner seems a bit scary, although I do think his bark might be worse than his bite.' Screwing up the paper bag, Kate looked for a waste bin and sighed when she immediately couldn't see one. 'The lady who works in reception, Gloria, reminds me of Grandma. And then there's Ben...' For a second, she gazed into the air as she thought about Ben. 'He's the owner's son. Similar age to me and get this: we have to share an office.' She began to laugh, spotted a waste bin and began walking towards it. 'Well, to tell the truth, I'll be sharing with him and two others, but the other two guys are out most of the time. They work on surveillance.'

'What, four of you in one office?' Eve began to laugh. 'I can't see you enjoying that, especially if the other three are really messy. Do they have any idea how OCD you are?'

'Eve, I am not, I just like things to be clean and tidy; there is a difference.' She threw the paper bag into the waste bin. 'And Ben's desk is tidy. It looks polished to within an inch of its life. So that's a good start. Isn't it?'

'You like him, don't you?'

Kate stalled. 'What... like who?'

'You like, Ben, Kate, why else would you mention him repeatedly? Is he handsome, sexy, do you want to—'

'Eve... enough.' She laughed. 'I don't want to anything. I live with Rob.'

Eve groaned. 'Kate, you might live with Rob, but do you love him?'

Kate thought back to the night before. The hushed phone calls, the aggressive manner. And then, that morning when he'd tossed her shoe into the air and even though she was sure he hadn't meant to hit the wine glass, he had and now the wine was all over the carpet. 'Eve, it isn't that easy.'

'Of course it is. You either love him or you don't.' Eve paused and Kate could hear the background noise of her fussing Max. 'And ask yourself this. What exactly do you get from this relationship because I know what Rob gets out of it,' Eve continued. 'He gets free board and free lodging. An all-inclusive deal. That's if and when he decides to come home.' The words struck a nerve with Kate. It was true, Rob did use the house as a hotel, he did live an all-inclusive existence and Kate tried to remember when he'd last contributed to a bill, or to the cost of the household shopping. Shaking her head, she once again looked up at the clock while trying to ignore the truth in her sister's words.

'Now, tell me more about you and Ben sharing this office.' Eve continued and for once, Kate was pleased she'd changed the subject.

'There is no me and Ben,' she laughed, made her way along the road and checked that her car was still in the parking space where she'd practically abandoned it just a few hours before.

'Come on spill the beans. I can tell you like him, and to be honest, who'd blame you? Rob isn't very nice to you, Kate. And I'd hardly call him husband material, would you?'

'Wow, back off,' Kate snapped as Eve's words hit every nerve in her being. 'Rob might not be perfect. I know that. But unless I'm mistaken, he never did anything wrong to you. Did he?'

'Of course he hasn't, but I love you, and we don't like the way he treats you.' She paused. 'Do we Maxy? And let's face it, Rob loves himself far more than he'll ever love anyone else, he's just unbelievably full of his own shit and you damn well know it. If I were you, I'd tell him to bugger off and find some other mug to put up with him.'

Kate shook her head. To Eve, life was literally that simple. Before the accident she'd have had three different boyfriends at any one time. They came and went like buses. Normally at speed and always at Eve's request. And if they were nice, they might get to stay around for just as long as Eve needed them. Her whole attitude to men had been brutal.

'Eve, Rob loves me.' Kate said as convincingly as she could. She wished it were true. But couldn't be sure. The change in his mood was more than obvious. The nights of him sleeping on the settee had increased without explanation and the time he spent away from home was becoming more and more suspicious.

'Yeah, sure. Now... come on, humour me and dish the gossip. Just how tidy is this Ben?' It was as though someone had flicked a switch and knowing that she'd said as much as she could get away with, Eve had changed the subject.

Kate laughed but didn't respond. She just thought about Ben, and the expensive suit that he wore, the open neck shirt that gave him a casual but intriguing persona. Then, there was the smile that lit up his face as he spoke, but only for a moment before his gaze turned distant and thoughtful and even though he'd stolen her parking space that morning, he did seem to be considerate. That, along with his uncluttered desk and organised approach, made him tidy.

'Yep, he's tidy,' she finally said, before picking up her water and sipping the ice-cold fluid from the bottle.

'I knew it,' Eve said triumphantly. 'Lucky you. You get a new job and a tidy new man.' Kate could hear the way Eve's voice dropped, the despondency that suddenly crept in. 'Kate, I've missed you today,' she whispered, 'Didn't we, Max?' The internal guilt surged inside Kate again. She already felt bad for leaving them to fend for themselves, but to hear Eve actually say it, Kate felt her heart break into pieces. The only saving grace was that Eve had Max and it was on days like today that even though Eve had resisted, Kate was glad she'd managed to talked Eve into getting him. Although still in training, Max could already retrieve the remote control or the telephone and had even managed to collect a newspaper from the specially designed post box.

'I know you do, hon, but we discussed my going back to work, didn't we?' Kate looked back across at Parker & Son. She knew that Eve needed her and started to wonder if she'd made the right decision. 'And watching daytime tv, was driving me senseless.'

'Well, some of us don't have a choice. We have to watch it whether we like it or not.' Eve said softly and Kate once again closed her eyes and thought of how boring and lonely Eve's daily life really must be.

'Look, why don't I pop over after work. We can take Max for a walk together, but I can't stay long.' Once again, her mind drifted to Rob. To the way he'd been acting the night before. The secretive phone call, the nasty attitude. None of it was conducive to a loving relationship and she knew that provided he actually came home, she had no choice but to sit down with him and have a conversation that neither of them was likely to enjoy.

* * *

Eve put the phone down and began to stroke Max. She was happy that Kate was coming over, pleased that her plan had worked and that even though Kate hadn't known it, Eve had gently manipulated her into doing what she'd wanted. And now, Kate would come. She'd promised to be here just after five and if she played her cards right, Eve would be able to get her to stay much later.

Maybe it was a twin thing, but Kate was the only one who understood her. She was the only person who knew what Eve had been through. She'd slept beside her at the hospital. Refused to leave her side and had held her hand through all the indignity of being poked, prodded and jabbed by multiple doctors and nurses. The endless invasion of catheters, enemas and drugs had gone on for months, until every inch of Eve's dignity had been stripped away and she'd found herself recoiling from everyone, except for Kate.

The weeks after James had died had been the worst. Everyone had mourned for him, including her, and even though everyone had been sympathetic that both she and Kate had been hurt, and that life as they'd known it had changed, neither had died and it had been made very clear to them both that James had suffered the most and that they should both be grateful for surviving. Only Kate had felt the hurt that she'd felt too and in the end, they'd clung together like limpets holding onto a rock which to them had felt like the natural thing to do. They were twins. They knew each other almost as well as they knew themselves. Although, from a very early age they had rebelled against the identical lifestyle that their mother had thrust upon them. Both had made a secret pact and had refused to wear the identical dresses, matching shoes or hair ribbons and they'd both gone out of their way to take their own path. They hadn't wanted to do anything remotely similar and had even gone as far as to hang around with different friends, which had ultimately led to them having different hobbies.

Kate had been the geeky one with little or zero dress sense. She'd spent hours in her room and had read books morning, noon and night. She'd been the perfect student. The one their father had nurtured in the hope that eventually she'd take over the family firm.

Whereas, Eve had been the wild child. The one who'd worn all the pink, had all the weird and wonderful hair do's, that had been dyed every colour. She'd been bright and creative and becoming a lawyer had been the last thing on her agenda and as soon as she could, she'd left school and trained as a beautician.

Stroking the black Labrador affectionately. Eve gave him a knowing smile. 'We did it Max. We knew we could convince Kate to come, didn't we, and now she is. Isn't she, Maxy?'

5

Kate walked back into the office and headed straight for the room she now shared with Ben. In her absence he'd moved the desks around and into a more uniform pattern and after making a comment that morning about the lack of filing space, she saw that a two-drawer silver grey filing cabinet had now miraculously appeared beside her desk and a bright pink chair stood behind it.

'Great, you're back. We have a client.' He tapped his fingers against a file, flicked it open. 'We've watched this person before,' he said as he read through the pages. 'Nothing came of it last time, and to be honest, I'm not sure we'll turn anything up this time either. But we'll see. It'll be a nice easy one for you to start with.'

Kate waited until Ben pulled a picture out of the file and passed it to her. It was of a casually dressed man of medium build, with dark, slicked back hair, thick, shaped eyebrows who, she noted, was fairly good looking.

'This... this is our person of interest?' She moved in her seat. 'Okay.' Kate nodded. 'Who is he?' She fiddled mindlessly with her pen, tapping it against her notebook. 'I mean, do you want to fill me in on his story?'

Ben laughed. 'Of course. He's called Luca Bellandini. He's a librarian. His employer thinks he's up to something, and he's probably right.'

'You say that you've watched him before. Is it worth doing again?' She questioned, 'Do we keep watching, do what you've always done, or do we take a different approach?' Kate was genuinely interested and felt as though her years in the police would help with her decisions and couldn't help but keep throwing questions out like bullets.

'First, we go to the library. We keep a low profile, we read and we study. We don't approach him. Not unless he comes to us. Just watch his movements.' He smiled, 'With your previous experience, I'll be interested in seeing what you spot about him. Which of our observations are similar.'

'Won't we be working together?'

Ben shook his head and picked up his coffee. 'Not all the time. I'll probably pitch my spot at the other side of the library. I might come over at some point and chat. But we'll act as though we've met in by chance. The most important thing is not to bring attention to why we're there. If he goes out, let him go.' Ben walked around the office and then sat back in his chair, making Kate wonder if he ever sat still. 'His boss says he's been acting suspiciously, which probably means he's getting mixed up in the family business.'

'The Bellandini family?'

'Yes. They're notorious. Always wheeling and dealing in something they shouldn't and all of them are in and out of jail like yoyos.'

He ran his fingers across the keyboard, read something that interested him on the screen and then looked back towards where Kate sat shaking her head.

'What's the bigger picture?' she asked.

'What do you mean?'

'The family – who runs it?' She stared down at Luca's picture and tapped at it with a long, pointed finger. 'This guy. Luca. If he's from an old Italian family then he won't be in charge. There will probably be an older, more established member that is.' She nodded, tapped again more determinedly than she had before. 'It's the older ones we should be looking for,' she said with conviction. 'Because in my humble opinion, that's where you'll find the answers.'

'Okay.' Ben lifted a hand to his chin, rubbed at the stubble that had just begun to show. 'Let's meet here in the morning, and we'll put a strategy together,' he said thoughtfully, 'Actually, why don't you put a strategy together. Tell me how you'd proceed, and what you'd look for first.' He stood up, smiled and with a look of amusement crossing his face, he walked towards the door. 'Oh, and if I see your car lurking around in the street, I promise not to steal your parking space, although you could always use the car park. There's a private one, behind the building. It's much easier to park in.'

6

'I'm so pleased you're here.' Eve smiled, held out her arms and hugged Kate, before turning her chair and wheeling herself into the kitchen. 'I've made a quiche, I thought you'd be hungry,' she pulled open the oven door, wafted the heat away with her hand. 'Oh, and if you open the fridge. You'll find a salad to go with it.'

After throwing her jacket over the back of a chair, Kate made a fuss of Max who excitedly circled her. 'There's a good boy,' Kate ran a hand down his back until affectionately Max rolled onto his side, lay on the floor and exposed his belly. 'Oh, you like that, don't you?' Kate said with one eye on where Eve had wheeled herself up to the oven and had visibly recoiled as the heat hit her.

'Do you want me to...' Kate jumped up. She desperately wanted to help her sister, but resisted the urge to rush forward and nervously, she watched as the quiche was lifted from the oven and placed on a wooden board that had been conveniently positioned on the lowered worktop.

Breathing in appreciatively, Kate pulled the salad out of the fridge and carried it into the dining room where the table stood adorned with pretty napkins, two plates and a small vase in the centre that had been filled with hand-picked flowers that Kate knew would be straight from the garden. 'Wow. That smells good. I'm starving.' She'd had every intention of going home early and speaking to Rob, but it was more than obvious from all the effort Eve had made, that she wanted her to stay and once again, Kate thought about Eve's day and how being here alone for the most of it, must be soul destroying. 'Here, do you want me to carry that?' Lurching forward, Kate went to make a grab of the dish and stopped when she saw the look of determination that crossed Eve's face.

'Kate. I'm fine. I can manage,' Even snapped, 'I might not be able to walk, but I'm not incapable. I just have to get myself organised and do things a little differently.' She precariously placed the quiche on a lap tray. Then balanced the bean bag base across her legs and with a confident smile, she wheeled herself into the dining room. 'After dinner, I thought I might do your nails. You will let me, won't you?' she pleaded, 'I really need to practise with the acrylics, it's been too long since I did any and you don't mind being a guinea pig for me, do you?'

Kate looked through the glass doors and into the living room where Eve had set her old nail station up. A table, a long UV lamp clamped to its side, the soft towels and a selection of polishes that Eve had obviously picked out. 'Oh, Eve. I can't stay long. I need to get home. We have a new case and Ben's asked me to come up with a strategy.' She sat down at the dining table, waited for Eve to wheel herself into position but saw the look of disappointment that crossed her face.

'It won't take me long. An hour at the most.' Eve looked at Kate with hopeful eyes. 'Besides, I have some news.' A huge, infectious smile crossed her face, her eyes sparkled and Kate noticed the way she looked at her, waiting for approval. 'I've made a decision. I know it's going to take a bit of work and I'll need to get a builder in to sort out the floor, a ramp and the heating. But...' she left a dramatic pause. 'I'm going to turn the garage into a nail bar. There's plenty of room and God knows, I don't need the garage to put a car inside. So, you know... I'm going to start my own business.' She nodded enthusiastically, and continued without taking a breath. 'I'm lonely, Kate. No one comes, not since the accident.' She picked up the salad bowl and with a pair of wooden spoons, she dished some onto her plate. 'All my friends, they used to come and visit at first. But now that they know that things won't change, that being in a chair is a part of my life, they don't know what to say. So, instead of just talking about everything and nothing like we used to, they avoid me. I thought that if I opened the nail bar, right here where I can access it easily and don't have to travel to go to work, people will come, won't they?'

Nodding. Kate felt the pride surge through her. Her eyes filled with tears and she knew that running a business would do Eve good. It would give her something to focus on, a way of meeting people and being less lonely. It would be crazy to try and deter her. 'Eve, if that's what you want to do. Then I think you should do it,' she said the words with conviction, but inside she was worried about the affects it might have and thought back to their twenty-seventh birthday, the night of the accident. There had meant to be a big party. A meal organised by their mother, that all the family would go to, including all the aunts and uncles, some of the cousins and her father's aging parents. It had been a party that neither her, James, or Eve had wanted to attend.

'Can't I get off?' James had pleaded. 'Me and Lucy have a date night planned. I've promised her we'll go to that new club in town, the one with the bouncers that are all dressed up in a tux.' Closing her eyes, Kate could still see the look on his face. The way he'd held a finger to his lips to indicate keeping it a secret from their mother.

'You mean the club where the barmaids are topless and the bouncers turn into strippers?' She'd laughed and then saw the appeal. 'Actually, I wouldn't mind going too.' She looked across the room at her sister, who had her arms above her head, dancing to the music. 'What do you say, Eve? Are you up for a club?'

'I'll take you both, but you need to get yourselves ready, and quickly,' he'd yelled as she and Eve had run up the stairs. Then, as they'd done on so many occasions, they'd climbed into his car, waved to their parents who'd stood on the doorstep and with laughter and banter bouncing around the vehicle, they'd set off into town, for a wild night out.

Then, everything had happened so fast. There had been a screech of brakes. The sound of metal upon metal. The car had spun and turned over and over. Air bags had exploded and covered the windows and she'd been thrown heavily against the side of the car. Then the car had begun filling with cold, icy water that had overwhelmed her with fear. Her body had tried to scramble, to move. But unable to do anything to save herself, her mind had descended into a long, silent darkness that was only disturbed by her sister's scream.

Suddenly, forcing her body to move, Kate had crawled out of an open door, and up the embankment where she found Eve looking pallid and terrified. Her eyes were pleading for help. Her hands were sporadically curling in and out of fists, and her mouth was forming words she could not say. It was more than obvious that something was terribly wrong, and in her panic, Kate screamed for James. She searched the darkness and through tired, confused eyes she saw him lying with his face partially below the water's surface, his body lifeless. For a while, she simply stared at the scene in front of her; her whole body had fallen into a daze and she couldn't move. Then, as though someone had pressed a restart button, the world had begun spinning again. Eve was still screaming and an indescribable pain tore through Kate's face, like a scythe slashing her. With her fingertips touching her chin, she felt blood gushing from a wound and a long, piercing noise that filled the air, came from within her own body and sounded deep and animalistic.

'Kate, what's wrong?' Eve asked. 'Do you want some salad?'

Eve's voice brought her back to reality. Once again the accident had been at the forefront of her mind and without warning, a single tear dropped onto her cheek.

'I'm fine. Honestly and yes... yes please.' She took the dish, held onto Eve's hand for a moment too long, and stared into her sister's eyes. For what felt like the millionth time, she threw her mind back to that day and tried to remember the moments before she'd found Eve. She was sure that James had been incapable of dragging Eve up the embankment but in the absence of anyone else being at the scene, she tried to work out whether she'd somehow managed to drag Eve herself and without realising, had caused her life-changing injuries?

7

If Kate had thought that watching daytime television was boring, then she soon realised that sitting in a library, watching Luca Bellandini was worse. Up to now, he'd done nothing more than stamp books and make polite conversation with numerous small children and adults over the age of fifty, who simply looked as though they'd got nothing better to do.

Looking at her watch, she counted the minutes and wished she were back in the office going through strategies with Ben. They'd spent most of the morning going through Luca's social media. His posts had been searched, records had been made along with lists of friends who he regularly interacted with.

'Facebook, any other Meta accounts such as Threads or Instagram. Twitter, X, whatever it's now called,' she'd said as she'd stared directly at the computer. 'There has to be something on one of them or all of them. Most people post the same thing to multiple platforms and hopefully something would give us a clue as to what he's up to.'

'And what if he doesn't use social media?' Ben had thrown in. 'Maybe he's a recluse. A geeky librarian. One who doesn't go out.'

Sighing, Kate had begun typing his name. 'Luca Bellandini,' she mouthed as she wrote. 'Come on, prove me right, show me who you are.'

Tapping her pen against a notepad, Kate felt herself hone in on the six women who sat on the table next to hers. One of the women, a thin lady with short spiky blonde hair, kept mentioning biscuits and another talked constantly about a book she'd just read.

'Are you studying law?' The enquiring voice of Ben Parker came from behind her, making Kate begin to tremble inside. Her eye began to twitch all by itself and with a nervous smile, she looked over her shoulder in his direction. 'Act naturally,' he whispered sitting down across from her. 'Do we have anything?' He looked at the six women, who were now sat nudging each other and smiling simultaneously.

'Nada.' She flicked the page of her book, pretended to read. 'What are you doing here? Shouldn't you be at the other side of the room?' Laughing surreptitiously, she pointed to another table and then frowned as her mobile bleeped, making everyone turn.

'I'm so sorry,' she whispered and grabbed at the bag. 'I thought I'd switched it off.' She shook her head in annoyance, rummaged around in the bag and after grabbing the phone, she flicked at the screen.

Don't wait up. I doubt I'll be home.

The message was from Rob and for a moment, Kate didn't know whether she should be happy or sad. Half of her wished that he'd pack a bag and leave of his own accord. But the chances of that happening were non-existent and she knew that a conversation would have to be had, and annoyingly, her eyes filled with tears.

'Hey, your private life is none of my business, but... are you okay?' Ben questioned in a soft whisper while his eyes never left the book that he continued to flick through.

Kate began to fold her books and stack them neatly. The last thing she wanted to say to him was that her private life was none of his business. Especially when he was paying her by the hour, which meant that anything she did during that time was definitely his business. 'It's nothing.' She felt her bottom lip tremble with emotion. 'It won't happen again.' She looked around, spotted the toilets. 'Do you mind. I... I need a minute.'

With the light inside the toilets coming on automatically, Kate sniffed at the air and pulled a face as she peered inside one of the cubicles. It was small, hardly enough room for a grown adult and had a cistern that looked as though it were about to fall off the wall and for a moment, she considered finding somewhere else to go but couldn't bear the thought of leaving the room, and walking back out to Ben, who was probably having serious doubts as to who he'd employed.

Leaning against the sink, Kate caught her reflection in the mirror, saw the disturbing image that presented itself and with a quick dig around in her bag she pulled out a make-up bag and set to work correcting her face.

* * *

'Are you still here?' Kate smiled jokingly as she walked back to the table, where Ben pretended to read.

'Of course I am.' He winked, then smiled and Kate was grateful that he hadn't mentioned the message she'd received that had obviously upset her. 'And you could at least try and look pleased to see me. The women over there are convinced we were flirting.' Ben's whole face lit up, and his eyes sparkled with mischief.

'Here, pretend to look at this.' Ben turned the reference book around for her to see. Then stood up and gave her a pleasant smile. 'I'll head back to the office.' He pointed to a paragraph on the book as though explaining something about it. 'He disappeared for just over ten minutes into a room at the back of the library. You might want to keep an eye on it. While I head back to the office and give that social media another look. There has to be something we're missing.'

* * *

'Have you finished with these?'

Even though Kate had been more than aware Luca had approached her, the sound of Bellandini's voice made her jump as his hand landed on the pile of books that she'd already dug through.

'You're studying medicine?' he picked up one of the books and absentmindedly began to flick through it. It was something Kate wasn't sure she liked and without knowing what to do, she began to explain.

'My sister, she has a spinal injury. I'm doing some research.'

'Have you tried *Spinal Cord Medicine* by... Wait a minute.' He suddenly disappeared and returned a few minutes later. A large book held in his hands. 'Here you go, it's by Vernon Lin. Loads of information. Covers everything from surgical procedures to rehabilitation.' His Italian accent was strong and Kate found herself enjoying the rhythmic tone.

'Thank you,' she said sincerely and took the book from him. 'I'm Kate.'

'Luca.' He shook her hand and smiled. 'You be sure to shout me if you need any more help. I'll be right over there.' He pointed to the reception, smiled again and walked away.

With the lights flashing on and off, Kate knew that the library was about to close and with a final look at her book, she gathered her pens and notebook, then carefully placed them into her rucksack. Heading down the stairs, she watched as people filed past her. They were all leaving for the night, and enviously, she thought about her own home and the welcome that awaited her. It used to be a place where she felt safe and happy. Whereas now, she just wanted Rob gone. And even though he'd messaged to say he wouldn't be there, she dreaded the thought that he could just walk in unannounced. With a sigh, she pulled her mobile out of her bag and checked it for messages. She was about to call Ben when her screen flashed with a number she didn't recognise and automatically, she swiped at the screen to answer it.

'Hello? Kate Duggan speaking.'

'Darling, is that you?' The sound of her mother's voice caught her by surprise. It had been a call she hadn't expected and with a quick look at the screen, she tried to work out if she'd seen the wrong number. 'Why are you being so formal?'

'Mother, I wasn't being formal,' she cringed. 'What's wrong?' It was a well-known fact that her mother rarely called and when she did, she normally had something cruel or nasty to say. She was practically the world record holder for backhanded compliments and even though she'd be mortified if she thought she'd offended anyone, the words seemed to fall out of her mouth without any effort.

'I'm fine, darling. Where are you?' The words and tone of her mother's voice hit her like a thunderbolt. Her mother asking where she was could only mean one thing and Kate sat down on the steps, put her head in her hands and pulled frantically at her long auburn hair.

'I'm at work,' Kate responded. 'Where are you?'

'I'm outside your little house, darling.'

Kate screamed silently and could instantly imagine her mother walking up and down the front of the property, checking the windowsills with the swipe of a finger.

'Mother, I'm working. I'm sure I mentioned to you that I was starting a new job, as a private investigator.' Kate really wanted to be calm and cheerful, but she began to suck deep breaths of air into her lungs and with a hand against her chest, she hoped that her heart would stop beating quite so quickly.

'Darling, I've been stood outside this tiny little cottage for the last twenty minutes. I thought you'd be here.'

The words had been said in a cold and patronising tone and Kate worked out that even if she left immediately it would take ten, maybe fifteen minutes to get back to the cottage and the thought of facing her mother was suddenly worse than the thought of facing Rob.

Turning, she spotted Luca Bellandini walking down the stairs and out of the door and with a sigh, she closed her eyes. She knew that the opportunity to thank him for finding the book would be missed and annoyingly, she had to watch him disappear down the street, while her mother was rambling on and no doubt, sneering at the hanging baskets while pulling at the dead heads.

'Mother, had... had you said you were coming to visit?' Kate asked as politely as she could, while racing towards her car. She was positive that her mother hadn't mentioned it, and knew that if she had, she'd have definitely remembered an event so big and so very unbearable.

'Coooooey.' The voice of Mrs Winters came like a blessing from God and Kate heard a muffled sound as her mother momentarily put a hand over the phone, 'Isn't it Kate's mum? Oh, it's lovely to see you again. How are you, dear?'

Mrs Winters was Kate's eighty-five-year-old neighbour and the exchange of words told Kate that her mother was being hugged and hounded into her house for both coffee and cake. No one ever emerged from Mrs Winters quickly and more often than not, it would be hours before her mother managed to escape. This would give Kate ample time to get home and sort out the mess. She might even get time to wipe the windowsills in the hope that they hadn't already been finger swiped. But not before she stopped off at the village shop and bought some supplies, along with a bottle of much needed wine.

8

After calling at the shop, Kate drove home to River Cottage, where she walked to the back of the house and let herself in.

It was half past six and with a deep sigh of relief she could see that her mother wasn't stood waiting for her. It was exactly what she needed and with a glance across at where Mrs Winters lived, she whispered a thank you, along with a prayer that her mother wouldn't escape before she'd at least had to drink the third cup of tea.

The thought that her mother was right next door made her nauseous and with a quick glance around the house, she summed up what she did and didn't need to do.

As always, Rob had left the house in a mess. His dishes were all over the kitchen. His abandoned clothes had been tossed all over the floor and she set to work filling both the dishwasher and the washing machine before attacking the bathroom with copious amounts of bleach and hot water.

It was all she could do to prepare the cottage for her mother's imminent arrival and even though she'd been running around at speed, she still felt cold. A shiver went through her and quickly she lit the wood-burning stove, along with scented candles that she scattered haphazardly around the room. Taking a moment, she closed her eyes and took in in the aroma. The cottage was now filled with a warm and homely feel, so why did she feel so cold inside and why did she have such an overwhelming sense of anxiety at the thought that her mother was visiting?

Walking back up the stairs, Kate headed into her bedroom. The stain that covered the carpet now looked worse than it had before and with her hands on her hips she considered the problem. She wished she had the time to have it cleaned professionally and after staring at the patch for much too long, she ran into the spare bedroom and with considerable effort, she dragged a rug out and into her own room where she dropped it over the stain.

'It'll have to do,' she announced to herself, 'because like it or not, she's here.' She knew that her time was up as she heard her mother's traditional three taps on the glass, followed by the sound of the back door opening and banging to a close.

Swallowing hard, Kate attempted to stay calm. Her stomach still turned and with a final check in the mirror to ensure the foundation still covered her scar, she walked down the stairs where she was met by the ever so perfect Elizabeth Duggan.

'Hello, Mother,' Kate said as sincerely as she could, but not before taking note of the huge suitcase that stood at her feet. It was a sight that made her stomach drop to the floor, in the knowledge that the suitcase could only mean one thing. Her mother was here to stay and not only was she staying, but by the look of the size of the case, she was just about to move in for good.

'Kate, only fish walk around with their mouth open,' her mother said as she tapped her daughter under the chin. 'Now come here and give your mother a hug.'

'Sorry, Mother.' Kate responded.

'Now then, dear, let me look at you.'

Kate watched as her mother stood back, placed a hand on each of her hips and looked her up and down with a determined gaze.

'Katie, darling, you've had your hair cut,' her mother stated as Kate waited for the insult that would surely follow. She felt herself being spun around while her mother took a better look. 'Never mind, it will grow.'

There it was. The insult that she knew would come. If nothing else, her mother was more than predictable.

'Coffee?' Kate asked as she walked into the kitchen. She suddenly felt the urge to do something with her hands and clicked on the kettle before once again picking up the antibacterial spray and giving the worktop a generous squirt.

'No, thank you, dear, I had a cup of herbal tea with Mrs Winters. I like to watch the calories you know.' She tapped her perfectly flat stomach as though proving a point before adding, 'You probably should start watching the calories too, Katie, dear. You may be slim now, but you are almost thirty and like it or not, those extra pounds will start to make a difference.'

Elizabeth Duggan promptly turned around and walked around the house as though checking its suitability for her stay. Her nose was in the air, as she swept her hand along all flat surfaces including the top of the freezer that stood in the space below the stairs. Then, with a flounce she walked into the living room only to stop abruptly in front of the sideboard, where an oak framed picture of James had been placed. 'There he is, my beautiful boy.' Her finger touched the picture and for what felt like an eternity, she stared directly at it. 'You've changed the carpet, darling,' she said after she'd inspected the room. 'I'm sure you had your reasons. Did it look nice in the shop?'

'Yes, it did, and what's more, Mother, it looks nice in my front room too,' she growled at her mother's ability to throw out an insult.

'I liked your grandmother's carpet, it had history.'

'What it had was moth holes. Even Grandma didn't like it towards the end and one of the last things she ever made me promise was to take care of the cottage and to get rid of everything that was old and threadbare.' Her mother ignored her comment and walked back to her suitcase. For the briefest of moments, Kate thought that she was going to pick it up, leave and stay anywhere in the world for the night apart from at River Cottage. But to her dismay, she simply tapped it on top, like a puppy dog waiting for its reward.

'Darling, get that no-good boyfriend of yours to bring that upstairs for me. I think I'll go up and take a shower. You know, freshen up before dinner.' She sauntered up the stairs with her hand barely touching the banister. 'Oh, and don't bother trying to cook tonight, dear. We'll go to that nice pub in Bedale. Give Eve a call, tell her we're all going out.' She spoke with an air of authority and Kate shook her head in disbelief.

'Did Eve know you were coming?' Kate hauled the case up the stairs behind her. Rob had said he wouldn't be home tonight, which meant that if she didn't carry it up, the suitcase would be stood at the bottom of the stairs overnight. Besides, her mother taking a shower was perfect. At least if she were upstairs, Kate wouldn't have to listen to the continual insults. She'd quickly worked out that up to now her mother had insulted her hair, her figure, her carpet, her tiny cottage, her cooking and her boyfriend. And only the latter did she want to agree with.

Back down stairs, Kate made herself a coffee and as though out to make a point, added extra sugar. No matter what her mother thought, she didn't need to lose any more weight; in her opinion, she'd lost quite enough. Smiling as the aroma of coffee filled the small kitchen, Kate moved around flapping her arms up and down hoping that the smell would drift up the stairs and into the bathroom, where her mother was probably examining the shower for its suitability before she used it.

Hearing the shower burst into life, Kate used the opportunity to leave the cottage and walked back towards the shop. The two bottles of wine that were stood on the kitchen worktop suddenly didn't seem to be nearly enough and she had a sudden urge to drink until she was unconscious, or at least until her mother had got sick of her constant bitching and had taken herself back to York.

Kate pulled her phone from her bag and flicked through her address book until she came to Ben's number. She paused, before giving him an update. 'Hi, it's me, it's Kate.' She kept walking towards the shop as she spoke. 'I... I just thought I should let you know that Bellandini spoke to me after you left.' She took a breath. 'And yes, before you ask, he approached me.'

'Did he really?' Ben asked, 'Any chance he chatted you up, or offered you a pile of drugs and you know, made our job easy.'

'No, don't be daft. You should know better, life isn't that simple.' She laughed, but her bottom lip began to tremble, and she tried to pull as much air into her lungs as she could. 'And why the hell would someone like Bellandini chat up someone like me?'

'Kate, he's a red-blooded male, and you...' he paused, thoughtfully. 'Well, you're a beautiful young woman, why wouldn't he?' She could hear Ben walking from room to room, a series of doors slamming to a close behind him.

She blushed at the compliment, but stayed silent. She wasn't used to men being nice to her, especially men who were as charming and charismatic as Ben.

'Kate, are you okay?'

Nodding without speaking, Kate stared at the pavement. Each step was taken with precision. Her foot central to each slab. Not stepping on any of the lines had been a game she'd played with herself since childhood, another random act she couldn't explain.

'Kate, answer me.' She could hear the panic in Ben's voice and wished she were sat in the office, drinking coffee with him and Gloria. The two people she'd only met the day before, but already felt more comfortable in their company than she did with her own mother.

'I... I'm okay.' She sighed.

'Are you sure?'

'Yes... No... I don't know.'

'Okay, well tell me to mind my own business if you like but you haven't been right since that text landed on your phone this afternoon. It obviously upset you and now, I'm worried,' he professed thoughtfully as the sound of a sigh emerged from his throat. 'Did I do something to upset you?'

Kate laughed. 'God, no. Sorry. It isn't you. Far from it.' She paused as she tried to decide whether to tell him all about Rob and her mother or not. 'Look, earlier, my so-called boyfriend, was acting like a dick and I can cope with that because he's always a dick. But it's more than obvious that my family hate him and for some reason only known to herself, my mother's turned up, unannounced and by the look of the suitcase, she's practically moved in.' An involuntary sob left her throat.

'And I take it that isn't a good thing?' Ben asked.

'I think she blames me for my brother's death,' Kate continued. 'And, to be honest, if I were her, I'd blame me too.' She paused and took a deep breath. 'The thought of her staying, well, it's unbearable.'

The sound of a door banging closed vibrated through her

handset and Kate pressed her trembling lips tightly together and did all she could to compose herself before speaking again. 'Look, I'm sorry, you don't need this. I'm gonna go and well... maybe I should probably phone my father. If I beg, he might just come and get her.' She pulled her long auburn hair over her shoulder, deliberately twisted it around in her fingers.

'Do you think he will?'

'Oh, I don't know.' She sighed. 'I'm sorry, you don't need to hear all of this, do you? I shouldn't have said anything.' She held back the tears, but failed miserably.

'Kate, where are you?'

'I'm just up the road from home but I'm fine.'

'Well, you don't sound fine. Just say the word and I'll come and get you?' Looking down at the phone's screen, she heard his engine start, his phone switch to hands free and with every ounce of energy she had left in her body she allowed her gaze to move upwards and towards the sky. The clouds were swirling around above her, all grey and moody and even though she wasn't too far away, the thought of Ben turning up and just taking care of her for just a few minutes was more than appealing but instead, she shook her head. She felt angry with herself for being so weak. 'No, Ben. Don't.' She held onto a lamp post, closed her eyes and imagined those deep, dark eyes, the way they sparkled when they caught the light and the way his mouth turned up at one corner. Especially when he looked in her direction. 'Look, seriously. I'm just moaning and I'm fine. But... thank you.'

* * *

After arriving back at River Cottage, Kate hid in the front room, sat herself down next to the ornate fireplace and with the phone in her hand, she whispered to her sister.

'Eve, she's practically moved in. Says she's going to stay here until she sorts things out with Dad, which, of course, could take forever. He's away on business, which means that it could be a week before he even realises that she isn't home. Oh, and get this, apparently we're all going out for dinner. She's in the spare room, with the hairdryer on, so I suspect that food could happen at any point between seven and nine. If you want to get ready, I'll phone you back when we leave.' Kate had to think on her feet. 'Oh, and Eve, help me out. You were right, things between me and Rob are fractious. But she'd have a field day if she found out and...' Kate opened the kitchen door and listened to make sure the hairdryer was still on. 'It would really help me out if she could stay with you?'

Eve began to giggle. 'I have a better idea. Why don't you come and stay with me. You could leave Mother with Rob in the house together. They hate each other so much it'd only be a matter of time before they killed each other and saved us all a huge problem.'

It was true. Her mother and Rob did hate each other and with a smirk, Kate wondered which of the two would draw the first blood and actually considered the idea of staying at Eve's. They could watch DVDs, eat chocolate and drink a bottle of their favourite wine between them. It was something they often did. But, now, with their mother here to stay, these nights would have to come to a halt until she went home.

'You will come out for dinner, Eve, won't you?' Kate asked, still wishing that their mother hadn't arrived and that right now, she was sinking into a bath and ignoring the world. 'Please. I simply can't stand the thought of a night alone with her. What would we talk about?'

'Okay, I'll come, but under one condition,' she added quickly. 'Don't you dare even suggest that she comes to stay here. Besides, there wouldn't be much point, she's already moved into your spare room and it'd be silly to move her out now, wouldn't it?'

Kate sighed. 'Fine, she can stay. But if she's still here at the weekend, Eve, I'm telling you now, she's coming to yours.'

9

Placing the phone back down in the cradle, Eve pulled herself out of her wheelchair and with the aid of the worktop that she used for support, she marvelled at the secret she kept. With her eyes on her toes, she stared disbelievingly at the movement so many had said would be close to impossible.

With one eye on the clock, she guessed that she had at least an hour before Kate would arrive and their mother would trounce in and the circus would begin. Which meant that she still had just about enough time and in her haste, she forced her feet to move just one inch at a time, until she stood before the bowl of bread mixture that she'd left rising for the past couple of hours.

Removing the cling film, she punched down the dough. Then she turned it out onto the worktop, and began to knead it with force taking great pleasure in the full body work out that kneading gave her. The aches and pains of sitting all day were replaced with something different and with an irritated look at the wheelchair, she prayed for the day when maybe she could throw it away for good.

Pummelling the dough even harder, Eve felt her legs suddenly give way. She grabbed at the worktop, felt her fingertips miss and breathed in deeply as she dropped to the floor. An act on its own that would have once left her traumatised, but now it was the dough slipping from the side that made her scream.

Alerted by Eve's squeal, Max rushed into the kitchen and stopped, waiting for his command. But when Eve simply began to laugh, he bounced around like a tiny pup and looked completely undecided as to what he'd jump on first – her or the dough. It was a tough decision. Eve being sat on the floor normally meant work. But today was different and he ran to her, checked that she was okay and then rolled onto his back, and waved his feet in the air.

'Oh, Max. What would I do without you?' She tickled him and laughed as he playfully rolled from his back to his front. For a moment, Eve stopped tickling him as her thoughts drifted off, until a short, sharp bark caught her attention. 'Oh, Maxy, we don't want Mother to stay here, do we?'

In Eve's mind, her mother staying with her wasn't even up for debate. She was annoying and interfering, and the moment she found out that she could stand, she'd insist on more physiotherapy and more medical interventions. Neither of which Eve wanted. This time, she was determined to do things her way, at her own speed even if that meant it took her longer. She shook her head and with a final stroke of Max, she pulled herself back up and into her wheelchair, determined that she'd be able to walk unaided, before anyone found out.

Angrily, Eve thought back to how independent she'd been and cursed inwardly that she'd been the one to end up in a chair. She hated the way people looked down at her, pitied her and spoke over her, as though by being in a chair she was less capable or intelligent than anyone else. And even though it had been the accident that had put her where she was now, she resented the chair and all that went with it.

So why, when the sensations had returned in her feet, had she hidden it from everyone? Deep down she knew that Kate would be more than delighted: so why had she felt the need to keep this a secret from her twin sister?

10

Kate and Eve sat in one corner of the Fox and Hounds pub, which was crowded and busy.

'I tried to make some bread earlier.' Eve admitted. 'I dropped it on the floor and only just managed to wrestle it into the bin before Max ate it.' She laughed and gave her mother a sidewards glance. Since arriving at the pub, her mother had been chatting to an older lady who'd sat herself down at the table right next to theirs.

'I'm a member of the WI too,' their mother had said, 'Last week we did a fabulous gift-wrapping course. The lady, Joanne, from More Pretty Things was from Sheffield; she'd travelled all the way to York just to give us a lesson.'

'Oh, I love learning new things.' The elderly woman replied. 'But I bet you're too busy to do things, you know... with your daughter like that?' She lifted her eyebrows and stared at Eve. 'Poor thing. Must be hard on you, having to look after her all the time.'

It was a statement that infuriated Eve and for a few minutes she waited for their mother to correct her, for her to say how wonderfully her daughter managed on her own and was totally independent. But of course, she didn't. Instead, she nodded and took the sympathy that the older woman offered.

'As I was saying earlier,' Eve growled the words, tried to ignore what their mother was saying. 'Zoe came over and walked Max earlier. He came back from the quarry smelling of the fox poo that he'd managed to roll in and he ended up with an impromptu hosing down in the back garden.' She spoke as loudly as she could, felt determined to prove to the woman that she wasn't incapable.

'Don't rise to it...' Kate whispered, and patted a hand against Eve's knee. 'She isn't worth the effort.'

'What's she really doing here, Kate?' Eve asked under her breath. 'Do you think she's fallen out with Dad again? I mean, it's not like she wants to see us, is it?' She gave her mother a sideward glance, could hear the way she told the elderly woman about the accident and of how she'd unfairly lost her only son. 'She's barely spoken to either of us all evening. In fact, I'd say that the only way we could be of any interest to her would be if one of us morphed into being James.'

Kate shook her head angrily. 'I'd just be happy if she buggered off home...' Once again she tapped Eve on the leg, and Eve caught her breath as her leg gave out an involuntary movement. She felt sure that Kate had seen and felt herself swallowing hard and half closing her eyes while waiting for the questions that would inevitably come. '...I'd much rather she used your house as a hotel and not mine.' Kate concluded.

'Not a chance.' Eve chipped in and felt the relief pass through her. 'And you know she only goes to yours because the house used to belong to her mother,' Eve smirked. 'She's probably highly pissed off that Grandma left everything to us, rather than to her.'

Laughing, Kate picked up her drink and took a sip. 'And, she probably feels as though she's still got a right to be there. I just wish she wouldn't fall out with Dad quite so often.' 'Kate. Don't look right now, but...' Eve wheeled her chair a few inches backward. 'There's a man. He's sat at the bar over there.' She lifted a hand, and used the smallest of finger gestures to point to the area directly behind where Kate sat. 'He's wearing jeans and dark rimmed glasses. He's waved at me a few times and I'm suspecting he's someone that knows you, rather than me.' She moved from side to side, lifted her eyebrows with interest. 'I'd say it's a case of mistaken identity and unless that's your new, tidy Ben, I really need to know who he is, because I'd say he's really cute.'

Kate laughed as her eyes searched the crowd. 'Eve, there is no "my new, tidy Ben"! But you have a deal, whoever he is. I'll introduce you.'

Impatiently, Eve fidgeted in her seat. Being identical twins, they were used to people waving at them and mistaking them for the other. It was a reaction they encountered on a regular basis, and before the accident they'd simply waved back rather than explain. But now, with the wheelchair, doing that was no longer possible and Eve felt her heart sink as she realised that unless she found a way to walk, unaided, she'd never again be the other half of an identical twin again.

Watching as the man glanced over his shoulder, Kate caught his eye and smiled as a look of confusion crossed his face. His eyes quickly went from her to Eve. Something that never got old and made them both laugh with amusement.

'Oh right, I know who it is.' Kate said, 'He works at Parker & Son. We met in the corridor yesterday. I couldn't work out where Ben had gone, and Mr Parker was waiting and...' she tried to think. 'Nope, I have no idea of his name.'

'Hi there.' Kate hurriedly pushed her plate to one side and stood up to greet him as he tentatively walked towards her. 'I'm so sorry,' she said. 'Yesterday, I didn't catch your name.' She turned, held a hand out in her sister's direction. 'I'm Kate, and this, this is my twin sister, Eve.'

The man pushed his glasses up his nose. 'Wow. You're so...'

'Yeah, identical... right?' Eve smiled, patted the chair beside her. 'Please...'

'Eric...'

'Right. Well, please Eric. Why don't you sit down and join us.'

11

Kate munched on her second packet of crisps as she'd walked from the car park and into the library. She was determined that she didn't need to go on a diet, not at her age, no matter what her mother kept saying. Although, the night before she'd hinted constantly at how many calories were in a plate of fish and chips, not to mention the sticky toffee pudding both she and Eve had eaten for their desert.

Their mother had continued her conversation with the woman on the next table and Eve and Eric had chatted non-stop. Kate had felt like nothing more than a spare part and in the end, she'd excused herself and left them all too it. Which had meant that their mother had had to drive Eve home and with every morsel of her soul, she hoped their mother might drop in for a nightcap at Eve's, drink one too many and stay for the night.

The fast escape had given Kate the chance to get back to the cottage before her mother. It had been quiet, peaceful and free of Rob, too. The cottage had been the one place in the world where she used to feel happy and surrounded by memories. The good times she'd shared there with her grandmother had seeped out of every brick and with a heavy heart she knew that her sanctuary had been spoiled; that while ever Rob stayed there, it would never be the same. A thought that had disturbed Kate's thoughts as she'd sank into her bed for a torrid and restless sleep.

And now, Kate was back in the library that was full of children that ran up and down the aisles, pulling books off the shelves and discarding them on each of the low tables or scattering them all over the floor. Bellandini, to his credit, smiled and picked them up, and without saying a word, he put each of the books back in their correct position.

Annoyingly, Kate looked down at the blank page on her notebook. She hadn't seen or heard anything of interest and frustrated with the lack of action, she dug around in her bag, pulled out her mobile and immediately noticed the twelve missed calls that had come from her mother. Purposely, she placed the phone on the table, face down and only curiosity made her turn it back over to see the screen light up and flash repeatedly. She wondered how long she'd get away with ignoring her mother and only when the phone rang for what would have been the fifteenth time, did she leave her bags where she could see them, and walk into the foyer to answer the call.

'Finally, Katie.' Her mother sighed. 'I've been trying to get hold of you all morning. It was quite rude of you to leave me to watch your sister's love life unfolding last night, and by the time I got back to the cottage, you'd gone to bed.' Her mother paused but didn't slow down long enough for Kate to answer, give explanation or apologise. 'Anyway. I need to know where your mousetraps are?' she demanded. 'I've found a dropping under the kitchen cupboard.'

Kate held the phone away from her ear and stared at the handset in disbelief.

'Mother, what the hell are you doing under my bloody kitchen units?' she snapped with annoyance as it occurred to her that not only had her mother had to remove the kick boards to look under them, but would have also needed a screwdriver to complete the job.

'Darling, I'm just cleaning and it's a good job I am. One dropping could lead to an infestation. There's no wonder Robert stays out most evenings, especially if you don't clean the house properly. Now, where are those mousetraps?'

'Mother!' Katie snapped. 'For goodness' sake. Why don't you go and annoy Eve for a few days?' Kate felt like a petulant child and angrily she closed the phone down. The last thing she wanted was to argue with her mother and she certainly didn't need to be accused of not cleaning her house.

Walking back into the library, Kate sat down heavily in her chair. Her shoulders slumped and it now occurred to her why she'd left Yorkshire in the first place. Why she'd happily moved her life to London and joined the Met and had only come back because of her love for her grandmother. If she hadn't taken ill and hadn't needed looking after, Kate knew that she'd probably still be in London. Her life would have been different, and the accident might never have happened.

Closing her eyes, she wondered if she should phone her father. She'd resisted calling the night before in the hope that their mother would see sense and that by now she'd be on her way home. With an air of resignation, Kate sat back in her chair, turned her phone over and over in her hand and tried to decide what to do.

But then as she glanced around the library, she saw a different librarian sat behind the desk and realised that Bellandini was no longer there.

12

Ben knelt by the gravestone, carefully emptied the stale water from the flowerpot and walked the short distance to where the water tap hung from a pipe. Using a cloth, he cleaned the pot, filled it with fresh water and then carried it back to the grave where his wife and unborn child both lay.

Ben wiped his eyes and pulled a bunch of extravagant flowers from a large bag. 'Oh, Julia, I still miss you,' he said, and paused. 'I miss chatting to you about everything, and nothing and I miss the way we'd laugh at the ridiculous things life threw at us.' He paused and flicked at the cellophane that surrounded the flowers. 'I miss the silly things, like arguing about the right way to pronounce scone or bath. You had your typically southern way, and me, the northern. We would argue so much, we laughed till we cried.'

He thought of his wife. She'd always wanted the best for them both, and had created a beautiful home, a life and a child. Yet, in one day, the meningitis had overtaken her body and in a matter of hours, she was gone. Taken from him. Along with the child he'd never have the privilege to hold.

He glanced up at the sky; the clouds had formed and with his eyes closed he sat down and his mind drifted to Kate. He thought of how much he enjoyed the time he'd spent with her. But felt guilty each time he attempted to laugh or be happy.

'Hey, you'd think I'd get better at this. Wouldn't you?' He turned back to the grave, fiddled with the flowers. Slowly, he placed them in the pot, one by one. 'But I don't. I doubt I ever will.' He stumbled over his words. 'You see, I never know what I'm supposed to say. Except that I miss you. But that's just more than obvious.' He searched through the carrier bag looking for scissors. 'And you'd kind of think I'd get better at remembering the stuff, wouldn't you?' He began to snap the stems, then lifted a single flower up to his face. 'And do you know what's worse. I miss your nagging. I miss you telling me to get my shit in order and yeah, yeah, I miss you telling me what to do. How to do it and when to do it.'

After he'd finished putting the flowers in the vase, Ben stood up. He pulled a tissue from his pocket, wiped his eyes and blew his nose. 'That was the last thing I said to you wasn't it: "stop nagging me, I'll do it."' A tear dropped down his cheek. 'Jesus Christ, Julia, I wish you were here. I'd love to hear you nagging me now and I hate how torn I feel every time something happens and you're not there for me to tell you about it.' Ben momentarily walked away from the grave and threw the cellophane and the carrier bag in the bin.

'But that's the question, isn't it? How do I feel?' He walked back to place a hand on top of the marble. 'It's what everyone asks, and do you know what, I have no idea how I should answer.' He paused. 'What I want to say is that I'm suffocating inside, and sometimes there are days when I can't breathe at all. I feel as though someone placed a vice on my heart and every so often, they squeeze it just a little bit more. That's what I should say. But, of course, I don't. What I say is that I'm fine. That I'm doing okay. Which I'm not. But telling the truth about how we feel isn't the

British thing to do, is it?' Ben looked up, and then took in a shallow, stilted breath.

He glanced around the graveyard, at the other people, crouched by headstones. It was so peaceful, yet so unbelievably disturbing, all at once. Was this it? Was this all there was in the end?

'Julia. I feel bad. But I need for someone to be there for me, for someone to boss me around.' He paused and placed a hand on the stone. 'And if I'm totally honest, for a long time now, I've missed being loved and giving love in return,' he whispered through painful, gritted teeth. It was as though he was fearful of saying the words out loud and he looked over his shoulder, in the hope that no one was listening. 'I know you can't give it. But I guess I'm asking for your approval.' He gulped and lifted his fingers to his lips, kissed them tenderly before placing the fingers on top of the stone. 'Please don't hate me for wanting to be happy. I loved you so very much.'

13

'I've lost him,' Kate frantically balanced the phone between her shoulder and her ear as she ran down the steps of the library and onto the street. 'I feel so damned stupid. One minute he was there. The next he'd gone.'

'Okay, let's think,' Ben said in a calm, unruffled manner. 'Could he still be somewhere in the building.'

Kate cast her mind backwards to when the call with her mother had ended. She'd been furious that her mother was in her house, digging around under the kitchen units and had stamped back into the library and scooped all of her possessions into a bag that had been yanked up from the floor and dropped on the table. The commotion had attracted the attention of at least ten pairs of eyes, all of which had turned around and impaled her with their hard, indignant stares.

'Shhhh...' The noise had come from a young woman who had been sat at the closest table to her. Her exaggerated finger had been held up in annoyance and lifted angrily to her proffered lips. 'You're in a library,' she'd snapped in a voice so loud that even more people had turned and glared.

'Yes. Yes... I'm so sorry.' With a nervous smile, Kate remembered pointing to the door. 'I'm just going to... you know... go.' As she'd said the words, she'd tipped her head to one side, quickly searched the area where Bellandini normally sat.

Kate shook her head as though Ben could see her. 'Not a chance. There was a woman, she was sat in the seat he normally occupied and I overheard her telling someone behind the counter that he'd gone.'

Pacing back and forth outside the library, Kate mentally kicked herself for taking the call. It was something she shouldn't have done, not while she was working. Although, since the accident she'd found it more than difficult to ignore a call. Especially when she'd had first had experience of how fragile life could be and how quickly things could change.

Looking back into the building, Kate heard a ping. Saw the doors of a lift, open and close. 'Oh my God. There's a lift....'

'Look, let's move on,' Ben said firmly. 'I've been going through his social media accounts. He isn't too communicative, however he does post once or twice a week. And get this... at least three times in the last month he's placed a similar post. Always on a Tuesday, always at the same time of day, which hopefully gives us a clue as to where he might be.'

'Go on.' Kate anxiously swapped hands with the phone and moved away from the street and into the doorway of a boarded-up shop. It was still early afternoon and the town was quieter than she'd have expected.

'I'm going to send you the pictures.' Ben finally said. 'They're all similar and they might just give you a clue as to where he goes and if I'm right, it's not too far.'

Staring at her phone, Kate eagerly waited for the pictures to drop in. 'Right, they're here,' she announced as she flicked from one picture to the other. Each picture was abstract, just one side of a large, brightly coloured coffee mug. A plate covered in Italian meats and brightly coloured fruits, all of which had been perfectly placed. There was a white bookcase, crowded with books and ornaments. Then a wider shot of it stood next to a navy-blue tub chair. 'Jack, this is the coffee shop that's...' She stood on her tip toes. 'It's a bit further up the road, opposite the pub.' Kate announced, 'I've been with Eve, it's lovely.' She paused as she left the relative privacy of the shop doorway. 'Ben, I'm on my way. I'll call you back.'

Wearing heels that would have been better suited to a night around town, it took Kate around twenty minutes to reach the coffee shop and just as Ben had suggested, Luca Bellandini was sat outside, staring into his coffee mug while skimming through his mobile phone and taking photographs of the stacked sandwich that had just been placed before him.

Kate crossed the road and without attracting any attention, she headed into the bar that stood opposite. It was traditional, with a part of the floor covered in a grey, plaid carpet. The other half of the bar had a solid oak floor. A pool table with the balls still scattered across its surface stood as though the game were waiting to be played. The walls were panelled half way up and in the window that overlooked the coffee shop was a small mahogany table, with four dark brown, buttoned leather stools standing around it.

'Now then Bellandini, show me what you're up to?' She perched on one of the stools and peered inquisitively across the road. The sight of Bellandini tucking hungrily into his sandwich made her stomach rumble. It had been hours since she'd sneaked out of the house to avoid her mother, once again without eating breakfast.

'What can I get you?' The voice made Kate jump. She almost fell off the stool and quickly spun on the spot to where a male bartender hovered beside her. He had a small, white cloth loosely held in one hand, which he dropped onto the table. Smiling, he quickly lifted the condiments, and the small white pot that held an array of plastic flowers, before wiping its surface.

'Oh, erm... maybe just a diet coke. No lemon,' Kate said as her eyes glanced across the room and hovered over the specials board. Deciding against the much-needed food, she threw her attention back to the window, tipped her head to one side and felt the adrenaline hit her square between the eyes as a tall, slender woman approached the table where Luca sat. She was wearing a white trouser suit and a striking pair of bright red, heeled shoes and without thinking, Kate lifted her phone and took a photograph, quickly enlarging the image to take a better look.

'Isobel Reed...' she whispered to herself with a smile. She'd instantly recognised the woman and gave her a curious look. 'What on earth are you doing here in Bedale, with Luca Bellandini.' She watched the interaction, the way she offered him a cheek, turned her face away as he kissed her.

'Your drink.' The bartender walked up to her side. Her glass of coke balanced on a tray. 'Will you be dining with us today?' he asked hopefully.

Turning, Kate saw the way he waved a menu around in the air and with a look over her shoulder at the coffee shop, knew that her earlier indiscretion needed making up for and with a sigh, she shook her head. 'No... thank you,' Kate replied. 'Just the drink. If... if that's okay?' She hesitated as she spoke, wanted nothing more than to order a sandwich and to dig into it, just as Bellandini had done.

'Of course it's okay.' He tucked the menu under his arm and pointed to the window. 'They sit there every Tuesday. Same time every week.' The bartender said, 'Unless it's raining of course and then I don't see them... because, well I'm guessing they sit inside.'

It was a comment that made Kate blush. She'd been naïve to

think she could sit and take photographs without drawing any attention to herself. She closed her eyes and quickly went over her options. 'The lady,' she said. 'She has the most beautiful suit on and...' She picked up the drink, took a sip and stalled for time. 'My sister's getting married,' she lied, 'I was admiring it and I'd love to get something similar.'

'Oh, well with that, I can't help you.' He ran a finger up and down his own attire. 'Don't have a clue where women shop. Only men.' He shook his head. 'The only thing that is obvious, is that the suit is expensive. No one wears a cheap suit with a pair of Louboutin shoes, now do they?'

Kate looked back at where Isobel sat with her sunglasses on, her hair perfectly coifed, and her legs stretched out in front of her. The tell-tale bright red soles of her shoes pointed directly at her. Once again, it was a reminder of how much she had to learn, and in an attempt to reconcile her earlier mistake, she lifted her phone and messaged Ben.

I've found Bellandini. He's in the coffee shop, just as you thought. And he's with a woman. Kate x

Automatically, Kate pressed send before rereading the message. Then, through horrified eyes she noticed the kiss she'd dropped in at the end. It was an automatic gesture she'd used on messages for years but now kicked herself for the informal indiscretion. Now, with one eye on the phone and the other on Luca Bellandini, her mind went into overdrive. She nervously bit down on her lip and wondered what Ben would think.

Ps: I recognise her. She's Isobel Reed. She was all over the news after her husband was shot on his doorstep.

This time, she omitted the kiss. Breathed a sigh of relief and with her phone's camera pointing directly at the table where Luca and Isobel sat, she watched, waited and clicked away as Isobel reached into her bag, and pulled out a small package which she discreetly dropped into an open shopping bag that stood beside Bellandini's feet.

Can you speak? x

Reading the message. Kate smiled at the gesture. Ben had obviously realised her embarrassing mistake and to make her feel better, he too had dropped a kiss on the end of his text.

'Hey,' she whispered.

'Hey, to you to,' Ben replied.

'You do know who Isobel Reed is, don't you?' She pressed her lips tightly together and watched Luca Bellandini, who gazed lovingly into the woman's eyes. He was obviously smitten with her perfect face and although she didn't seem to share his mutual desire, he didn't look away. Not for a moment. 'She's the widow of that drug dealer. The one that was shot on his own doorstep, in broad daylight, around two years ago,' Kate explained, 'and get this, I've just watched her passing something to Bellandini. It really wouldn't take a genius to guess what it might be...'

14

'Okay, so we have our next person of interest.' Ben said the moment Kate walked back through the front door of Parker and Son. It had only been around twenty minutes since they'd spoken on the phone but enough time for her to grab a sandwich from next door, along with a small box of bright pink donuts, which she dropped on the table beside Gloria.

'To share,' she whispered, as she dropped her coat off her shoulders, sat down on the settee and took the picture from Ben's hand, that he hurriedly passed to her.

'Here you go,' he said with a smile. 'Good work this morning, really good.' He paused, and passed a set of the photographs to Gloria. 'Now, as you well know, our person of interest is Isobel Reed and if Kate's photographs are anything to go by. She's taken over her husband's company.'

Kate looked up from the pictures and caught Ben's eye. 'Why would she do that?' She shook her head thoughtfully. 'She has more money than most of us could dream about, which tells me that once again there's someone above her. Someone else is pressing the buttons and running the show.' Holding Ben's gaze, she thought back to the previous night's phone call, the way she'd wanted to hear his voice, and the gentlemanly way he'd responded.

He continued. 'Every law enforcement agency in the country has tried to catch her. Ever since her husband was shot she's become quite a target, so much so that there's a million pound reward for bringing her to justice. And thanks to you, Kate, we may just have found a way to earn it.'

'That's a lot of money,' Kate said, as she stood up and fanned her face with a hand. She'd always lived in a rich household. One where money had never been an issue, and although he'd never admit to it, she suspected that after her father had hit the millionaire status – though by the way their mother acted, it wasn't apparent.

'As far as we know, she's dealing. And with what you saw at the coffee shop, Bellandini is either taking the drugs or dealing them. Which explains why his boss has become suspicious. And as far as Isobel is concerned, she's not the kind of dealer that would stand on a street corner selling her goods.' Ben shook his finger in the air and then pointed upward. 'Although here she is, sitting on a street corner passing over something that looks suspicious.' He paused, tapped the picture. 'Word has it that she's right at the top of the food chain, which means she's the one that's importing the drugs.' Ben caught Kate's eye, held the look that passed between them before blinking and looking away.

'So how does she get the drugs into the country?' Kate chewed on the last of her donut, then watched as Gloria poured the coffee and handed each of them a mug. 'Or more to the point, who brings them in for her?'

Ben laughed. 'Well, if we knew that, we wouldn't have any reason to stake out her house for the next few days, would we?'

'A stake out, that's great.' Kate responded eagerly, feeling pleased that she wouldn't spend another day sat in the library and with an excited smile, she sipped at her coffee.

'Yep. We sit. We watch. We do nothing. Not unless we have some evidence. Once we get the evidence, we pass the information onto the police. At that point, we register our claim on the reward.'

'So, we're bounty hunters?' she asked with a sense of disappointment. She'd worked on drug raids before. Had loved the adrenalin rush and the way that each of the officers knew exactly where the other would be, at any given time, keeping each other safe.

'Something like that,' Gloria whispered.

Ben nodded. 'We have no power to arrest them, Kate.' He raised his eyebrows as though looking for her approval. 'We find the clues, but we can't intervene.'

Ben sipped at his coffee. 'So tomorrow, once again you'll be out on surveillance. We'll be watching her house from a vehicle but I can't promise that it'll be me that's with you. I have things to do tomorrow, so I'm sending you out with Don and Patrick. Both are good. Both are very experienced.'

'Thank you,' Kate said with a nod, and although she felt disappointed that she wouldn't be working with Ben for the day, she gratefully leaned forward to take a thick blue file from his hand.

'You'll need to do some research,' Ben said as he looked away and closed his eyes and sighed. His brow became instantly furrowed. His face tormented. 'I had her followed this time last year,' he opened his eyes and continued, 'but we couldn't prove anything. She appears to be a serial adulteress, as well as a drug dealer. I think the two have gone hand in hand for years and it was quite apparent that the Louboutin shoes are not being bought out of her widow's pension. But other than that, we found nothing.'

'Becoming a widow so young is probably an occupational hazard,' she said thoughtfully. 'Did they ever find out who shot him?' As she spoke, she passed a picture of Isobel's deceased husband back to Ben, accidentally brushed her hand against his leg, and felt an electric shock cut through her. Every part of her arm tingled and didn't stop until it reached her fingers.

'It was a deal that probably went wrong. Nothing was ever proved, the killer never caught.' Ben got up and began to dig in a filing cabinet. 'I have a file on his death in here somewhere.'

Kate stood up, peered over his shoulder and into the filing cabinet where all the files looked neat, tidy and in a carefully organised order. 'Why were they dealing from the house?' Taking the work home was something that most the dealers avoided. 'It would make it far too easy to watch and catch them, wouldn't it?' She pondered over the thought, took the file from Ben's hand. 'Unless of course, the dealers were family.'

15

After just two hours of going through the files, Kate had worked furiously to set up an evidence board. She'd pinned as much information as she had to it, along with pictures that she'd either downloaded or printed from the internet. By the time she'd finished, she knew exactly where Isobel's hairdresser was, along with her immediate friends that had all been found on her social media channels, and not to mention her beautician and gynaecologist. She'd studied MCAT and had found out about the numerous names they now used for certain drugs: mephedrone and meow meow. She wrote the names on the board, and underlined them twice before adding pictures beside each of them, to show exactly what they looked like.

Standing back, she felt her energy deplete. 'You do know it's up to you to get this scum off of the streets, don't you?' she barked and shook her head. Had absolutely no idea how she would do that and felt thankful that Ben was sending her out with experienced agents. With a quick glance at the two empty desks, she wondered what her colleagues would be like, whether or not they'd like her but then she shrugged her shoulders, knew she wasn't there to be liked. What she was here for was to stop the dealers selling drugs to teenagers under the guise of them being a 'legal high'. The side effects were dangerous; the drug – highly addictive; the kids – much too young to know what they were doing.

There was a knock at the door and Gloria walked in, coffee in one hand, sandwich in the other. 'Here, I thought you'd need this,' she said with a smile. 'You haven't moved since you got back.' She looked up at the evidence board that Kate had created and gave a look of approval at the perfectly positioned photographs that had all been laminated, along with the typed sheets of information. 'Gosh, you have been busy.' She walked to the board, studied the information.

'It's what I used to do in the force,' Kate said proudly. 'They always gave me the job of organising the evidence board, knowing that my OCD would ensure that it would always be neat and tidy.'

Gloria tapped at one of the pictures. 'Is this what they're selling?' The photograph showed two types of drug, one was a small coloured tablet, the other an ampule of fluid with a syringe by its side.

Kate nodded. 'It is. They sell it in two forms. Dependant on who the buyer is. It can cause fits, hallucinations and panic attacks,' she said, as Gloria pulled out a chair and sat down. 'Ketamine can actually stop you from breathing.'

'Where do they get the money, that's what I would like to know?' Gloria stood back up, sauntered across the room and came to a stop beside where Kate sat at the computer.

'They're selling the tablet form really cheap,' Kate said, 'for just a few quid each. Most kids have access to that sort of money these days.' Kate pointed to the screen.

'It says that they're closely related to amphetamines,' Gloria said, as she read the screen over Kate's shoulder. 'Similar to drugs such as speed and ecstasy,' Gloria tutted, 'it's renowned for being a dirty drug, and can be mixed with just about anything.' She shook her head emphatically. 'I'd heard that before. But would have no idea what they'd mix it with?'

Moving her chair to one side, she looked up at where Gloria stood. 'It's normally mixed with soap powder or rat poison. We had a time in the Met, when the kids that lived around the city were dropping like flies. A few of them died.'

'One unnecessary death is one too many, which is why we have to put a stop to what they're doing and fast.' Ben snapped as he re-entered the office. 'People have no idea how death affects others. Especially when it's unnecessary and could have been avoided.' The words came out with emotion and sounded just a little too personal and Kate looked down at the floor, wondered who Ben had lost. She looked towards Gloria, hoping for answers.

'Right,' he said, as he dropped a small box on the desk. 'Van keys are in here. There are three sets and three vans. They're all kept out the back.' He lifted a hand and pointed through the window. 'We need to be inconspicuous.' Ben continued. 'We have various vans, in various sizes and with various signs. All are magnetic and fix to the side. One day the van could be dressed up as a plumber's van with ladders and plastic piping on the roof. Another day it could be TV licensing with an ariel and another it could be double glazing or window cleaning. We park in different places daily and the surveillance team stay in the back. The driver takes you to the site and then gets out of the cab and walks away. It gives the appearance that they've left for the day and hopefully no one would guess that there are agents in the back.'

'I saw this happen in the Met, but I wasn't on the team that went out with the vans. We were the legs on the street, so to speak.' She paused. 'But just a thought. If they are working vans, wouldn't they be parked on people's drives?'

'Not necessarily,' Ben replied. 'Lots of workmen park on roads so as not to block drives. Sometimes, they even park and get into other vans, especially if they're going into town to work. Saves them paying double for parking.'

'And what about toilet breaks, or is there one of those in the back too.' Kate was joking but the look on Ben's face answered her question and with her mind racing she had the urge to run down to the yard and check the cleanliness of all the toilets.

16

Looking at her watch, Kate realised how late in the day it was and felt herself yawn. She'd been sat in the back of the van with Ben for the past two hours, curiously examining one piece of equipment after the other.

The length of the van was filled with computers and screens to one side. At the other side stood two chairs and to one corner was a curtain that pulled around a ceiling mounted rail, surrounding a toilet that, in Kate's opinion, stood far too close to the transmitters which sent signals out and the receivers that brought the signals back in.

'I take it that these make recordings?' she questioned with a slow, thoughtful nod. 'Ones that are listened back to, later?' It was a question that didn't really need answering and with the determination of a camel, she knew that crossing her legs for as long as she remained in the van, was preferable to using the toilet.

Jumping out of the back and into the yard, Kate kept her eyes on the dry wipe board that was attached to the back door of the van. Ben had artistically drawn a map on it. 'These are the areas where you'll be parked. Either here, or here.' He drew a street, the houses that stood along it and three crosses to show the positions where he wanted them to park. 'I'll get Patrick to position the van carefully. No one gets in unless you know them and if you need to get out, you need to use common sense, wear a high-vis jacket, a hard hat, gloves and boots. Use the props to help you.' He looked her up and down thoughtfully. 'As I said before, you'll be working with both Don and Patrick. They're good guys, and very experienced. If you need anything, you ask them. Is that understood?'

'Understood.' She'd initially felt disappointed that she wouldn't be working with Ben, but knew that something was on his mind, and watched the way he gazed across the yard with eyes that were fixed and hands that were twisting in and out of tight, angry fists. 'Ben.' She rested a hand against his shoulder. 'Are you okay?'

Shaking his head apologetically, Ben sighed, turned and smiled. 'I'm sorry. But yes, I'm fine.' He looked down and away. 'Just thinking that it's probably a good thing that Joe Public doesn't have a clue what we're up to or what technology we really have.'

Kate rolled her eyes skyward. 'We really are spies, aren't we?'

Ben locked the van. 'Of course we are, this is what gaining intelligence means. This is what we do, albeit as my father said, it's important that we always stay within the law.' He rested a hand on her shoulder, looked her directly in the eye. 'And this.' He stopped and handed her a mobile phone and charger, 'it looks like a normal phone. Keep it charged and keep it with you.'

'What do you mean by looks like?' Kate turned the phone over and over in her hand.

'Have a play with it sometime. It has some interesting apps and features. Most importantly, it has an emergency code which Gloria will give you and if you ever need assistance fast, key it in. It has a tracking device built in and we'd find you really quickly. All our operatives have one. Now, go on. Get yourself off home.' He stopped, gave her a long, genuine smile, 'Tomorrow is going to be a long day. Be here for seven. That way you'll have the van parked before anyone else is around.' He rocked backwards and forwards. 'And Kate, be careful,' he finally said.

17

Walking to the front of the building, where her trusty yellow Beetle was parked, Kate climbed in and looked at her watch. It was just after five and she knew that she'd have to go home and face her mother, who after the earlier call about the mouse dropping, would be waiting, and ready to pounce.

Unless of course, she'd deemed her house unfit to live in and had done just as Kate had suggested and climbed in her car and gone to Eve's or maybe, just maybe, she'd gone back to York, where she belonged.

'Kate?' Ben's voice caught her attention, just as she was about to drive off.

'Yes,' she carefully lowered her window and looked up at him. He looked tired and washed out. His crisp white shirt was undone at the collar, his tie had long since been abandoned and his hands dug deep down in his trouser pockets. The day had obviously taken its toll.

'I... I owe you an apology,' he blurted out, but then looked down at the floor. His face full of pain and emotion. Taking in a deep breath, Kate wondered what she should do. It was more than obvious that he was hurting, but she didn't know why, all she did know was that if he was one of her girlfriends, she'd be offering them a hug right now. But Ben was not a girl or even close to being a friend, he was her boss, her colleague. There was a difference and deep inside, she had no idea how to handle a situation like this.

'What are you apologising for?' She smiled, turned off the engine and climbed out of the car.

'Earlier. I snapped at you,' he said, 'I shouldn't have done that.' Leaning forward, he placed both hands on the bonnet of the car, looked as though he were doing all he could to hold it still. 'It's hard to explain,' he whispered. 'You see, I lost my wife... she died.' Again, he paused. 'It was four years ago... four years ago today actually... meningitis.' He looked down at the floor and studied his shoes. 'She was pregnant... I lost them both.'

Kate's mind exploded. She'd known something was wrong; known that something had been on his mind, and it had occurred to her that Ben must have lost someone. What she hadn't known was how huge and life changing it had been.

'Oh my goodness.' She felt awkward and quickly searched her mind for all the platitudes she'd been given after her brother had died, knew how useless they'd been. 'Look, do you...' she looked at the wine bar that stood next door to the office. 'Do you want to get a drink?' It had been all she could think to say and Kate found herself also looking at the floor, nervous of what his answer would be. All she did know was that she really hadn't wanted to go home and by the look of Ben, he hadn't wanted to go home either.

Looking up and into Ben's eyes. Kate saw the sparkle that looked back at her. He had eyes that were full of tears that wouldn't fall and a gentle smile that crossed his lips. The anger and frustration of earlier had gone and in its place was a tired, but peaceful expression.

'Do you know what?' he replied with a definitive nod. 'I could murder a drink. Where do you want to go?' He held out an arm and laughed.

'Well,' Kate said a moment later. 'We could drive all the way into Richmond, there are great cocktail bars there, but then, it'd be a shame not to keep the business local, wouldn't it?' She pointed to the wine bar and laughed. 'Think this place is a bit closer, don't you agree?'

Ben laughed and they walked inside together.

18

Heading into Vino's, Kate immediately noticed the décor. It was traditional in style, all oak with deep red walls and soft, golden lighting, which was all accentuated by the lively hustle and bustle that only a crowd of happy, relaxed and halfway to intoxicated people could bring.

Friends and couples sat intimately together. They chatted, laughed and shared bottles of wine. One couple opened a bottle of champagne and smiled intimately. Whereas others stood by the bar, clinking glasses that were all filled with various cocktails and without exception, they were all making the most of each other's company at the end of what had been another long, working day.

Making their way through the crowd, Kate kept her eye on where Ben went. She saw him approach a fair-haired waiter. He seemed to recognise Ben and with an understated, but respectful handshake, he led them to an area at the back of the bar to a small, private booth.

'Bottle of Rioja, if you don't mind, Graham. The nice oaky one,' Ben said with a smile and then gave Kate a look of concern. 'Actually, that's if Rioja, is okay with you?' He held a hand in the air, halted the waiter and waited for Kate to respond.

'Rioja is perfect,' she said with an appreciative smile. To her, wine was wine. She drank whatever came and she could have spent the next twenty minutes looking through the list, only to end up waving a finger around in the air and with her eyes closed, she'd point at the menu and hope for the best.

'So, Parker and Son.' Ben suddenly questioned. 'Is it what you expected?' He hovered outside the booth, held a hand out in a clear indication that she should take a seat first. After dropping her handbag down on the seat, she slid along it, rested her elbows against the table and watched as Ben proceeded to empty his pockets. His phone, keys and wallet were dropped onto the table and pushed to one side.

'Well,' Kate gave him a half-smile, and in an attempt to keep the conversation light, she bit down on her lip before speaking. 'Well... On my first day I was a little scared of the boss. But now, I'm just terrified of his son.' She gave him a wink, searched his eyes with hers, then laughed as she saw the amusement sparkle within.

'Oh, terrifying, am I?' Pausing as the waiter approached, he cheekily held a finger to his lips and waited for the wine to be poured, checked and tasted. Then, with a look of amusement crossing his face, he picked up both glasses and mischievously pulled them towards him. 'Well, in that case, I guess I'll be drinking the wine all by myself.' He looked deeply into her eyes, rolled his jaw thoughtfully. 'But then... I guess you have had a long day and, well...' he laughed. 'Hopefully, I'll get to change your opinion of me.'

'Thank you,' Kate tapped her glass against his, lifted it to her lips and took a long, and much needed drink. 'That is so good,' she whispered, 'and you're right. It's so very needed, especially tonight.' She thought of how close she'd almost come to driving away and of how her mother would be pacing around the house, waiting for her return. 'And I hope my car will be okay parked out front, because this wine.' She pressed her lips tightly together. 'It's just too good to have the one glass.'

As the evening began to draw in, the soft amber lighting created a warm and comfortable ambience. The conversation between them was effortless. The self-assured confidence that Ben had shown in the office had disappeared and he now came over as being just a little more than vulnerable, making Kate wonder what his story really was. Up to now, he'd spoken about work, cases he'd worked on and with a genuine interest, she listened to each of the stories in turn while sipping at the wine that trickled down her throat with a warmth that only came with a full-bodied red.

'So, tell me all about you?' Ben sipped at his wine, kept his eyes fixed on hers.

'There's nothing much to tell,' she responded. 'I'm just Kate. The geeky one of the family.' A blush flooded her cheeks; she'd never previously referred to herself as geeky. It had been a name that the others called her. But now she'd said it. It was probably true. She did prefer books to people. She liked the emotions a book could bring and even though some of them made her sad, the books didn't purposely hurt her, not like people and subconsciously, she thought about the accident. About the cruel comments that had been thrown at her since. Everyone had insisted how lucky she'd been. Out of the three siblings that had climbed into the car, she'd been the only one that had walked away and as though someone had slapped her in the face, she turned her face away from Ben's gaze and consciously lifted a hand to hide her scar.

'Don't let it define you,' Ben slowly lifted his hand to hers, pulled it away from her face and held it tightly. 'The scar, yes, it's there. But it doesn't make you any less of a woman.' He held her gaze. 'You're a beautiful woman, Kate. You shouldn't ever let anyone tell you differently.'

Kate pulled her hand out of his and once again she used it as a shield to hide the scar. 'I can't help it.' She scanned her handbag, knew it contained her makeup, all the tools she needed to cover the scar and even though she couldn't hide it completely, she always felt better when it had been freshly covered.

'You don't need to hide it.' He spoke gently and once again, he took hold of her hand, and pulled it away from her face. It was a simple gesture, but one that immediately turned her fingertips to fire. Pins and needles rushed through them and with short, sharp intakes of breath she stared at the table, where their conjoined hands were so perfectly linked together. She swallowed hard, looked over her shoulder and with a heat moving through her fingertips like fast-moving lava, she tried to explain.

'The accident.... It was the worst day of my life.' Once again, she pulled her hand out of his and forcefully pressed her hand between her knees. Her hand felt cold without his touch and she wished she'd left it resting in his but now she felt awkward. 'I feel guilty. The accident, it was all my fault. It was me that wanted to go into town and because of that, my brother died and Eve was left disabled.' She paused, felt her eyes glaze over with tears. 'She'll be in a wheelchair for the rest of her life.'

'Who says it was your fault?' Ben asked, angrily. He moved back in his seat, threw an arm in the air. 'No one should have ever put that on you. You didn't ask for that to happen.'

Kate sighed. 'But it doesn't make me blameless either.' She looked down at the table, composed her thoughts. 'I remember the crash, the airbags and then nothing. I think I must have passed out or somehow blocked the next few moments out but when I realised what had happened. Eve was already half way up the embankment. I must have pulled her out of the car. It's my fault she's got the injuries she has and my brother... for some reason I left him to die. What kind of a sister would do that?'

'What makes you think you did that?'

'Because there was no one else there.' Kate closed her eyes and felt her stomach turn. She could still see the darkness that had surrounded the car. The trees that had hurtled towards them. 'And my mother, the person that seems to blame me the most has turned up at my house. Just like that. Uninvited. Before the accident, I'd have been pleased, we'd have driven each other nuts but spending time together would still have been fun.' Kate rolled her eyes in the knowledge that her mother would be stomping around in the kitchen, slamming pans on and off the cooker. 'I know I should be more welcoming. More understanding. But I can't help it.' She lifted a hand to her chest. Used a fist to bang against it. 'I can't help but feel this giant knot of pressure in my chest that feels as though it's going to explode, all the time she's there.'

Shaking his head. Ben gave her a knowing smile. 'Kate, you're bound to feel resentful. No one wants to be blamed for something that was so catastrophic and your home, well that should be your safe space. The one place where you can escape from everyone else.' Once again, he picked up her hand and held it tightly. 'And what makes it worse is that none of this was your fault.' He breathed out heavily. 'It's easy for me to say. But try and put the past behind you, because there's a whole lot of future to live for, Kate, and living in the present is a whole lot better than living in the past. Trust me. I know.'

Kate raised her eyebrows. She knew that Ben was talking about his wife, about her death and about the loss of his child and for a moment she wondered what his wife had been like. Tried to picture him with a woman, but couldn't.

'One day everything was normal,' he said slowly. 'Everything. Then the next, it had all changed. It was as though my heart skipped a beat, and my whole life as I knew it had gone and there was nothing I could do to get it back.'

Kate felt her heart lurch forward. She could see the glassy texture of his eyes. The tears that wouldn't fall and knew that he was hurting, more than he'd ever really admit.

'Could I ask you a really personal question?' Ben asked.

'Of course,' Kate answered just a little too quickly. Nervously picked up her wine and took another sip.

'Kate, your boyfriend. Do you love him?'

'Wh–why would you ask me that?' Kate questioned.

Ben stared into her eyes. 'Do you?'

Kate breathed in slowly. The knot she'd described as building up in her chest was back. Swirling around and pressing against her heart and her throat. The question should have been an easy one to answer. But she couldn't. Not when she didn't know the answer herself. Rob had come into her life by chance. He'd been parked next to her at the hospital, helped her when her car wouldn't start and for the weeks that had followed, he'd pursued her relentlessly. He'd been charming, charismatic and caring. Her whole body had trembled with excitement when she'd known she was about to see him. But for some reason, he'd changed. He was a very different man to the one she'd first met, the difference demonstrable. And she had no idea why.

Shaking her head slowly from side to side, she looked up and as a single tear slipped down her face, and she saw the look of concern that crossed Ben's face.

'You're unhappy,' Ben said gently, 'and I know it's none of my business, but Kate, you deserve so much more.' He looked down at the table, thought about his words. 'I saw the look on your face, when he messaged you in the library. I could tell that he'd hurt you.'

Kate stared at their hands that were still held tightly together.

His thumb gently moved back and forth over hers in a slow rhythmic movement.

'How about you, Ben?' she carefully asked. 'Don't you deserve more?'

He nodded thoughtfully. 'It's taken me four years to try and come to terms with what happened to her, to us, to my life.' He let go of her hand and leaned back in his chair. 'Some days, I'm not sure I'll ever move forward. On others, I know that I have to.'

'Did you say it was meningitis?' she finally asked.

'It was. I'd been working away, as normal, and when I got home, she was laying on the floor, unconscious. They tried to save her. But couldn't. The sepsis had taken them both and I still can't believe that they're never coming back.'

Kate picked up the bottle of wine, refilled their glasses. She needed something to do. Something to concentrate on, that wasn't the sound of Ben's shaking voice or hands, or the deep and profound sadness that had taken over his eyes.

* * *

As she sipped the last remnants of her wine, Kate checked the time on her phone and began to panic when she saw that it was already eight o'clock. Her mother would be furious and would be waiting with a full vocabulary of insults and for a moment, Kate closed her eyes and considered the idea of not going home. However, she quickly realised that other than going to Eve's, she had nowhere else she could go.

'Look, I'm so sorry, I really have to go. I'm going to have to go and face my mother.' She rolled her eyes, 'Let's hope she got bored of waiting and if I'm really lucky she might have buggered off to Eve's, like I told her to.' She stood up abruptly, dug in her bag for her purse and quickly pulled a twenty pound note out of the back. 'For the wine.'

Ben shook his head and gently placed his hand over hers. 'No arguments, the wine is on me.' He jumped up to his feet, and beckoned the waiter. 'Actually, let me organise you a taxi.'

'No.' Kate jumped in. 'It's fine. I'm fine. Honestly. There's a taxi rank just up the road and you know, the fresh air and all that. It'll do me good.' She laughed, winked before shuffling out of the booth in a way that had taken far more of her concentration than she'd have liked and with a concerted effort, she weaved herself through the crowd, until she reached the door and stood with her hand pressed against the glass. If she opened it, she'd have to leave and with a moment's hesitation, she looked back over her shoulder to see that Ben was still standing, watching her. His eyes pierced hers. It was more than obvious that he hadn't wanted her to go, and she knew that right then, at that moment in time he needed her company so much more than her mother did. With a new, challenging negotiation of the crowd she made her way back towards him and sat back down at the table.

'I thought you had to go?' Ben asked.

'Well,' Kate replied. 'Had to. Wanted to. Semantics,' she laughed. 'I came to the conclusion that I have a choice. I could go home, and face Mother and be in trouble for being late. Or I could stay here with you and still be in trouble for being late. So, I'd rather stay here,' she paused, 'that's if you want me to?'

She held her breath as she waited for him to reply.

19

Standing in front of her bedroom mirror, Isobel Reed studied her reflection with an appreciative glance. The dress was long, and white, with a deep cowl at the back that swished as she walked. The nude stilettos gave her foot the perfect arch, and her calves an elongated look. It was an outfit that would have normally made her happy, as did anything that was lush and expensive and bought in Monaco. She'd spent a whole weekend there, carefully making her way from one boutique to the next and had loved being in an environment where the Monégasques looked after their customers. She'd felt rich and successful. But tonight, she had no time to feel the pleasure of the purchase. Tonight was business. Nothing more. And with a flick of her skirt, she knew she had to pull off the event of the century if she were to get the experts on board and she gave herself a steely gaze as she once again went through the guest list and which of the men were more important than the others.

She shifted uneasily.

'Roberto, is he still coming tonight?' She took in a long, deep breath and looked across the expanse of the room to where Giancarlo lay stretched out on her queen-sized bed. It was stood on a platform, with a half tester draped in a long, deep pink curtain. It had been a colour she'd liked, but now it didn't look quite right. Not with a red-blooded Italian laying across it.

'Why the hell wouldn't he come?' Giancarlo's strong Italian accent echoed around the room. 'He's family. He knows what has to be done and tonight, he has to be here.' He pushed himself up against the mountain of crisp white pillows, held a Liga Privada cigar between the fingers, and slowly, he lifted it to his lips and inhaled.

'Maybe because you sent a woman to do a man's work,' Isobel threw back in his direction. 'You embarrassed him, hurt him. And then, you expect him to turn up here and sit across the table from you drinking wine.'

Annoyingly, his hand flicked repeatedly at a bow tie that had been loosely hung around his neck. It was more than obvious how much the bow tie annoyed him, yet he did nothing to remove it. 'Ah, don't worry yourself *la mia cara ragazza*. He isn't hurt too badly.' He slipped from the bed, and with slow, seductive footsteps he sidled up behind where Isobel stood. 'His pride is hurt, that's all. And I can assure you, he will turn up. He knows what the consequences are if he doesn't.' Pushing an arm around her waist, he rested his head on her shoulder like an oversized puppy dog, vying for attention. 'So, don't you worry about tonight. You let me do the worrying for the both of us.'

'Talking of worrying.' Isobel looked up, paused, and pierced his gaze with hers. 'Your wife, Elena. I presume she's still coming tonight?' Moving out of his hold, Isobel impatiently waited for the affirmation she knew he would give, before rolling her eyes like a petulant child. 'Giancarlo. I don't want her here.' She pouted childishly, swished her skirt angrily with her hand and flounced across the room in the hope that Giancarlo would notice her outburst.

'Isobel, you don't need to be like this,' he said, gently. 'You know I love you. That's all that matters.'

'Is it fuck, Giancarlo. This is my house, and my rules. I get sick to death of the way she always picks at her food like the smallest of mice and does all she can to steal my glory.' It was true Elena had a way about her that most of the men adored. She could capture a room in her hand, and get them all turning to listen.

'My darling, Elena balances the room.' His hand came to rest on her shoulder and with her chin lifted up high, she held her nerve. 'Without Elena there, you'd be the only woman at the table.' Once again he nestled in behind her, and moved his lips sensuously down the side of her neck. 'Besides, you know that Elena is suspicious. She doesn't like us spending time together. And who could blame her,' he whispered, 'By inviting her to the parties, it alleviates her suspicions. And you know what they say, if you have a happy wife, you have a happy life.' He laughed riotously.

'Giancarlo, I was a good wife,' she growled. 'And I don't like being a mistress.' She took a step back, purposely dug her heel into his foot. 'Maybe it's time I found myself a new husband. Someone who could care for me, and for only me.' Isobel threw back with a laugh. 'I quite fancy the idea of a new lover in my bed.' She liked Giancarlo's company but no matter how hard she tried, he would never leave his wife. Which had left her with only one alternative, and that had been for her to take other lovers. Most had been men he didn't know, but recently she'd broken her own rule. She'd taken a lover within their circle and with a blink of regret, she wondered how long it would be before Luca confessed.

'My dear.' He moved his black tuxedo jacket to one side, flashed his gun and gave her a disingenuous smile. 'You take another lover at your peril.' He said angrily. 'I don't share my women.'

'But they're expected to share you.'

'How dare you.'

Turning back to the mirror, Isobel ignored his outburst, and lifted a pair of diamond earrings beside her face, studied the effect they had next to the dress. Then, determined to look better and more elegant than Elena, she dropped them heavily on the carved oak dressing table, picked up a different pair that were bigger, with double the amount of diamonds.

'Maybe Roberto will like these?' she whispered under her breath, thought about the proposition he'd made her the other morning and considered the challenge.

'Pardon?'

'Nothing.' She turned from left to right, kept her eyes on the mirror and with her mind spiralling with excitement, she tried to work out whether or not the catch would be too easy, or, after the way she'd walked away that day and left him to brawl with her minders, would he hate her and make the chase worthwhile. With the self-imposed challenge burning fresh in her mind, Isobel thought through her options and with the flicker of a smile, she tried to imagine Roberto lying on her bed. His young, muscular body leaning up against her pillows, the dolphin tattoo that stretched itself around his bicep.

'So, you think you're only a mistress, do you?'

'Darling. I deserve to be a wife.' She went to stand behind him, took the two ends of the bow tie in her hands, crossed it over and just for a second, she considered pulling it tight, but instead, she tied it with precision. 'And once I am...' She paused, caught his eye in the mirror. 'We could go back to Monaco, it was our happy place.' Pouting, she moved her hand down his chest, knowing that the last thing she needed was for Giancarlo to turn against her.

'I never promised you anything. Not marriage, and definitely not Monaco,' he said, arrogantly. 'And it's true you were a good wife, too good.' He gave her a guarded look. 'If you'd come to me sooner, and allowed me to take you, your husband might still be alive and you my dear, would still be a wife.'

Feeling her heart rate accelerate, Isobel spun around on the spot. She narrowed her eyes at the man who had been one of her husband's friends. Except he hadn't been. Not really. A real friend wouldn't have pursued another man's wife. He'd been powerful. Charismatic. And she'd been flattered by all the attention. She'd also been fearful of what her husband would do if she'd dared to stray. Closing her eyes against the memories, Isobel flicked an imaginary calendar over in her mind, realised that it had been just two days after she'd rejected Giancarlo that Scott had been murdered. A thought that made her catch her breath and take refuge in the en suite.

'He wouldn't...' She shook her head, and allowed her fingers to trace the marble decorations on the walls. This had been the last place that she and Scott had made love and she tried to understand what had happened to her life and whether her initial rejection of Giancarlo had been instrumental in her husband's death. Like a kick in the gut, she realised how easily Giancarlo must have engineered it all. How he'd killed to get what he wanted. Either that, or Scott had simply been in the wrong place, at the wrong time, but Isobel seriously doubted it.

Opening her eyes, she stared intently at her reflection and bristled as she suddenly saw the woman she'd become, and with a deep intake of breath, she came to the conclusion that she didn't like her at all.

'This isn't the time to fall apart,' she whispered to the mirror, ran a hand across her hair, and with a small piece of tissue, she blotted her lip colour a little more vigorously than she'd intended.

'Keep him sweet, just keep him happy. It will soon be over and then...' she whispered, 'then you'll have more money than sense and if you want to go to live in Monaco you can... with or without Giancarlo.'

20

Knowing that it was almost time for her guests to arrive, Isobel paraded the dining room. It was a long, narrow room at the back of the house, where double doors led onto a garden that was now bedecked with fairy lights, fire baskets and comfortable seating. She had every intention of bringing her guests out here after dinner, allowing them to relax.

She glanced skyward, saw the dark, looming clouds and gave herself a congratulatory grin as she looked across the lawn to where a weather proof gazebo had been erected. It had drapes at the front, that could easily be closed. But if the weather remained good, they could stay open to give her guests a perfect view of the pool house, where long bi-folding doors and small café bar style tables and chairs now stood, along with small silver buckets of champagne that had been scattered in between them.

Turning her attention back to the dining room, she took one step at a time. Checked every part of the table setting. Tall candlesticks had been placed centrally and between them, floral displays had been expertly arranged.

'Waiter?' Isobel called. 'This plate.' A small speck of dust caught her eye and with an agitated finger, she pointed directly at it. 'Quickly – it needs changing,' she snapped. 'Check the rest.' The anger rose in her voice, and a young man immediately ran into the room. Watching, she saw the way he looked, the animosity that crossed his face and then he picked up the plate and disappeared back into the kitchen where a flurry of angry voices all yelled back and forth.

Needing a moment of calm. Isobel picked up a decanter and poured herself a generous measure of brandy. Swirling it around in the snifter, she watched the way the dark, amber liquid circled the sides. 'My guests,' she shouted, 'they'll be here in less than ten minutes and everything needs to be perfect.' She stamped across the room, threw open the kitchen door. 'Is the soup ready?'

'Yes, madam.' A tall, ginger-haired man turned. He wore a white hat, not as tall as the one a chef would normally wear and nervously, he pulled it from his head, twisted it around in his fingers. 'It's all ready to go, Mrs Reed. Just as soon as you say the word.'

'Then it's ready much too early. Make sure it doesn't split.' Flouncing into the hallway, she cast an eye up the grand staircase. It had been decorated with garlands that were all lit with bright, golden lights. It reminded her of Christmas. A time of year she hated the most and with a frown she stood and watched as Giancarlo began to descend.

'Damn chef is going to ruin the soup,' she growled. 'It's taken him all day to make it and now he's ready, much too early.' She tipped the glass anxiously from side to side. Then in a show of agitation, she tipped the glass backwards, took a mouthful and swallowed.

'Okay. That's enough.' Giancarlo lifted the glass out of her hand and gave her a look of annoyance. 'Tonight is dangerous. These men can be unpredictable and you... you need to stay on top of your game.' He pointed to the doorstep, to the exact spot where her husband had been murdered. 'You know how quickly things can go wrong, don't you?'

* * *

Still bristling as the first of the men approached, Isobel switched on her smile. If nothing else, she was the perfect hostess. She knew exactly how to act, how to react and how much time to spend with each of the guests.

'There you are, my darlings.' With her arms open wide, she welcomed each one of them in turn as Simon, Jason and Martin all strode towards her. 'Did you all travel together? How very sensible, and Simon, I love the waistcoat, is it new?' She lifted a hand, tentatively ran it across the satin, embroidered material. It was a gesture. An act worthy of an Oscar nomination, rather than a blatant invitation. After all, Giancarlo would be watching and with her stomach turning in anticipation of the night ahead, she kissed each of them on the cheek and then smiled as a second car pulled up. 'There's champagne and canapes. They're in the library,' she said as Giancarlo appeared in the doorway, 'Ah, here he is. The man himself. Now, please, go through and help yourself...'

The hurried slamming of car doors made her take a step backwards. Automatically she pressed her body behind the bullet proof glass that surrounded the doorway. Having it fitted had been one of the stipulations she'd insisted on after Scott had been killed. Yet still, every unusual noise made her bristle with nerves and while staring at the floor, she took a few measured breaths, before honing in on where Luca now stood.

'Gentlemen...' she threw herself back into her performance, smiled affectionately. 'Luca... how good to see you again.' She moved in close, lifted her lips to his cheek. 'He liked the quality of the gear, yes?' Inching backwards, she caught his eye and watched for the wink. It was a sure sign that their efforts had paid off and that the new buyer was already on the hook.

Moving around the room in rotation, Isobel kept her back to the carved oak bookcases. They stretched from floor to ceiling and were full of books she'd never get to read and ornaments she'd never grown to like. It was a room that screamed of Scott. Large leather armchairs stood to each corner, where soft amber lighting softened the mood. It was a room he'd used for business and ironically, it had been the very room he'd been sat in, just a few moments before he'd been shot on the doorstep.

Counting the guests, Isobel knew that one of them hadn't arrived and with a nod to the waiter, she anxiously kept one eye on the hallway while proudly watching as the champagne began flowing. 'That's right, my darlings. Drink up,' she whispered under her breath in the hope that the conversation would soon turn from pleasure to business and that each of the men would agree to her terms.

Sidling up to her, Giancarlo leaned in and whispered. 'Roberto, he's late?' He gave the room a smile, sipped at his champagne and carefully watched the way his wife worked the room. 'The men, they must have hurt him more than I thought,' he continued. 'I'll send someone over to the gym. We need to know where he is.'

With her eyes on the door, Isobel noticed the chef she'd spoken to earlier. He moved frantically from foot to foot, and with a frenzied wave of his hand, he beckoned to her.

'What is it?'

'It's the soup, Mrs Reed. I'm so sorry but if we don't serve it soon, it'll split and Chef, he's already pacing around the kitchen as though his heads about to explode and told me to say, that if we don't serve it soon, he'll have to make a new one,' he rambled at speed. It was more than obvious that the young chef had been sent to relay the message and for a moment Isobel felt sorry for him. Once again, she was looking in the mirror, wishing she could be a nicer person and with the thought in mind, she placed a hand on his shoulder. Felt his whole body tremble with fear and like an all knowing parent, she looked over his shoulder and glared directly at chef, before speaking.

'Gentlemen and Elena, would you like to follow me to the dining room. It appears that the soup will wait for no man, not even for Roberto,' she paused and smiled. 'I'm sure he won't be long.'

A low moan travelled around the room. The sound of discontent went from man to man and the previous buzz of happy people immediately turned to low, aggressive grumbles. All of them had an opinion, and without exception, none of them appreciated Roberto's absence.

'I think we should wait.' Martin stepped forward. Dropped his half empty champagne glass onto a large silver tray. 'I don't know about everyone else, but I'm not happy about doing business, not until he gets here.' He paused and looked at his watch. 'Rule is, we all arrive on time.'

'Something must be wrong,' Simon added. 'What if he's been arrested. Or talked.' He took a long, hard look at the door. 'The fact that he isn't here, doesn't sit well. Not with me.'

'We could all be sitting ducks,' Colin, one of the newer members of the group added. 'We're all under one roof, it'd be the arrest of the century. The damn papers would have a field day.'

'Hold your nerve.' Giancarlo said confidently. 'He's my nephew, he knows the way this family runs.' Running a hand up the inside of his jacket, he checked for his gun and then, nonchalantly, he rested a hand against the sideboard. 'He wouldn't talk to the police. He knows what would happen if he did.'

Without warning, the door flew open and bounced dramatically in the architrave. The whole room took a step backwards, and several weapons were drawn, Elena screamed and then a moment of silence filled the air as Roberto took a step forward. With a swollen lip, and a face that had a full range of colours, he was still wearing his gym wear that was covered in blood and with a forced, painful smile he looked across the room to where his uncle stood. 'Sorry, I'm late,' he chided and glared without blinking. 'I had a problem. A & E, they were a little bit busy.' He nodded slowly. 'The two guys that jumped me, they're in a worse state than I am.' He watched, waited for his uncle's reaction, but then allowed his shoulders to drop as Giancarlo walked towards him. 'Ah, you poor boy. Come... let me get you a drink and...' He slipped out of his tuxedo, and slipped it around Roberto's shoulders. 'There you are, my boy. Now you're dressed for dinner.' He patted him heavily against his back, saw the wince that crossed his face. 'And unless anyone else wants to object. I think it's time we let chef serve the soup and we... we should take our seats at the table.'

21

Wriggling around on a camp chair in the back of a very small van and with her eyes fixed to the monitors, Kate began to feel claustrophobic. The space was not really big enough for two, especially when Don was over six foot in height and almost the same in breadth.

With nausea threatening to overwhelm her, she pressed her fingers to her temples. It certainly wasn't the environment in which to have a hangover. Her head was still pounding and her mind reeled with unanswered questions. And regretfully, she thought about the wine. Knew she should have stopped drinking after the first large glass. Not two hours later, or after a third bottle had been happily consumed. The taxi ride home had passed by in a blur, and she'd dozed off at one point then woken herself up with a snort. Then once back at her cottage she'd spent half the night listening for Rob, just in case he came home.

Lifting a hand to the dial, she watched the way Don pressed a number of buttons, then as he had so many times already that morning, he gripped his stomach in anguish. 'Oh, boy. Thai curry last night,' he said, 'It was a bit on the spicy side and wow, do I know about it today.'

Kate grimaced at the thought. She wished she could open a window and took deep breaths inwards, in the hope that the oxygen would fill her lungs and that her mind would stop the merry go round from spinning around in a relentless fashion.

Turning her attention back to the surveillance screens, she watched as the odd bird or two flew into the frame. It had been the same monotony ever since Patrick had driven them to their position, climbed out of the driver's seat and walked away. Since then, her legs and bottom had become numb and painful, not to mention her bladder that screamed out for a toilet.

'What do we do about toilet breaks?' she asked, hopeful that Patrick would come back and drive them to a different location. One preferably with a public toilet, food and something non-alcoholic to drink.

Don pointed to the corner where a very small chemical toilet stood behind a curtain that hung from a rail. 'The curtain was put up in your honour. If you pull it around you, you should get some privacy.' He chuckled, 'But not much and if I'm honest, you might want to go before I do.'

Kate recoiled. They'd begun the stake out just before eight. It still wasn't noon and the lack of anything to watch on the monitors had given her far too many opportunities to drink juice and to think about the conversation that had passed between herself and Ben. They'd laughed and joked effortlessly and had shared far too much information, that only a bottle of wine or three could release. But now, she regretted the fact that she hadn't waited until Friday, and made a mental note that going out on a work night wasn't something she fancied repeating. Not anytime soon. Although the night itself hadn't been that bad, the fact that Rob hadn't come home had given her mother ample ammunition to throw around over breakfast. Not to mention the snide, cutting comments about a single mouse dropping, which had instantly turned her home into a health hazard.

'It's a wonder the cottage isn't totally infested.' Her mother had said, as she'd chewed on her toast. 'You really need to clean once in a while, Katie dear, there's no excuse. If you don't have time; make time. But then again if you go to the pub every night after work drinking wine, there's really no wonder that you don't have time to clean, is there?'

'Mother, give it a rest. I've been to the bar once for God's sake. I've only worked there for three bloody days. It's hardly a habit.' Snapping back had made Kate feel guilty. She normally tried not to retaliate, not where her mother was concerned, but the constant jibes made it difficult to stay quiet. Especially when she knew that her house was perfectly clean and that no one other than her own mother would have turned up and pulled the kick boards off to check behind them. And what's more, she seriously doubted that there were any mouse droppings at all. Just her mother trying to be difficult. It was something she'd done on a regular basis since James had died.

Her attention shifted back to Isobel's home, Honeysuckle House. She longed to go for a walk, to look around and to see for herself what kind of house Isobel Reed really lived in. What's more, Kate wanted to know if the other woman was at home. She still hadn't emerged and the chances were that she'd simply stayed indoors. Which wouldn't be surprising as it had begun pouring with rain and by the looks of the dark, grey clouds, the rain wasn't going to stop any time soon.

'Don, I'm going to go and have a look around,' Kate said as she stood up and turned towards the back doors of the van.

'Ben said we should stay with the van.'

'I'm just going to have a walk around, try and see if anything is happening. Firstly, it will give you a chance to... you know.' She pointed to the curtain. 'I'll head towards the lane at the back of the house. Give Patrick a call. Get him to come back and meet us here in twenty minutes.'

Grabbing a high vis vest, just as Ben had instructed, Kate pulled it on, jumped out of the van and immediately felt the fresh air hit her like a wave. It was cold and raining, but fresh and with a long, deep breath she pulled the air into her lungs, and stretched her aching legs.

All the houses on the edge of the National Park were exclusive mansions, with long, tree-lined drives, between six and eight bedrooms and hallways that would have been bigger than half of her house.

'Why would anyone want to sell drugs if they lived here?' Kate mumbled to herself as she admired the properties. 'Or, here's a thought, are the drugs the reason they get to live in a house like this?' She pulled the hood up on her jacket and with her clipboard in hand, she made her way from house to house until she sided onto Honeysuckle House. It was the biggest and impressively stood back, in its own grounds. Huge oak and cherry trees stood close to the building giving the upstairs windows a degree of privacy. Which was lovely for the occupants, but not so lovely for her, who could barely see any movement at all.

Shuffling past trees and bushes, Kate noticed an extension at the rear of the house. It had glass bi-folding doors that ran along its length and to one side, a white gazebo that still had empty bottles of champagne stood on tables, along with half-empty glasses. 'Wow, a party and a pool house.' She nodded her approval, inched around the property and while hiding in trees and bushes, she took a better look at the house. For a moment, she thought back to what Ben had told her. 'Ugathwaite was the Viking word for Owl Meadow.' She nodded thoughtfully and even now in its newly developed status, Kate could easily imagine a long, sweeping meadow, with owls living and hunting these meadows for food.

Hearing a car approach. Kate slid behind a tree and watched as a silver Mercedes drove past her. It had blacked out windows, looked more than suspicious and with a wide swerve it pulled into Isobel's drive.

'Okay, who are you?' She carefully squatted, pulled off her high vis and hid it in her rucksack. Then, through a pair of mini binoculars, she watched, and listened, as the man, who was dressed in a tight leather jacket and jeans stood pounding relentlessly against the door with fingers that were covered in dark, skeletal tattoos.

Lifting his phone to his ear, he tried to make a call and aggressively punched at the door again as he held the phone out, and stared at the screen in annoyance.

Putting the binoculars down, Kate took out her mobile, took a couple of pictures and hoped that one of them would capture his face and give them an identity but she felt her heart sink as she flicked through the pictures and saw the result. 'Stupid,' she said the word much louder than she'd intended and cursed herself. Both pictures had caught a perfect image of the back of his head and in an attempt to get closer, she began to sneak along the edge of the bushes, and around its edge.

'What the—' A hand went over her mouth, and she was dragged rapidly down to the floor. A scream began and stopped in her throat and as she grabbed at her attacker, she struggled to breathe and a frenzied panic took over her body.

'Shhhhhhhush.' She heard a man's voice eventually growl. 'You're going to get us both killed. Now if you calm down, I'll let you go.' Feeling the pressure released from her face, Kate spun around. There she saw Eric in his black-rimmed glasses with his piercing blue eyes and a finger held against his lips, demanding her silence. With her heart pounding audibly in her ears, the sound of a car door slammed in the distance and she held her breath as the car drove off.

'Eric, what the hell?' Kate took a moment to get over her shock, before looking down at the mud that was now smeared all over her jeans. 'My jeans, they're ruined.' Anxiety rose inside as she brushed against the mess, her hands were making the dirt worse and the more she rubbed, the more she panicked. 'What are you doing here?'

'That man,' he replied angrily, pointing towards the house. 'I think he had a gun, and you, well you were about to get yourself killed.'

Kate ducked back down, and even though she knew that the man had driven away, the mud and dirt suddenly became secondary to the idea of being shot. 'Are you sure?'

'Of course I'm sure. And he was huge.' Eric held his arms out to prove a point. 'Wore a brown leather jacket that he nearly burst out of and he had knuckles the size of...' he took a breath, 'When I saw you, I panicked and all I could think was that neither Ben, nor your sister would ever forgive me if you got killed, and that I'd watched it happen.'

Kate looked up at the sky as Eric's words sank in. She thought about what she'd seen and felt sure that the man had only held a mobile phone, and not a gun. 'He's gone now.' She rested a hand against his forearm, saw how pale he'd suddenly become. 'Are you okay?'

'Yes. Yes of course,' Eric said as he leaned against a wall. 'Her husband got shot here you know? Well, there actually.' He pointed to the front door, to the pathway that meandered between the trees. Eric's face had gone pale. It was now beyond the pallid colour it normally was and with a sigh, she dug around in her bag, looked for her phone and wondered whether or not she should call for help.

'Eric,' she asked. 'What did you actually see?'

'The man, the gun, and then you. I was fine about looking after myself, but couldn't bear the thought that I couldn't protect you too. It took me ages to make my way around the garden. I hid behind there.' He pointed to the large thick laurel bush, the size of a small car.

Kate closed her eyes. Last night she'd been so pleased to call herself a private investigator. She'd really enjoyed her time with Ben and had begun to feel as though being part of a team would be a huge benefit to her confidence and to her lifestyle. But today she couldn't feel more different, and her whole day couldn't get any worse, not unless Eric was right and she could have been shot and now, she was sat on the pavement, in the rain, covered in mud, with Eric who was quivering like a jelly. 'Come on, I think we should get back to the van.' Kate nodded sympathetically.

'Oh my g-goodness, I am s-so s-sorry.' Embarrassed, Eric began to stutter. He hurriedly jumped up, pulled a tissue from his pocket and with long, sweeping movements he began to wipe the tissue across his brow and inadvertently smearing the mud across his face. 'I was so scared. He could have easily shot you.' He shook his head, kept looking over his shoulder. 'Besides, I only just met Eve. She's lovely, by the way and she'd hate me if you got shot and I were there.'

Kate softened towards Eric. She liked the way he mentioned Eve. He obviously cared and she did all she could to reassure him. 'Eric, you can calm down. Neither of us got shot.' She patted herself up and down. 'Look.' She was desperate not to smile and even though she was initially amused by the mud that had been smeared across his face, she bit down on her lip and then remembered the mud that had been all over her own hands and clothes. Standing up she pulled a wad of tissues from her rucksack. The mud seemed to rub in rather than rub off and even though every part of her mind screamed to be clean, she did all she could to remain calm.

22

'I swear that if there wasn't a million pounds up for grabs, I'd say we were wasting our time,' Kate jumped out of the van, took in a deep breath of fresh air and practically ran through the back door of the office. 'Nothing can be seen from the road and most of the windows are at the back of the property, which was probably done by design.' Kate gratefully accepted a steaming mug of hot coffee from the tray that Gloria brought in and passed a second one to Eric. He stood leaning against Ben's desk, with his back to her, frantically studying the dry wipe board. Looking for clues.

'Did Don go home?' Eric asked as his eyes quickly processed the information before him.

Kate pulled a face. 'Well, if he didn't, I don't think it'll be long before he does. The Thai curry he'd had last night hadn't agreed with him. He didn't look too well in the van and as far as I'm aware, he made a dash for the bathroom.' She sat down in the new pink office chair that stood behind her desk, pulled a pad and a pen from her drawer and along with Eric, she looked up at the evidence board.

'So, how do we get inside the house? Maybe I could knock on

the door, pretend my car has broken down and see if she'd let me use her phone?' Kate gritted her teeth as she spoke, did all she could not to look down at her jeans. Being dirty and covered in mud sent her OCD into overdrive. She felt hot and nauseous and made a mental note to carry spare clothes with her from now on. She could easily keep a set in the boot of her car, or leave some at the office but what she really wanted was to sink into a deep, hot bath, clean her mud smeared face and apply a fresh set of make-up. 'See if you can come up with something while I...' she looked down at her clothes. 'Well, after being rugby tackled, I need to clean myself up.'

Checking her reflection in the mirror, Kate felt a surge of relief. Her make-up wasn't as damaged as she'd thought and with a dab of foundation, she quickly repaired it.

'Kate.' Eric addressed her as she walked back to her desk. 'You do know that knuckles could come back, don't you?'

Kate laughed. 'Knuckles. That's a good nickname and well, it certainly suits him. He did have huge knuckles, didn't he?' Kate threw him a tissue. Pointed to the patch of mud that remained on his face. 'But to be honest, Eric, if a guy like him wanted to do some damage, I doubt he'd need a gun and as I said before, I really don't think he had one. All I saw was a mobile phone. Honestly.'

They both pulled faces, as the door opened and William walked in. 'How's it going?' He walked up to the evidence board, clasped his hands behind his back and studied it.

Kate sighed. 'I took some pictures, but they're all a bit distant.'

'Let's have a look. Maybe I can enlarge them or something, try and see his reflection in the windows or door, maybe?' He sat down at Don's desk and fiddled with the keyboard then clicked on print.

'Damn it,' she cursed. 'They're still not clear enough and we still can't see his face or what's in his hand.' She threw her head back, closed her eyes and went over what had happened again in her mind's eye.

'No, you can't see his face,' William said as he tapped excitedly on the print. 'But you can see that Isobel Reed is upstairs. Look.' He tapped on the photograph. 'She's hiding behind the curtain. Which means she was definitely at home.'

'But we left. No one is watching.' Kate was puzzled, picked up the print and squinted.

'No, you're not. But the other team are. Patrick took a second van across and if there is something going on, we'll find out what it is.'

'And...' Eric shouted across the room, 'Take a look at what I've got.'

Leaning over his shoulder, Kate stared in amazement as Eric cleverly flicked through a series of diary pages. 'Am I to presume that they belong to Isobel Reed?'

'You presume correctly. Ben got me to hack into her computer and we retrieved her electronic diary.'

'What? How?'

'While I was in her garden I picked up her Wi-Fi and IP address. Hacked in. I then sent the information back to the office. It's easy; I'll show you how to do it.' He turned his attention back to the screen. 'Having these pages gives us access to everything she does.'

'Wouldn't her Wi-Fi need passwords?'

Eric tapped his temple with a pencil. 'My dear, I'm the best hacker in the north of England. Why on earth do you think Ben employs me, because it certainly isn't for my gun spotting skills.'

Kate laughed. Eric was geeky, but had a way about him that she liked and while smiling in admiration, she paid attention to how he analysed every piece of information. The way he went through the pages. Catalogued every clue and carefully worked out what relevance they had before drawing a timetable onto the drywipe board and with the information he'd already gathered, he began to fill it all in.

'We know what days of the week she has set appointments: hairdressers, beautician, etc. But what we need to do is to look at the gaps.' He indicated towards the board to the gaps that left clear blocks of time when Isobel had no visible plans. 'These are the times that Isobel would have the opportunity to go out or to take visitors. We also look for codes, you know multiple numbers, stars, repeated words. She could use these symbols to remind her of things that she didn't want to write down,' he said smugly as he looked at Kate with a 'why didn't you think of that?' look on his face.

Kate sat with her chin in her hands. 'Of course,' she said, nodding in agreement. 'So, what else did you see or do while rummaging around her bedding plants and – more to the point, what did I miss?'

'I saw that she'd had an overnight visitor.'

Kate jumped up. 'Really? Who was it?'

'Well, I don't know who he was. But he had been there overnight and he wore brown leather brogues. I could see them through the glass in her hallway.'

'Did you get a photograph?' William asked.

'Sure, on my phone,' Eric replied as he tossed the phone across the desk. 'I'd only just arrived and hadn't got all my gear organised. I only just avoided being seen.'

'So?' Kate questioned as she looked at the photograph over William's shoulder. 'How do you know he'd been there all night?'

Eric laughed and pushed his glasses back up his nose. 'That's easy. His shoes. It was raining and had been for at least a couple of hours. If he'd been out within an hour of my seeing them, they'd have been damp. Or he'd have had mud on the heels.'

Kate looked at him in amazement. 'Eric, that's very clever.'

Eric shrugged. 'It's not, it's easy. As I said, the shoes were dry, there was no mud and seeing as it was still early and not many people go visiting before eight o'clock in the morning, the probability is that he'd stayed the night.'

Kate suddenly jumped up from her chair. 'The brogues, Luca Bellandini wore brogues exactly like that, I saw them, in the library. Actually, I got a photograph, entirely by accident and they had a tiny tear in them, right on the top. Sorry, I have a thing about shoes.' She picked up her mobile and flicked through the pictures.

'The brogues I saw did have a slight tear,' Eric said and grinned at Kate.

'This suggests that it was most probably him that stayed the night, which means we solved a part of the case. The shoes were Luca's. So he's definitely involved.'

William shook his head. 'Not necessarily. Just because he may or may not have stayed the night, does not make him a drug dealer. I'm afraid you need a lot more proof than that, before closing a case,' he said, as the door opened and Ben marched in.

Ben looked Kate up and down. 'Hey,' he muttered, 'I hear you had an incident. Are you okay?' His eyes searched hers and with a smile, she nodded. 'Thank God, you're not hurt?'

Eric coughed. 'Hi, Ben. I'm okay too. I almost got shot too. But, hey, thanks for asking,' he said sarcastically and ducked as Ben picked up a pack of post it notes and tossed them at him with a smile.

'It was a phone!' Both Kate and William shouted in unison. A look was exchanged, followed by a smile, before William stood up and left the office.

'Right, fill me in on everything that's happened,' Ben said to Eric and Kate.

Ben sat at his desk and gave them his full attention, while both Kate and Eric told him what had happened that morning.

'So, you've solved one tiny part of the jigsaw.' He smiled, studied the dry wipe board intently. 'In summary,' Ben said. 'What we suspect is that Luca Bellandini is having an affair with Isobel Reed. It was him that led us to Isobel in the first place. So that confirms a connection. But if Isobel is supplying drugs to dealers, we need to find out who those dealers are and whether Luca Bellandini is definitely one of them. Once we've done that, we not only need to find out how she's getting the drugs into the country, but who her main supplier is. Then, and only then, can we claim the million pound reward. So we've still lots of work to do.'

23

Driving to work the next morning, Kate could still feel the anger surging through her veins. The night before had been a nightmare. Her mother had insisted that she was home in time for dinner. Then as though nothing had been said, she'd promptly gone out the moment Kate had got home. Which to be fair, would have been exactly what Kate would have wished for, until of course she'd taken a call from Rob, and some cock and bull story as to why he'd be late again. Which meant that once again they couldn't talk and by the time he had arrived home, it had been way past midnight.

Pulling into one of the parking spaces in front of the office, tears of frustration filled her eyes and Kate took a moment to compose herself. As she walked past the bakery the aroma of freshly baked bread, doughnuts and scones hit her. Taking a diversion, she chose a selection of pink and chocolate iced doughnuts, along with a few random cupcakes, to make her feel better about last night.

'That should cheer us all up.' She smiled gratefully, took the box from the assistant and carefully made her way through the front door of Parker & Son. Her eyes were immediately drawn to the brown leather settee, where Ben was sitting with a very young, slim, dark-haired woman, who may as well have been sat on his knee. Her hand rested close to his leg, making Kate's head spin.

'I... I brought doughnuts.' Was all she could think to say as she hurried past. 'I'm going to...' She felt her cheeks flush. 'I'm going to put them in the kitchen?'

'Thanks Kate. That's great,' she heard him shout out from behind her, but she quickly closed the door and stood with her back pressed against it and with a sigh much bigger than the situation deserved, she dropped the doughnuts onto the side. Even though she knew she shouldn't, she felt a huge rush of disappointment.

After a night spent with Rob, who had made it more than clear that he was only in their bed because her mother was in the spare room, she'd barely slept at all. And even though she'd woken up on the verge of exhaustion, she'd still got ready with a smile, because she'd been looking forward to seeing Ben. Which now she thought about it was ridiculous. They'd only just met. He was the boss's son and now feeling a surge of jealousy flying through her, she felt the need to berate herself. But the sight of seeing him with another woman had disturbed her just a little more than she'd ever admit.

Moving from the kitchen to the office, and so as not to be seen, she slammed the door behind her to see a puzzled looking Eric. He was stood at the evidence board, with his pen at the ready.

'How do you fancy a haircut.' He glanced across, gave her a smile and made Kate suddenly feel self-conscious. Her hand shot upwards and with an anxious sigh, she pulled a compact from her bag and checked her appearance.

'Why, what's wrong with my hair?'

'Nothing, but I've gone through Isobel's diary and she's due to have her hair cut later this morning and Gloria has secured you an appointment at exactly the same time. In the same salon.' He tipped his head comically from side to side, and added, 'With a different stylist, of course.'

'Oh?' Kate picked up the ruler that had been haphazardly thrown on her desk, lined it up with the keyboard, then shook her head, opened the drawer and dropped it inside.

Eric was laughing. 'Of course, Parker and Son will pay for the haircut and you, my dear, will be in the right place at the right time. Women tell their hairdressers everything, don't they? So I thought it would be a great way for you to listen in on her conversation.' He held his hands out, one to each side. 'Go on, tell me how ingenious I am.'

'Who's the woman in reception?' Kate suddenly demanded. 'She's draped all over Ben like a leech.'

Eric spun around on the spot. 'Wow. Okay...' He paused, took a step back. 'Oh my God. You're not jealous, are you?' His finger waved up and down in the air. 'Because that would be crazy.'

Kate shook her head. 'Don't be ridiculous. She looks like she's twelve. Not the type I'd have thought Ben would be into. Anyway...' She rolled her eyes upwards. 'It's none of my business.' She looked back at the door, realised that the woman was in fact much older than twelve, and growled internally at her own reaction. 'I brought doughnuts for everyone, that's all. Her being here took me by surprise. I didn't count on extra guests when I bought them.' She sat down and picked up the telephone, held it to her ear and then placed it back down. 'Does this thing ever ring?' she asked in a vain attempt to change the subject.

24

'So, you and Rob, you're all lovey-dovey again, are you?' Eve's sarcastic tone came down the line. 'Since when?' Kate could imagine her sitting in the wheelchair pulling faces at the phone.

Kate sat in her car and counted to ten. She'd arrived at the hairdressers early, parked her car and had decided to phone Eve to catch up on the gossip but after looking at her watch, she realised how close the time was to her appointment.

'We didn't exactly fall out, Eve,' she lied. 'He's been late home once or twice and stayed on the settee for a few nights. That's all,' she answered protectively, glanced in the rear-view mirror. She really didn't want to admit that her relationship with Rob was over. To admit it would make it more real and if Eve found out, then her mother would be next and an onslaught from her was the last thing she needed.

Kate closed her eyes, leaned back against the car's headrest and allowed the April sun to warm her face. She knew that Rob was self-centred. Just about everything he'd ever done, he'd done for himself and she still had no idea why he'd disappear for days that could easily turn into a week, without explanation.

'Maybe he's putting on a show for Mother's sake, you know, coming home, sleeping in your bed, playing happy families?'

Kate knew that Eve was angry, she could hear it in her voice. It was also Eve's way of trying to get a reaction from Kate – one she couldn't give. Not right at this point.

'Maybe he just loves me, Eve.' Kate rummaged in her handbag and pulled out one of the chocolate bars she'd tossed in there that morning. 'Have you ever thought of that?' she said, opening the foil packet and nibbling at the edge of the bar. 'Anyhow, have you spoken to Mother yet?' She changed the subject.

'Yes, she says she's staying with you for at least a week. Maybe longer.'

Kate closed her eyes at the thought. Having her mother for another whole week would drive her insane. She could imagine that by the end of it, one of them was likely to end up dead, and at this moment in time, Kate had no idea which one of the two might kill the other. Considering her options, she thought about phoning her father. But since the accident, their relationship had been strained and she doubted he'd care if her mother stayed for a month or not.

'Eve, please let her stay with you,' Kate begged as her sister went quiet and sulked. Kate knew that Eve had as much of a problem with their mother staying as she had, but Eve lived by herself, she always complained of being lonely and what's more she had a spare room with an en suite. Unlike Kate's cottage that only had two small bedrooms, paper thin walls and one bathroom between them.

* * *

'Okay, okay, she can stay here. I'll ask her later. Tell her it was my idea, but only if she's still here after the weekend. I'll make an excuse, tell her I need some help,' Eve relented and took in a deep breath. The last thing she wanted was anyone staying at the bungalow. It would mean disturbing her routine and the thought of her daily physio being interrupted, brought her out in a sweat. She couldn't allow her mother to know her secret. No one could know. Not yet. Not until she could stand unaided and be sure that she could without falling over.

'I don't really want her here, Kate.' Eve sighed. 'But, for your sake, I'll ask her. I think things are much worse between her and Dad than you think.'

'Why would you say that?' Kate asked. 'They've always fought, you know that. And it's harder for him now, working for another firm rather than working for himself, he's always under pressure and some days it gets too much for both of them, especially since James died.'

'She cried, Kate. I don't think I've ever seen her cry before, she said she was scared of the future, said she had nothing left and she sobbed for hours. I think she's having a nervous breakdown, or something. Some of the things she came out with were quite frankly weird and our dad can't do anything right, and you know how much she adores him.'

'Do you know what?' Kate said, 'You might be onto something.'

Eve's voice broke as she spoke. 'Kate, what if she does something, you know, something stupid?' It was a simple question. One Eve didn't know the answer to. All she did know was that for their mother to leave their father, even if it was for just a few weeks, it must mean that things were bad.

But for a short time, she had no choice. Mother needed looking after too, and with Kate and Rob's relationship being so difficult at the moment, Kate needed the time to sort it out. Which meant that whether she liked it or not, looking after their mother was down to her.

25

Isobel stared at her reflection in the mirror as Marcus lifted her hair and fastened the black vinyl cape behind her neck.

'And how's the lovely Isobel today?' His voice was soft and friendly with a slight Scottish tone. He was as thin as a sapling tree and his flower covered jeans gave him an animated appearance as his hands went up and down constantly pulling his fingers through Isobel's long, blonde hair. 'Would you like a tea? You take it black, darling, don't you? I'll get Miranda to make you one. Now, what are we doing today?'

Isobel smiled. Marcus barely took breath. 'Oh, I'm good, Marcus. And, yes, tea would be lovely,' she responded. 'I'd like it tidying up, just a little off the length. And straighten it for me too. I'm going to my therapist later. I like to look nice.'

'Oh, I know exactly what you mean, my darling. How is your therapist, still networking?'

Isobel smiled and nodded. 'He is. He's thinking of getting a new Porsche.' She began to giggle like a schoolgirl. 'Bright red with a cream interior, what do you think?'

'My dear, I think it sounds perfect. Will you be buying one too?'

Isobel nodded. 'I thought I might. I might name her The Red Lady.'

'What will your neighbours say when it's delivered?' His arms once again waved around and he used his hands to pretend he was driving a car. 'Can you imagine it?'

'Oh, I don't worry about the neighbours. I will have it delivered at midnight, so the neighbours don't see and preferably on a night when it isn't raining. I don't want it getting too wet.'

* * *

With the exchange still happening between Isobel and Marcus, Kate sat in the chair beside them while her own hair was washed and trimmed. Her hairdresser, Jackie had chatted on a relentless scale and Kate already knew about every part of a holiday she'd been on and had felt a sense of relief when the hairdryer had been switched on and the hairdresser's annoying voice had blended into the background.

Kate fixed her eyes on Isobel's mirror. She began cursing herself that lip reading wasn't one of her talents and did her best to pick up on as many words as she could. While Isobel sat calmly, her hairdresser waved his arms around in the air, occasionally blocking the view which was becoming increasingly annoying.

It was obvious that Marcus had heard Isobel's tales before. The expression on his face was one of boredom and he didn't seem overly impressed or surprised. But he did manage to smile politely in all the right places and continually repeated sentences that hadn't needed repeating, making Kate look each time he did. She also noted that Marcus had used a water spray to damp down Isobel's hair, rather than washing it over a bowl and Kate was disappointed that Isobel didn't get a drenching, or a towel wrapped around her head, with mascara dripping down her face and smudges of foundation missing from her oh-so-perfect face, like she had. With a comb, Marcus picked up tiny strands of hair, snipping away as he went. It was more than obvious that Isobel's hair didn't need to be cut. That every snip was nothing more than a titivation and that Marcus was playing with it more than styling it. An easy hour for an overpaid stylist.

'...next week, darling. I'll give you an update as soon as I can.' Isobel shouted out loud, looked pleased with her response and Kate bit down on her lip, wished she'd heard the beginning of this sentence and watched through the mirror as Isobel walked behind her until she reached the desk. It was all she could do not to spin in her chair, but Jackie had begun carefully pulling at the strands of her hair with straighteners, allowing each section to fall in soft, gentle curls around her face and made it impossible for her to see where Isobel had gone. Thinking as quickly as she could, she grabbed at her phone.

'Jackie. I've already missed quite a few calls. It must be important. Do you mind if I just call my mother back, she isn't too well.' She put the phone to her ear, walked to the area next to reception, pretended to make a call and listened intently as Isobel paid Marcus for the haircut she hadn't needed.

* * *

'Oh, nice hair,' Eric said, as Kate sneaked back into the office, via the back door. After her embarrassing encounter that morning, the last thing she needed was to walk into reception and find Ben entertaining another of his friends.

'Thanks, where's Ben? Still with his friend?' Kate felt stupid for having been annoyed that morning. She berated herself for acting so out of character and while standing on her tip toes, she looked through the door that led to reception, hoped she'd see him, but all she could hear was Gloria's voice as she answered the phone in a courteous and professional manner.

That's what you need to be, a professional, she told herself. He isn't interested and you of all people should know better. She thought of the times she'd worked alongside other colleagues, frowned upon working relationships and had seen how difficult keeping secrets had been. Some of the relationships would have stood a chance in the outside world, but in the force, it had been more than difficult, which should give her an indication of why it was so unbelievably wrong on all levels. Parker and Son was a small, intimate team and most of them were family, which was why she had to take control of her attitude, or face the consequences make an absolute fool of herself if she didn't.

'You do know who that friend was, don't you?' Eric pushed a large piece of a chocolate doughnut into his mouth and chewed while staring at his screen.

'It's none of my business.' Kate stomped out of the office and back into the kitchen where she picked out one of the doughnuts, carried it back to the office and began to break it into pieces.

Eric laughed. 'Okay, but, from where I'm standing, you look just a little too concerned with the fact that Ben may or may not have a friend and I just thought you might want to know who she is.'

'I'm not concerned.'

'Yes you are, otherwise you'd have already told me all about what happened with Isobel.'

'Give me a chance. I was just about to tell you.'

'Come on then. I'm ready.' Walking to the evidence board, Eric picked up a pen and poised it, ready.

'I didn't really learn that much. It's obvious that money means everything to her and she has a personal trainer that goes over most days, but other than that she didn't really say anything else.'

Eric laughed. 'Ah well, at least you got a haircut out of it. Now, tell me exactly what she did say.'

Kate shrugged her shoulders wondering how much she could remember. 'Well, she mentioned a red Porsche with cream seats. Her therapist is buying one and she's thinking of doing the same and calling it The Red Lady.' She stopped, paused and thought. 'Said she'd have it delivered at midnight so the neighbours didn't see. She also hoped it wasn't raining, because she didn't want it to get wet.' She picked up a pad and a pen, began scrolling on the page. 'Oh, and something was happening next week and she'd update him as soon as she could. Sorry, I missed the beginning of the sentence, blooming hairdryer blasting in my ear. Is any of this relevant?'

'Yes, of course it's relevant.' Eric began scribbling on the board, just as Ben walked into the office.

'Hey. Nice hair.' Ben tipped his head to one side, gave her a genuine smile. 'Okay, Eric, what have we got?' Ben watched intently as Eric completed the board.

'There's a shipment coming in next week, could be in a red car, boat or aeroplane. The leader of the organisation is taking one delivery, Isobel the other. I'd say it's a cream substance or drug. Possibly the MCAT mixed with a cream or white powder, which normally means soap powder. Whichever it is, it's coming in at midnight, under cover of darkness, so the authorities don't pick up on it. Oh, and she didn't want it getting wet, which I'd take a guess at and say that she's bringing it in by sea. So, by deduction, I'd guess we're looking for a boat that's called The Red Lady.'

Kate looked between both Eric and Ben. 'Wait a minute, how the hell did you get all of that from what I just said?'

* * *

Ben turned his back on Kate. He wanted to look at her, but couldn't stop himself from staring. She looked amazing and the last thing he wanted to do was make her or himself feel uncomfortable, especially in front of Eric. The haircut had added just a few curls to her long auburn hair, which now framed her face. She'd obviously altered her make-up and now lined her eyes with a smudged brown that made her eyes pop with colour.

'Okay, Eric. That's great. Anything else?' He tried to concentrate on the board and listen to what Eric had said. And for just a second, he closed his eyes. He needed to focus on the job, concentrate on the clues, and more than anything, he needed to bring this case to a close. It was fast beginning to cost more money than it would soon be worth, especially if they didn't bring Isobel Reed to justice. 'Do you think she'll take delivery at the house? Or will it be elsewhere?' He tried to think.

'As I said, she mentioned the name Red Lady. You might want to dig around and see if there's anything relevant about the name.' Eric gave Ben a knowing look. 'And in my opinion, my money would be on it being a boat.'

Ben quickly turned to his computer. 'Red Lady, okay, leave that with me.'

'And, Ben, the back lane,' Eric said quickly, making Ben look up from his computer. 'We should take a van to the other end, watch it from both sides. It's a second point of entry, easy to come and go without being seen.'

'So, if we take the van on the back lane, who gets to go in the van on the front?' Kate asked, as Ben noticed her move from her chair to stand at his side.

Eric jumped down from where he sat on the desk, joined them both at the board and put a hand to his chest. 'Well, seeing as there isn't many of us left, I think I'd be joining you in the van.' He nudged her with his shoulder playfully. 'And I promise not to have a Thai curry for tea.'

* * *

Pulling up just short of Owl Lane, Kate jumped out of the van as instructed, wandered along the street and carefully planned her next move. She could see Honeysuckle House and made her way around the side, where she looked for a vantage point, a place where she could leave a remote camera.

Crouching down, she pretended to tie her shoelace while scanning the terrain and with a swift move to her left, she placed the camera as far under an ivy bush as she could. It was close to the drive, but looked directly into the back garden and gave them the perfect view of the back door and the pool house, neither of which could be seen from the road.

Turning, she headed towards where Ben would have parked the van and bounded to the corner, but stopped as a familiar noise made her stop in her tracks. Once again, she was crouching behind a bush. Her knees were dirty and while trying to work out what she'd heard, she kept herself hidden until eventually, she crawled along the drive and made her way between the trees. Then, like a mirage, she saw Rob's truck. It was there. Right in front of her. Parked on Isobel's drive and for a few seconds, she felt confused.

'He's found me,' she whispered. 'But why, I mean how?' She shook her head, considered calling his phone but then as the realisation hit her like a thunderbolt, she worked out that Rob wasn't there to find her at all. He was there to see Isobel.

* * *

'Okay. Are you sure?' Ben pulled her into the van, sat her down and held onto her shoulders. 'Start again. Tell me what you saw.'

'It's Rob. It's his truck. But the question is, why the hell is he here?' Disbelief turned into frustration and Kate looked up, stared incessantly at the surveillance screen and sipped at a bottle of water that Ben had pushed into her hand. 'Isobel isn't on his list of clients, which means what?'

Crouching down beside her, Ben took the bottle from her and slowly, he took her hands in his as he stared up with eyes that were full of pity and concern. It was a look that made her uncomfortable. Rob being there changed everything and made it feel personal.

Taking in a deep breath, Kate's eyes moved from screen to screen. She'd previously been suspicious of Rob. She'd known he'd been up to no good. But never in a million years had she considered the idea that he'd be involved in drugs.

'Kate, let's think rationally. He's a personal trainer, right?' Ben asked, again looking directly at her. 'That house.' He pointed out of the window. 'That house is big enough to have a gym in it and Isobel Reed is rich enough to employ him. After all, didn't she mention having a personal trainer at the hairdressers?' He sat down on the van floor, his arm rested on her leg and she purposely turned her gaze away from his, began to turn the dials until the picture on one of the screens became brighter.

Seeing what she was doing, Ben jumped into action. 'Let's try and get some sound. This one cuts out the background noise,' he said as a green line flashed across a screen. 'When the line becomes irregular it indicates that a noise can be heard and if it's distorted, we turn this.' He pointed to another dial.

Kate nodded. Her hands still trembled, and in need of something to do, she picked up the water and took a gulp that hit the back of her throat and made her cough. 'Sorry. Wow. Okay. What do we do now?'

'We just wait,' Ben replied. 'We have till three o'clock, that's when Patrick will come back for us. We'd have normally waited until after four, but I have a meeting that I really can't be late for.'

'Is your girlfriend coming over again?' Kate tried to smile, but knew that her voice had sounded petty and childish.

'What girlfriend?'

Kate rolled her eyes. Not getting a straight answer was exactly what she'd deserved. He didn't owe her an explanation and whether she liked it or not, it wasn't any of her business who he did or didn't snuggle up to. She just wished she hadn't witnessed it, the moment she'd walked in.

'Sorry. Just ignore me. I just thought that the woman at the office must have been someone… you know.' Kate stared at the clock nonchalantly, tried to look calm but anxiously bit down on her lip when, after a five-minute silence, nothing had changed. Rob's truck was still in exactly the same spot. He still hadn't emerged from the house.

'She wasn't my girlfriend.' Ben looked down as he spoke. 'The woman in reception. That was Rebecca, Julia's little sister. I've known her since she was a baby. We used to babysit for her.' He laughed. 'We were all very close and with it being the anniversary of Julia's death this week, Rebecca wanted me to go to the cemetery with her. She wanted to take flowers and didn't want to go alone.' He explained thoughtfully.

Turning away, Kate felt the colour flood her cheeks. 'Sorry. It was none of my business.' She continued to look at the dials, considered climbing out of the van and taking a crawl around the flower beds.

'Hair looks really good, by the way.'

Feeling grateful that Ben had changed the subject she quickly pressed a finger to her lips. 'Wait, what's that?' She'd heard a noise. The green line had jumped repeatedly and reminded her of a machine in the hospital. One that would show your heart beat pulsating, until it didn't. It had been the sound she'd woken up to after the accident. A noise she'd never forget and for a moment she could still remember laying there. Watching. Holding her breath. Wondering whether or not she'd see it go flat. Whether a person saw that last second of life, before they saw nothing at all.

Lifting a hand up with his palm outwards, Ben held his breath as a rustling came through the speaker. A bang was followed by a giggle and for a while, the silence was deafening. Until the faint sound of footsteps were heard. A door opened. Then slammed. No words were spoken until a strange murmuring sound made them both move closer to the receiver, and with a swift click of a button, Ben began the recording.

'Oh, babe. Surely, you can't want it again?' Rob spoke. The sound of heavy, erratic breathing could be heard. A building of tempo that was interspersed by loud, animalistic grunts.

'I knew it,' Kate whispered angrily. Her mind raced and even though she didn't want to believe what she'd heard, every emotion flew through her body. The realisation hit her like a thunderbolt. Rob. Her Rob was in that house. And right now, he was having sex with Isobel Reed.

'That's... that's my so-called fucking boyfriend.' Kate moved to the far side of the van, where she crouched in a corner, pressed her body against the side of the van and pushed her fingers firmly into her ears. It was an attempt to block out the noise, but it didn't work. 'Do you know what, Ben. I can't listen to that. Can you...' she lifted her fingers into the air, turned down an imaginary dial. 'Please. For the love of God. Switch it off.' She didn't need to hear the tape. She knew what was happening and closed her eyes, in appreciation of the silence.

'Are you okay?' Sliding a foot towards her in the already cramped space, Ben rested a hand on her forearm, he then looked around the floor, picked the abandoned water bottle up and pressed it firmly into her hand.

'My boyfriend is in that house, having sex with another woman.' She glared angrily in Ben's direction. 'Of course, I'm not okay.' She could imagine Rob's arms encircling the perfection that was Isobel Reed. Holding Isobel in exactly the same way he'd held her, only this time the woman he was making love to had perfect features. She didn't have a scar that was carved into her jawline and Rob didn't have to look at it every time he kissed her. Kate felt herself heave.

'Okay, okay. Try drinking the water?' Ben lifted the bottle to her lips. 'It will help.' He rubbed his hands down his jeans and looked more than uncomfortable.

'Are they... are they still...' she gulped the water down '...you know?' She looked back towards the dials which had now been turned down.

'I don't know. I can review the tape later, when I'm alone.'

Closing her eyes Kate didn't know which was worse. The embarrassment of Rob cheating and of her finding out in front of her boss, or the fact that the same boss would listen to the tape, and to all the gory details. 'How could I have been so stupid, so god-damned blind?' She blinked back the tears. 'He's been sleeping on the sofa, it's been going on for months. I should have known.'

'I'm sorry this happened to you.' Ben reached out. Pulled her into a much needed hug. 'You didn't deserve this,' she heard him whisper as she allowed him to encircle her in his arms and just for a moment, she felt safe, and secure and with the same tight grip she hugged him back.

26

'What do you mean, you're getting divorced?' Kate demanded as she stared at Elizabeth Duggan in disbelief. Her mother had suddenly announced that she'd left their father and that she was leaving him permanently.

'I can't live with him any more, Kate. I think he's a sociopath. He's horrid to live with.' She looked down at the floor as she spoke. 'He just doesn't understand me.'

'But, you and Dad, you're a team. You've always been very much in love. Everyone says so. Besides, where the hell would you live?' Kate's mind reeled, the fact that her mother had chosen to run and stay at her house was enough of a warning sign.

'I've wanted to tell you before. But your father insisted that I shouldn't, he said you had enough guilt on your shoulders about what you did to both your brother and your sister, without thinking you'd split us up too.' She rambled on at speed. 'Besides, he's been working away. It would never have been the right time to tell you.'

'Wait a minute,' Kate took a deep breath. It was as though someone had just punched her in the stomach and she stared aimlessly, hoping she'd heard the words wrong. 'What did I *do* exactly? Why the hell is any of this my fault?' In her own mind Kate had always blamed herself for what happened, even though rationally she'd known that it was nothing more than a horrific accident. It had been no one's fault. And for her mother to actually accuse her had blown her mind.

Rummaging through the utensils, her mother began to lift them out of the drawer and onto the worktop. 'Darling, if only you hadn't insisted that James had driven you that night. None of this would have happened.'

Kate spun around on the spot. 'Why... why would you even say that?' she demanded. 'I couldn't have predicted what happened. I'm not responsible that he crashed the bloody car.'

'Darling, where do you keep the potato peeler? I can't find it.' Her mother slammed the drawer and opened another and Kate seriously wondered how on earth she didn't know which drawer the peeler was in, especially after she'd cleaned, and tidied and reorganised all of her drawers in the past few days.

Sitting down at the kitchen table, Kate simply watched as her mother continued to search. 'You really do blame me, don't you? Do you think I want you and Father to split up, because I'll tell you now, it's the last bloody thing I want, because if you did I'd hate to think where you'd end up living.'

Her mother turned and glared with annoyance. 'Kate, we don't always get what we want. All I know is what we are left with. We just have to make the best of it, don't we?' Again, she opened a drawer. Slammed it shut. 'And if you kept things in order, we'd all be a lot happier.'

'The best of it?' Kate shouted. 'Good God, Mother, how the hell do we make the best of what we have left?' She pointed to the picture of James that stood on the sideboard. 'James is dead. Eve is paralysed. And I have this... How can any of us ever put that right?'

'Katie, don't be so dramatic. I'm leaving your father, lots of people get divorced nowadays and that's that,' she said, as she hastily chopped at the carrots. 'I can't live with him, he's too bitter and twisted and I wish I knew why,' her mother growled as she stood facing the range. 'Every time he talks to me, he says something nasty, something insulting and I don't like it.'

Kate laughed out loud and thought of the irony. She looked at her mother's back and wondered if she actually ever listened to what came out of her own mouth and for just a moment it occurred to her how alike her mother and father really were.

'James was running late for his date,' Kate began to whisper. She was sick of shouting, her head pounded and after the day she'd already had, she really needed a drink. 'We were just doing what we'd always done. James always took us to town on our birthday; always made out we were too much trouble.'

Kate closed her eyes and thought of the times her brother had teased both her and Eve. He'd always moaned when they were in the same clubs as he was but had always invited them along anyway. 'Don't you dare be in the Alabama Alligator club tonight, especially around ten o'clock,' he'd tease with a wink. 'Last place I need to see you two is at the bar.' Which had been his way of saying, be there and I'll buy you both a drink.

'The car spun off the road, it was no one's fault,' Kate said as she thought back to the accident, remembered the way she'd been launched across the car at speed. How it had spun repeatedly, before turning over and over.

'That's right, dear, no one's fault. That's why my son doesn't visit me any more. You are scarred for life and my darling Eve now sits in a wheelchair,' Elizabeth said as she calmly continued to chop vegetables for the evening meal. 'Of course, if you want to believe that pulling your sister from the car and crippling her was not your fault, then that's fine. It's you that has to live with yourself and even your father said that if you'd only caught the bus that day rather than taking the car, none of it would have happened. He'd still have his precious law firm and James would still be working there. But because of you, he had no choice but to sell it.'

Kate was shocked. Eve was right, her mother really was having a nervous breakdown. She thought that James simply wasn't here, rather than being dead. And, even though she'd always suspected that both her mother and father had blamed her, it was the first time that either of them had actually come out and said it.

'I need to phone Eve,' Kate grabbed at her phone, thought of the conversation she'd had with her just the day before. She'd said that mother had been upset, crying, but now there was no emotion. There was no sorrow. No sign of tears and the words had been said with the same amount of feeling she'd have used when reading a weather report. 'Monday will have showers with a hint of sunshine,' Kate imagined her mother saying, 'and Tuesday will see a rather dramatic divorce happening around the vale of York.' Kate took a step back, felt stunned and had no idea what she should do.

'Do you want boiled potatoes, dear, or roast?'

'What?' Kate slammed her hand on the table. 'Mother, stop chopping the bloody vegetables like you're feeding an army and sit down. We really need to talk.' Her chest heaved as pain and realisation tore through her body. She'd tried to put the accident behind her, but now it was all she could think about.

Had she really been responsible for Eve's injuries? Was Eve in a wheelchair because of her? Had she pulled her out of the wreckage?

All the thoughts raced around in her head all at once. Like a huge tornado spinning violently through her mind. In the course of one day, she'd discovered that her boyfriend was a lying, cheating rat, that her parents were getting divorced and that they both blamed her for the accident that had destroyed everyone's lives.

'Mum, the accident. I think you should know...' Kate closed her eyes. She had no idea where to start. How to tell her that James was dead and not just refusing to visit?

'I know, dear, you're sorry. Could you pass the gravy jug?'

'Are you bloody serious?'

Elizabeth Duggan walked past Kate, picked up the gravy jug, and then walked back to the range giving the gravy her whole attention. It was an action that made Kate gasp. Her mother was most probably in the middle of a nervous breakdown, while throwing all the guilt at her daughter, but God help anyone who got in the way of her making the bloody gravy. Kate pushed her chair backwards, stood up and walked over to the wine rack, where she studied the three bottles of wine that had sat there for the past three days. Then, like it mattered, she pulled a bottle of red from the rack and without studying the label or caring what the contents were, she poured a large glass, and drank it in a single gulp.

'Yes, please, darling, I'll have a glass. Now did you say boiled potatoes or roast? I think roast are so much nicer with beef, dear, don't you?' Elizabeth Duggan looked up from the gravy boat that she'd been polishing with a tea towel and as though nothing had been said, she gave Kate a smile.

It was more than Kate could take. Her world began to spin and she sat down quickly as her legs began to wobble. 'Mother! After all you've just said, do you seriously want to know what bloody potatoes I want?' Kate growled as anger took over her voice. 'You do know that the accident ruined my life too. Don't you?' She snatched at a tea towel, viciously rubbed the make-up off her face. 'That day ruined everything.' Kate held her chin towards her mother, pointed at the red puckered ridge that lined her jaw and watched as her mother's gaze was averted.

In the last twenty-four hours her life had turned from being predictably boring, to being a complicated nightmare. It was now an intricate web of deceit, of secrets and lies, that spread out in every direction, and she had no idea how to control the outbreak.

Kate saw her mother's bottom lip quiver. 'I'm sorry.'

'Sorry? Does sorry even cut it? You need help, professional help. You need a doctor.' Kate gulped down the wine, went to stand in front of her mother and tentatively, gripped her hands. 'Mother, we need to phone Eve. She has a right to know what's happening, she needs to know about you and Daddy, and I can't cope with all this alone, not today.'

Her mother nodded, calmly. 'She knows, dear, I already told her.'

'She knows? So what did she say? Is she all right, should we go to her?'

'Don't be silly, dear, Eve's fine. She certainly didn't react like you did.'

With her mind reeling. Kate felt the pressure build up inside. She knew that her mother wasn't well or acting normally and Kate knew she had no choice but to take control. Somehow, she had to get her mother back to York and to do that, she knew that she had to speak to their father.

Taking in a much-needed deep breath, Kate walked to her mother's side, took the knife from her hand and pulled out a chair from beneath the table. 'Here you go mum. Take a seat.' She swallowed hard and cast an eye across the pile of vegetables she wouldn't want to eat. 'Here,' she picked up the wine, slowly poured herself a second glass, then lifted another glass down from the shelf and filled it for her mother. 'You have a drink and I'll... well I'll make the roast potatoes.'

27

Barely remembering the twists and turns of the country lanes, Kate drove into Bedale. The roads were uncharacteristically empty, and the weather was drizzly, cold and windy for mid spring. Everything about the journey completely matched her mood and she allowed the tears to roll down her face as she pulled up in front of the office, where she simply sat and stared at the Victorian building with its polished front door and bay windows.

A sharp knock on the car window made her jump, her hand grabbed hold of the steering wheel and with tired, unfocused eyes, she turned towards the noise.

'Hey, what are you doing here?' Ben's deep tone startled her and confused by his question, she pushed open the door, looked up and into his eyes and felt a sense of relief, when he pulled her towards him. 'Hey. What's wrong. Come on. I've got you.'

While holding her gently against his body, Kate told him about the conversation she'd had with her mother and how guilty she felt for leaving her alone. 'She's still at the house, she's alone. Anything could happen.'

'Is she in any danger?'

Kate didn't know the answer, but Ben's voice slowly bore its way through the thick mist that had overtaken her mind and as she stared into space, the tears continued, stopped and then started again.

'Come on, I'll get you a drink.'

'I don't need a drink.' Sighing, Kate realised how painful her eyes had become. They burnt with the lack of sleep. Her mind was surrounded by a deep, engulfing fog and her whole body blended against his, as a deep sense of exhaustion enveloped her.

'Where's Gloria?' Kate looked around reception. It was more than obvious that something was different. That there was no noise, no kettle boiling and no printer churning out the constant stream of paperwork that Gloria always did and with her mind drifting into her own thoughts, she tried to make sense of the day. Nothing felt real.

'Kate, it's Saturday. It's Gloria's day off, and yours. Patrick and Don are working the case, and I'm here in case they need some back up.'

'Oh. I didn't...?' A hand flew up to her mouth. She felt hot, flushed, and more than embarrassed. Not only had she gone into work on the weekend, it suddenly occurred to her that after only a week of working here, she'd felt safer coming here than she had staying at home.

She pulled a tissue from a box on the table and blew her nose loudly. 'Oh my God, I'm so sorry. Not very ladylike, is it?' She tried to smile, to lighten the mood. Then as she eased away, she became aware of how much she'd cried. That her make-up would have completely rubbed off and that right now, Ben would be able to see her scar in all it's ugliness.

'Look. I'm so sorry,' she whispered. 'I need to...' She wanted to say that she needed to cover her scar, to hide it from view, but with her eyes darting around every corner of the room, she couldn't find the words.

'Sorry for what?' A gentle, dazzling smile lit up Ben's face.

'Well, for bawling for a start. I shouldn't bring my personal problems here. You hardly know me and Jesus, this really would have been the last thing you needed.' She tried to smile and failed miserably.

'I think you had good reason. The past couple of days have been hard on you.' Ben sighed. 'Did Rob go home last night?'

Kate shook her head.

'He doesn't deserve you.' His words were calm and once again, Kate blew her nose.

'You're right. He doesn't,' she snapped. 'And I won't allow him to hurt me again.' Kate shook her head and with a determined gaze, she sat up straight and stared at the coving. 'I want him gone, Ben. I want him out of my life, for good.'

* * *

Ben sat back, pulled Kate into a hold and patiently waited for her tears to subside. He breathed in and out as gently as he could and allowed her to sleep, fearing that any sudden movement would cause her to move.

She'd been absolutely right. He didn't know her. But even so, somewhere deep within him made him want to protect her. It was a fine line he wasn't sure he could cross. Not without her permission and thoughtfully, his mind went back to Julia. To how helpless he'd felt as she'd lost her battle. And now, for the first time since Julia died, he felt helpless again. Other women had tried to get close and failed. He'd kept them away, but Kate was different: she was feisty one minute, yet vulnerable the next and more than anything in the world, he wanted to take her in his arms and look after her, but the last thing she needed right now was more confusion and with shaking fingertips, he lifted them to his lips, pressed a kiss against them and then gently touched her cheek with his fingers. He knew it was wrong. That now was not the time to make a move. And he wouldn't. For now, all she needed was a friend and with a nod, he realised that friendship was something he could happily give.

Stirring, Kate suddenly sat up. She yawned, stretched, and as though doing it by default, her hand immediately went up to her scar and subconsciously, she turned her face away, leaned against one of the cushions and hid it from his view.

'Hey, sleepyhead,' he muttered, 'Listen, Patrick is back and both he and I have to go out on location. And seeing as it's your day off, and you're here, I wondered if you fancied coming with us?' he tipped his head to one side, gave her a hopeful smile, then pushed himself up to stand beside the settee. 'We're going into Whitby to check out some of the fishing boats, see a few contacts and chat with one or two of the locals. And get this – apparently, there's a boat moored there, and it's called The Red Lady.'

* * *

Puzzled and concerned all at once. Kate sat up straight, looked at her watch. 'I can't. I really should go back to Mother. I need to make sure she's okay.' She paused, looked from Ben to the door. 'And, if it's our day off, who is following Isobel?'

Ben winked. 'Don't worry. Don just picked Eric up. They're on their way to Isobel's. They have a campervan. Anyone looking at them will think they're tourists, pulling up to make coffee and sleep. Besides, now that we know Rob could be around, we can't risk you being on site. And as for your mother. I've asked Gloria to pop round. As you know, she's normally very good at taking care of people.'

Relieved that her mother would be well cared for, Kate felt her whole body relax. Gloria would know what to do, she always did, and her mother was always fond of chatting away to another woman of a similar age. 'So, Don and Eric get the easy form of transport, do they?' Kate threw in and laughed at the irony. She'd been squashed into the back of a surveillance van, with no air, no hot drinks and no comfortable seating for the past few days and on the one day that she wasn't in the van, the men had coffee making facilities, a proper toilet, windows, daylight and soft seating. 'I have to say, I'm just a little bit jealous.'

Sitting back, she was quite pleased that she wasn't parked outside Isobel's and that the thought of doing something other than going home felt like fun and the thought of spending the whole day with Ben was more than appealing.

'They only work half a day today. They can't park all day in a camper van and surveillance can't stop, just because it's the weekend. So, are you coming?' He looked at the door, flicked his head towards it. 'Patrick's waiting and there's work to do,' Ben said as he picked up a folder from the desk, and tossed it in a briefcase.

'I can't. I mean, my face,' Kate gasped. 'I've made a mess of my face.' Catching her reflection in the glass cabinet, Kate cringed. Her nose was bright red, her eyes were puffy, her make-up non-existent and the scar on her face was bright red and puckered.

'Okay.' He looked down at his watch. 'Get a coffee. Use the bathroom. Do whatever it is you need to do, and I'll meet you in reception at... shall we say, ten o clock?' Without waiting for an answer, he briskly walked out of the room and into William's office, where Kate could hear him chatting to his father.

Making her way into to the cloakroom, Kate pulled her make-up from her bag and began the art of hiding her scar. Practice makes perfect and she was an expert at covering it up. But the puffy eyes were going to take some work and after some thought, she held a towel under the cold tap, applied the cool material to her eyes, and waited for the swelling to reduce. Fifteen minutes later she emerged: her dignity restored.

'Ben tells me you're going to Whitby?' William said with a huge grin on his face as Kate walked into reception. 'I love Whitby. Let's hope the sun shines for you.'

'Err, thanks.' Kate felt awkward. William was being nice and she wasn't sure how much Ben had told him, but by his new smiley mannerisms she got the impression that he was more than aware of everything that had happened.

'Oh, and make sure he pays for the fish and chips. On the company. I insist,' William said with a laugh, as Ben entered the room, sporting a pair of jeans, boots and a jumper.

'Dad, do me a favour, check on Don and Eric for me. A couple of hours should do it. If they need any help, get Steve and Joseph over from Hawes, they're the closest.'

Kate watched as William walked over to Gloria's desk, sat down and looked at the screen. 'Don't you worry. I know how to use the trackers. I can see who is closest. Now, off you go. Enjoy the fish and chips, and Kate, make him take you to one of those posh restaurants, not the rubbish back street ones.' He winked at her and with the thought that William wasn't half as scary as she'd initially thought, she smiled gratefully.

28

The wind in Whitby gusted over the cliff tops and right through the abbey car park where Kate stood waiting for Patrick and Ben to finish talking. She pulled her coat tightly around her, checked her mobile phone and considered texting Rob. She knew what she needed to say, but had absolutely no idea how to say it.

'Okay. Plan is – I'm going to ask some questions up there. There's a lady at the abbey that I've known some years. She works in the gift shop, and she'll know if anything's been going on in the harbour,' Ben said, as he too grabbed his coat and pulled it on.

Patrick looked over his shoulder. 'I'm going to go and speak to some of the shop owners down on the quayside. Not sure how long that will take, but shall we meet back here, at the car?' He lifted his phone, looked at the screen. 'Shall we say around four o'clock?'

Ben nodded. 'Sure, all the boats should be back in by then. I'll check them out, ask a few questions. Maybe we could take a tour on one. See what they know.'

'Great. What shall I do?' Kate zipped up her coat, looked hopeful and rubbed her hands together in anticipation of receiving a task.

'You should probably stay with me.' Ben cut in. 'Between us, we can create a good cover story,' he added. 'One person asking questions looks suspicious. But two, well they just look like nosey tourists and we...' he paused. 'We could pretend to be on a honeymoon.'

Kate blushed; she knew he was right and with a grin, she followed him to the top of the ninety-nine steps and began to think of the ways she could impress him. Playing the tourist was right up her street, but being a detective was what he paid her for and right now, she wanted to prove to him what she could do.

'Come on,' Ben said as he pulled her along beside him. He was smiling like an overgrown schoolboy. 'If you're nice and let me look at the ruins, I'll buy you those fish and chips.'

Kate laughed at his enthusiasm. 'I thought we were supposed to be working?'

'We are. But being undercover means exactly that. We need to look like tourists and act like tourists. We're here, pretending we're a couple. Doing things that couples do,' he paused, 'so looking around the ruins, that will be allowed. Right?' He led the way to the abbey and continued to talk. 'This is the home of The Whitby Gladiator.' He pointed to a statue that stood central in the courtyard. 'As well as being the home of Dracula, of course,' he joked with an over exaggerated and evil laugh.

'Yeah, right.' Kate playfully slapped his arm. 'You do know that it's just a story, don't you?'

'Is that what you think?' He grabbed her hand and pointed to the harbour. 'Many years ago, during a terrible storm, an old Russian schooner found its way into that very harbour. A man's corpse was strapped to the helm.' He spoke in a loud, spooky voice, stared into her eyes and nodded. 'It's true, there was no one else on the ship.'

'So, how did it get to the harbour?' She looked nervously up at Ben, just as the wind whipped around them, giving Ben a full authentic stage on which to perform. He spread his arms wide and took great pleasure in going into full storytelling mode, his voice spooky and realistic.

'The dead man steered it here.' He pointed to the sands. 'As soon as the schooner hit the sand, a huge dog jumped from the ship and ran up that cliff.'

Kate looked at the cliffs that Ben pointed towards. There was a sheer drop to the harbour and there was no way that anything could have ascended it. 'That's impossible. No one could get up there, and certainly not a dog.'

'Well, it's true.' He nodded enthusiastically. 'That night the killings began, and some say that Dracula is still here,' Ben teased, grabbed hold of her shoulders and pretended to hide behind her, as he indicated the churchyard that lay in the distance. 'They say his grave is in there. We could go and look for it if you like?'

Kate shook her head and shivered at the thought. 'I don't think so,' she replied. She stood looking up at the architecture of the abbey. She'd never been before and as Ben went into great detail to explain its history, she found the whole story more than amazing.

'Right. Wait here. I'll be back in ten,' he said suddenly, as a woman appeared in the doorway and Ben turned, hugged her and began chatting in an animated fashion.

Kate didn't want to watch Ben with yet another of his friends and with a new found interest in artifacts, she made her way around the room they'd wandered into and looked at every object in the tall, glass cabinets.

* * *

'Come on, let's go outside.' Throwing an arm over her shoulders, Ben led Kate towards the elevator. Once inside and only after the doors had closed, he spoke. 'There, no one can hear us in here. We're looking for a fisherman called Sharky. He's got a whole herd of children and has been working strange hours for the past few months. He's been seen fishing over the wreck of the San Georgic late at night.'

'What's wrong with that? He's a fisherman.'

Ben pursed his lips. 'Fishing isn't allowed there, so if he really was there, he had to be up to no good.'

'Maybe he was lobster potting or catching a few extra fish. I don't want to be sceptical, but just because he's out fishing at night, it doesn't really prove anything, does it?' Kate asked as the lift doors opened.

'Hey, sceptical is good,' Ben said as they walked back outside. 'It shows you're thinking, and it shows that you're not looking at the world through rose-tinted glasses.' He nodded, pulled his coat tightly around him. 'But these men – they work strict hours. Hours that would be dictated by the tides and the governments and for them to add more hours to their quota, they need a good reason to do it.'

'And good reasons normally mean lots of profit,' Kate added.

'Oh, and the other thing.' Ben pointed towards the harbour, 'His fishing boat; it's called The Red Lady.'

* * *

Heading back into the fresh air, they walked through the ruins, and even though the wind was bitterly cold, Kate realised that they were so much more than the pile of rocks she'd imagined. There was an old, arched stone window with great spaces where there had once been glass and a view of sky where previously the most amazing roof would have been.

'Wow. I wish I'd been here before, it's amazing,' Kate said as she huddled into her coat, pulled it tightly around her and walked towards the cliff edge, where she took in the impressive sight of the bay of Whitby, its harbour and the open expanse of the sea beyond.

The rain once again began to drizzle and hurriedly, they ran for cover as the tiny spatters turned into huge globules of water, falling heavily and then splashing up from the puddles as they ran.

'At least the rain has spared us looking round the gravestones,' Kate said with a laugh as they hastily, but carefully, ran down the ninety-nine steps and towards the street below, where the water followed them in torrents.

'Mind, the steps are slippery,' Ben cautioned, as he held out a hand to grab Kate's before leading her onto Henrietta Street, where he pulled her behind him into the doorway of a small shop. Huddled together they took in the long, cobbled street, the smell of smoked fish that drifted towards them from a tiny shop a little further along the street and the medley of cottages stood in rows. They were all similar, yet each looked individual. They were the types of cottages often seen on postcards with white washed walls and brightly painted windows and doors in every colour.

Pulling a handkerchief from her bag, Kate carefully dabbed at the rivulets of water that ran down her face and eventually, when she could stand it no more, she pulled out her compact and checked her make-up, making sure that her scar was still covered.

Ben started walking again and Henrietta Street quickly led onto other narrow, cobbled streets with small galleries, cafes and curiosity shops.

'In here,' Ben said, quickly pulling her towards one of the shops as he ducked through the low wooden doorway. The shop was quaint and sold old-fashioned sweets, all in tubs symmetrically lining the walls. Each tub was filled with sweets of all colours and sizes. It was the kind of shop that reminded Kate of being a small child, one that was searching the shelves for her favourite sweets.

'Go on, pick some,' Ben said, his eyes shining like Christmas tree lights as he scanned the shelves. 'Look, there are flying saucers, winter mixture, bonbons and humbugs,' he picked up each of the tubs in turn and handed them to the rotund, grey-haired lady who stood behind the counter. She smiled. Her cheeks were as red as beetroot and her glasses reminded Kate of the jewelled ones her great-grandmother used to wear.

'I like liquorice allsorts,' she finally said, after scouring every shelf, looking for her favourite. 'They all taste just a little similar, but in reality, you never know quite what you're about to get.'

Standing back, Ben let out a riotous laugh. 'Wow, that's a surprise. For someone with the worst OCD ever, I'd have thought you'd have picked something quite different.'

'I do not have OCD.' She turned and glared, then saw him wink. 'Okay, maybe I do. A little. But I've only been this bad since the accident. It made me self-conscious and now I can't bear for anything to be out of place.' She laughed, poked him in the side and watched as the sweets tumbled effortlessly into a stainless-steel weighing scale, before falling from the bowl and into a small, white paper bag.

'I've noticed. Everything with you has a place. Even Don and Patrick have begun tidying their desks since you moved in.' Pulling open his wallet. Ben passed the lady a ten-pound note, thanked her and told her to keep the change. 'I think you've scared them into being tidy.' He poked Kate in the ribs, just as she had to him and pushed one of his humbugs into his mouth, before once more ducking to avoid the low doorway, as they both stepped back out onto cobbles beyond.

Kate was relieved that the rain had slowed down to a spat and leaned just close enough into Ben that she could reach into his bag and steal one of his sweets.

'Hey, eat your own,' he grumbled.

Kate shook her head. 'Nah, forbidden fruit is much more fun, isn't it?' She pointed to the seagulls that were hiding under the eaves of the terraced cottages. 'You see, it's much more fun to steal one than to ask for permission.' She grinned, winked and moved to his left-hand side all at once, before happily skipping down the street beside him.

Arriving at the quayside, they paid plenty of attention to how many fishermen had moored their boats and while pretending to pose for photographs, they took pictures of what the boats were called. Some of the fishermen were throwing their loads up and onto the quayside, whereas others sold rides on their boats and made promises of seeing a great coastline. One said that he always saw seals, dolphins and other spectacles, most of which were probably never to be seen.

Discreetly, Ben chatted to one of the fishermen, and as Kate pretended to look in a shop that sold everything from Whitby rock through to Dracula capes she saw money changing hands, which meant that information had just been given.

'This way,' Ben said, as he reappeared by her side, then steered her along the quayside and down some steps towards one of the boats. Before Kate knew it, she was being dragged onto a large fishing boat that was empty, other than the captain.

'Private tour, please,' Ben shouted as he jumped on board The Red Lady. 'And some rugs for our legs, if you don't mind.'

'Ben, no,' she tried to protest. 'Couldn't you do this alone? I'm not sure my sea legs are up to it. Besides, I can see the cliffs from here.' She pointed to the cliffs and then to the sea, its rolling white water crashing against the rocks at the base of the cliff. 'I... I don't much like the water,' she lied, but knew the game they were playing.

'Where's your sense of adventure?' Ben whispered just loud enough for the captain to hear. 'It's our honeymoon and we have to do something crazy, find ourselves a few stories, things we can tell the grandkids.' He flashed her a smile. But not just any smile. It was one of those smiles that lit up his whole face. It radiated a warmth that Kate had never seen and for just a moment she melted into it, wondered how it would feel for a man like Ben to smile at you, every single day.

Searching the boat with her eyes. Kate knew how much they needed to get the information. This was The Red Lady. The very same boat that Isobel had mentioned and if the captain was riding the waves at night, she had every intention of finding out why.

'But...' She looked at Ben, hoping he'd play along. 'I'm nervous. I kind of need to go to the loo.' She hopped from foot to foot, 'Maybe you could go on the boat trip alone and I'll pop to the toilets...' She headed for the steps, went to haul herself up them.

'We have a toilet on board, miss, they're right in there, just through the galley.' The captain pointed to the doors. He obviously didn't want to lose the fare and under the pretence of reluctance, Kate excused herself, and went in search of the toilet.

Stepping back onto the deck, Kate saw Ben handing money to the captain. 'Darling, we're going to go right along the coastline and the nice captain is going to bring us some rugs.'

Reappearing, the captain placed one of the blankets on the wet seat to make them a dry, comfortable area and then carefully he tucked the other over their legs, whilst Ben was still looking like an over-excited child at the prospect of a boat trip.

'How much did you pay him?' Kate said under her breath as she pulled the blanket around her and smiled. It was clean, fluffy and Kate doubted it would normally be used, not unless the price had been right. Like the rest of the boat, the toilets had been spotless, as had the galley. Even the deck was clean and tidy and painted bright red, with black and white stripes that surrounded a bright yellow winch that stood on the stern. Everything looked far too pristine for a working boat and with another inquisitive look into the cabin, Kate doubted that the boat had been used for fishing in a very long time.

'You have a very beautiful wife, sir,' the captain commented as he tipped his hat, then turned to steer the boat out of the harbour.

'Thank you,' Ben replied. 'I think so too.' He pulled Kate towards him, kissed her on the cheek and for a moment, Kate felt herself blush but then reminded herself of the game they were playing, of the pretence of a honeymoon that the captain had obviously believed.

With the sound of the wind making it difficult to hear, Ben leaned in close to Kate. 'I doubt he gets more than a couple of private tours a day and out of what he earns, he'll have expenses. You know, the fuel, the harbour costs, etc.'

'Which means he must be making a living doing something else?' Kate looked over to where the captain stood. He was quite young, but extremely competent, and Kate admired the way he easily steered his boat through the waves and around the coastline.

'He probably does other jobs on the side,' Ben whispered as the boat took a dip on the waves making Kate shriek with nervous laughter.

'Just playing devil's advocate here, but what if there are no extra jobs?' she whispered back.

Ben pondered her question for a moment. 'Well, he'll do what he can. Sometimes work is slow. Sometimes it's non-existent. Men like our captain here would have learnt how to take the good with the bad. It's like the rain, some people would be miserable and see it as a hindrance, others would take the opportunity to splash and dance through the puddles.' Ben had replied with a metaphor that Kate knew was directed at her. The past days had been difficult, but Ben was right. She should dance in the rain. For her own sake she needed to put the bad things behind her. After all, as the saying goes, what doesn't kill you makes you stronger.

She thought of the accident, of what her mother had said the night before and of Eve. 'Oh no, I didn't call Eve.' She jumped up from her seat as Ben pulled her back under the blanket and put his arm protectively around her. The touch of his hand sent an electric shock down her spine, her legs trembled and her stomach did a somersault.

'Don't worry,' he said, as his eyes searched hers. 'Eric said he was going over after work. He has an early finish today.'

'Seriously. Why would he do that?' Kate's voice was concerned. 'They've only met the once. Haven't they?'

'He said something about taking her to join his book club.' Ben smiled. 'Eric's harmless and probably very good for Eve. Trust him.'

'But she barely knows him?' Kate said as she searched frantically through her bag, looking for her phone.

'Kate, she's fine. Stop fussing.' Ben said with a laugh, and pointed to the sea. 'Because if you think you'll get a signal out here, you're kidding yourself.'

Kate hesitated before settling back down under the blanket. 'But they're so different, in fact, I'd say they're poles apart. I mean, do they even like the same kind of books?'

Kate settled down in the arc of Ben's arm. They were pretending to be married and Kate had begun to quite enjoy the role play. Besides, it was the perfect excuse to curl up close in a situation where she felt secure, comfortable and wanted.

Feeling her stomach lurch, Kate felt herself squeal and held onto her breath as the boat bounced up and down on the swell. Gulls swooped overhead in the hope that they might find some food and the abbey loomed impressively above them on the cliff top. It rose up out of the rock, high above where they now sailed and beside it stood the car park where they'd left Patrick earlier that morning, which reminded Kate that those steps would have to be climbed.

* * *

Ben looked down as Kate slept. He'd hated seeing her so upset that morning. His heart had gone out to her and if he could have, he'd have taken the pain away and now, for the second time that day, she slept against him.

Enjoying the moment, he wondered how safe she felt. Or whether, she'd simply been so exhausted that the movement of the boat had made her collapse into a deep, and meaningful sleep. It was a question he couldn't answer. He just hoped for the former and that she felt comfortable in his presence. Like him, she was a little broken and hurt. She might never come to terms with the scar on her face, the crippling of her sister, or the death of her brother. Especially when her whole family seemed to blame her and Ben took the opportunity to glance down at the left-hand side of her face; at the scar that was clearly visible and thoughtlessly, he lifted a finger, and gently drew a line across her jawbone. For some reason, he felt the urge to magic it away. But to do that would change her which was something he wouldn't want to do.

As the boat came to a halt in the harbour. Ben looked up at the captain, indicated to him that he give them some time and Ben mentally kicked himself. He was supposed to be talking to the captain. But to do that would mean waking Kate, and with a deep, inward breath he hugged her more tightly. It was far too soon to wake her, far too soon to let her go and even if he sat there for the whole afternoon, he was more than content to sit it out and to allow her to wake up, in her own good time.

* * *

Kate stirred. She'd felt Ben's finger lightly touch her face and the way he'd drawn a line along her scar. It was a sensation that made her catch her breath. Never before had she been so comfortable with anyone being so close and no one but a doctor had ever been allowed to previously touch the scar. But for some reason she didn't move.

Taking into consideration the movement of the boat, she noticed that it rocked now rather than bounced. She presumed that they were back in the harbour and that the boat had come to a stop. Which meant that both she and Ben would have to move. It was a feeling that made her both happy and sad. She'd told the truth earlier; that going on boats was not her forte. Buy laying here, in Ben's arms, was a feeling she wanted to keep, for just a few moments more.

Warm and comfortable, she felt Ben's face lower to hers. His lips gently brushed her mouth and she opened her sleepy eyes to look into his that were jet black, deep, welcoming and sparkled like ebony. She held his gaze lovingly. 'You... you kissed me,' she whispered. The words were all she could manage to say as her fingers went up to touch his lips.

'I did.' He paused and Kate knew that he was thinking of his next words carefully. 'What was it you said? Better to steal one, than to ask for permission.' He nodded. 'Well, I was testing your theory and I think you are right.' He kept his eyes on hers. 'Forbidden fruit, it's much more fun.'

She smiled. 'Touché.' Sitting up, she looked around to see where they were. 'I'm sorry I fell asleep again. I... I barely slept, you know, last night.'

'Don't worry. It's fine. You've had a horrid few days.' His hand reached up, gently touched her face and for a moment, Kate thought he'd repeat the kiss. But instead, he smiled, stretched and folded the blankets before winking playfully and adding just loud enough for the captain to hear, 'Oh, and by the way, I think you should know. You snore like a train.'

* * *

'Oh you're horrid, why on earth did I marry you?' Kate shouted as Ben jumped from the boat. She knew that the captain was watching and while still wanting to play her role, she climbed onto the quayside, pulled Ben towards her and mischievously but firmly placed a kiss on his lips. 'And I'm starving, so if you don't buy me some fish and chips soon, I may have to consider divorce.'

Ben took the hint and steered Kate further along the quayside.

'Right. Wait here, just for a few minutes. I need to go back and pretend you lost an earring or something,' Ben announced as he turned back towards The Red Lady.

Kate caught his arm. 'Why?' she searched his eyes with hers, with a look of amusement crossing her face.

'I need to get some answers. I was so content, sitting there hugging you, I totally forgot the investigation. I should have been looking for clues. If he is involved, there would have to be something. I won't be long.' Ben began to walk away and with a burst of laughter, Kate held up her mobile phone.

'Do you mean like photographs of maps, and compass points?

Along with Isobel Reed's phone number, and a date and time of a meeting, along with quantities of drugs that are about to be dropped. I found it all scribbled on a pad, in the room beyond the toilet. It was locked at first, but it's amazing what a safety pin and a nail file can do.' She smiled, and looked pleased with herself as Ben studied the photos. 'What do you think I was doing? You know, when I went to find the toilet? Oh yes, that's right,' she laughed out loud. 'I was doing what you were supposed to do, and I was being a private investigator.'

* * *

With a sparkle in her eyes, Kate chatted all through lunch about her love of North Yorkshire, the visits she'd made to her grandmother's cottage as a child, along with both Eve and James. They would have days when they would all drive for miles, just looking for the perfect picnic spot after going to the creamery.

'Grandmother would sit on the rug with a loaf of homemade bread, a pack of butter, our newly bought cheese and a really big knife.' She laughed. 'She'd butter the bread fresh because she knew I liked it and between us, we could eat the whole loaf if we wanted.'

Ben smiled. He liked the way her face came to life when she spoke, how her hands became animated as she described how her childhood and teenage years before the accident had been. It was as though her whole life had been split in two. There was her life before and her life after the accident.

Smiling, he thought of the kiss he'd stolen, of how Kate had reacted. She'd questioned it, but hadn't looked surprised or offended and he wondered for a moment if she'd thought that it had been a part of the act, of their pretending to be newlyweds. But then, as they stood together in the quayside, he'd considered kissing her again, but this time in a real, more loving way. But hadn't. It wouldn't have been right. Not there. Not while they were working. A real first kiss just had to be special, full of hope, passion and trust and with a sparkle in his eye, he began making a plan. One he knew that Kate would like.

29

'Come on then, tell all. How was your afternoon with Eric?' Kate asked inquisitively. She was busy spreading a picnic blanket out on the grass, but looked up to see Eve's smiling face and the sight of Richmond Castle behind her.

'Max, come here,' Eve shouted, as a very energetic Max, being out of harness, was taking every opportunity to chase his ball and with a zoom, he ran around in circles, and carefully dodged the empty wheelchair while constantly sniffing and searching for newer, more interesting scents.

Unlike the day before, the sky was clear and the sun shone brightly. The grass had dried, which made it a pleasure to sit on and both she and Eve kept one eye nervously on the shop their mother had disappeared into just a few minutes before.

'Eric's lovely,' Eve said, excitedly. 'We went to a book club. Which would have probably been a lot more up your street than mine. But I actually got out, Kate. I met people. And for the first time in a year, I didn't feel like the disabled one that everyone pitied.'

Sitting back, with her arm outstretched. Kate took a loaf of fresh bread out of her basket, sliced it freehand and slathered on the butter, just as her grandmother had done. It was a memory she'd always loved and with a smile crossing her face, she unwrapped the ham, coleslaw, scotch eggs and lastly, the quiche. It was a sight that made Max stop running around. He instantly sat down and patiently waited to be given a treat.

Eve lay back on the blanket. 'We're reading *The Secret Keeper* by Kate Morton. It's really good. It's two stories, set in different times. A young girl witnesses a crime while she's hiding in a tree house and fifty years later it all comes back to haunt her.'

'Eve, I'm not interested in what you're reading, silly. I'm interested in you and in Eric. You only met the other night and now you're going out on dates. I mean, come on. How did that happen?'

'Kate, I have been on a date before.' Eve said sarcastically. 'Quite a few, for your information. Eric asked and I said yes. It wasn't a secret.'

'Will you be seeing him again?' Kate asked hesitantly, hoping that Eric had enjoyed the day as much as Eve had.

'Of course I am. He's taking me out to dinner tomorrow,' she responded enthusiastically and flicked her hair backwards in a way that Kate hadn't seen her do in a number of years. 'We're going for a carvery, over at the creamery in Hawes.' Eve lifted herself back up into a sitting position. Leaned against the wheel of her chair. 'So, what happened with Ben?'

'Nothing.'

'Don't lie.'

Kate sighed. She thought of the lovely day they'd shared. The trip to the abbey. The boat ride. The stolen kiss followed by the fish and chips and the way he'd playfully chased her up the ninety-nine steps, even though the run had just about finished them both off.

The whole day had made her think about Rob, about his

involvement with Isobel and about moving on. After what she'd heard outside Isobel's house, she wanted him to leave, and as far as she was concerned, the sooner he went, the better.

'I'm back,' her mother's voice bellowed as she weaved her way between other groups of people who lay on the grass of the castle grounds. She had a bottle held tightly in her hands. 'Mead, darling, your father and I love it.' Kate stared in disbelief as she watched her mother carefully place the bottle into her bag. 'I thought I'd buy him a bottle; it'll make him so happy.'

Once again, Mother was acting strange. It was as though nothing had been said and with a look at her sister, Kate wondered how long it would be before their father came to get her. Kate crossed her fingers. She knew that her father would know what to do. That he'd persuade her to go to a doctor and she also hoped that, with any luck, he'd be here soon.

'So, does this mean you're going home?' Eve asked hopefully, saying exactly what both of the twins were thinking.

'No, dear. Your father's working away. He's told me to stay here. He thought it would be better for me than staying home alone and it's only for a few more days.' She sat down on the grass. 'He has a reason for everything, dear, you know it's easier not to argue.'

Both Kate and Eve had a way of communicating without saying a word and both had picked up on the news that their father was away. Which was why he hadn't been answering the phone. But at least their mother was no longer threatening divorce, nor was she calling him a sociopath, and just one look between them created a silent acknowledgment to keep quiet on the subject.

Kate's mobile buzzed and she checked her messages.

Hope you are having a good day. Ben x

A smile turned the corner of her mouth. It was only the second text that Ben had ever sent, and what's more, for the second time, there was a kiss at the end of it and with a heat travelling thorough her cheeks, Kate felt herself glow. She liked him, but still found it hard to believe that a man like Ben would like her too, and wondered if she'd somehow mistaken his affection? Brushing the thought to one side, she picked up the phone and quickly replied.

Today is a good day, but yesterday was better x

She pressed send and wondered if it were better to take a chance and to say exactly what was on her mind or whether she should play it a little more casual.

'Mmmm, looks like you had a good day too.' Eve picked up Kate's phone, tapped in the passcode and read the text message.

Grabbing the phone out of her hand, Kate laughed as they both simultaneously pulled a face just as the theme tune on her mobile rang out and Eve began to quietly hum the wedding march, and Kate glared across in her direction. She wished for her to be quiet and then felt her heart drop to her feet as Rob's name flashed up and onto the screen.

'What do you want, Rob?' She took in a deep breath. She'd once been told that the only way to not break down was to stay in control and right now, that was exactly what she intended to do and with the memory of him and Isobel being together clear in her mind, she had every intention of telling him exactly what she thought.

'Hey, baby, what's wrong? I just called to check you were okay and there you go biting my head off.'

'What are you up to, Rob?' She stood up and walked across the grass. She wanted to be out of her mother's earshot and took note that she was currently leafing through a glossy magazine. 'You haven't been home for days, again.' She had to be careful what she said. Isobel was still under investigation and Kate couldn't confront him, not about her. To do so could blow the whole case, and if it did, the million-pound reward would most probably be lost.

'So I haven't been home for a day or two. It happens. You know what I'm like.'

'Yes, I do know what you are like, Rob, and I don't like it. Not any more. What are you hiding?'

'Me? Why would you think that, baby?'

'As the saying goes, Rob, tell me no secrets, and I'll tell you no lies. Problem is, I can't keep up with all your bloody lies, and I no longer want to.' The words were spat down the phone like venom. She'd had enough and this time he wasn't getting away with feeding her the normal bullshit that fell from his mouth.

Rob had gone quiet; Kate knew she'd caught him off guard, and knowing Rob, he was contemplating the situation and deciding what retort he'd come back with. 'What's got into you, Kate?'

'I'm only going to say this once, Rob. I want you out.' She couldn't help herself. The words had just fallen out of her mouth like an erupting volcano. 'I want you out of my cottage and I want you out of my life. Do you understand?'

* * *

'Err, what? Where the hell...?' Rob shouted. 'Why the hell would you say that?' Feeling the panic rise within him he couldn't understand where the 'grateful to be loved' Kate had suddenly gone. She seemed different. Angry. And he knew that he had no choice but to calm her down.

'Baby, don't be like this.' He walked slowly, purposely and stared across the open fields that stood opposite his gym. To the outside world he was a personal trainer. A man who lived with a barrister's daughter, which had given him a certain standing within the community. Men trusted him with their wives and if he were single, the trust would be lost and the drugs wouldn't get sold.

'Look, I'm sorry I didn't come home. You know I love you,' his voice quivered, and desperately, he tried not to lose his temper. 'We're good together, Kate, you know that. What about the other night, when I made love to you in the bathroom? It was good, wasn't it?' He tried to sound authentic but in the bottom of his heart he knew that a woman like Kate should be grateful. Especially after the accident that should never have happened. In reality, no one should have been injured. No one should have died. A simple spin on the road should have resulted in Rob saving the day. But there had been oil on the road. The car had gone into the stream and James being killed hadn't been a part of the plan. The plan had been for Kate to love him, for her to provide him with a home. A safe house from where he could work. But all good plans didn't always work and the moment he realised that things had gone wrong, he'd pulled both Kate and Eve out of the wreckage. But James had already been dead and he'd had no alternative but to abandon the plan and just a few weeks later, he'd followed her to the hospital, tampered with her car and turned on the charm.

* * *

'Rob, you need to be gone before I get home.' Kate's voice was angry but controlled and with her stomach twisting with a deep-seated anxiety, she looked over her shoulder and checked on her mother. The last thing she needed right now was the 'I told you so' talk and purposely moved away.

'You don't mean that.'

'Oh, yes, I do,' she snapped. 'Get your things and get out. It shouldn't be hard for you to find somewhere to stay, you don't normally have a problem.' Closing her eyes, she thought of all the times he'd been warm, tender and affectionate. Moments she'd clung onto for far too long. But she wasn't clinging to them now. He didn't love her. That was more than apparent and with tears filling her eyes, she wondered how many women there really were and mentally she went through all the women she knew of and the constant showering and changing of clothes.

'Rob, did you hear me?'

'Oh, I heard you,' he shouted angrily, and Kate pulled the phone away from her ear. 'You can't do that, you bitch. I stood by you, Kate. It was me that had to look at that disgusting scar, me that had to make love to you looking like that, yet still, I stayed.' He paused, and Kate took the chance to draw breath.

'Had to? Had to?' She couldn't believe her ears. 'Get out... I want you out, and I want you out now!' she screamed. At this point she didn't care who heard, she just wanted him to realise that she meant what she said. 'At least then you'll never have to look at this disgusting scar, ever again you bastard. Will you?'

'Ohhh, I get it. What's his name, Kate? Who are you shagging?'

'Don't turn the tables on me, Rob, I won't justify myself to you. Now I want you out of my cottage, before I get back. Is that clear?'

Rob suddenly went quiet and Kate pulled the phone from her ear and checked the screen. For just a moment, she listened to nothing but silence.

'Have you been dieting, Kate?' Rob said completely out of the blue. 'The jeans you have on, they're looking too loose?'

The words made her panic, her jeans did look loose, but Rob hadn't seen her for days and he couldn't have known what she was wearing and with that thought in mind, her breathing escalated and she spun around, searching and looking for Rob.

'Where are you, Rob?' she murmured in a soft questioning voice as she searched the castle ground, the turrets and the battlements, but as she did, she heard Rob's response and her stomach turned as he erupted with a loud, evil laugh that went on forever.

'I'm everywhere, Kate, and don't you ever forget it.'

She stared up at the sky, did all she could to clear her mind. What if he'd been in Whitby, what if he'd seen her with Ben? But, then again, why would that matter and why should he care?

'You're everywhere are you, Rob? Well, you might think you are, but in reality you are nowhere. You are no one. You're not important. Not to anyone. Especially to me and I really do want you gone and what's more, I never want to see your evil, ugly face ever again.'

'Who's telling you to do this, Kate? Is it that new boss of yours, or your good for nothing mother?' He paused. 'Or, actually, I bet it's your pathetic, crippled sister? It's her, isn't it? She's never did like me. Did she?'

Kate reeled at the multiple insults. 'Do you really think I don't know my own mind, Rob? Do you think I can't live without you?' She laughed. 'Well, I've got news for you, I can. Now get your filthy cheating backside out of my fucking house before I get home.'

'Cheating? Is that what you think?' He paused. 'What the hell makes you think that?'

Kate inhaled and bit down on her lip. She couldn't reveal what she knew and had to be careful. 'Rob, you don't come home at night and I'm clearly not stupid.'

'Well, you do know that no one will want you, because your face is a mess. Do you know that?' The words had been carefully chosen, vindictive and meant to hurt, but Kate was past hurting. She knew her scar was ugly and didn't need him to tell her for her to know it were true.

But she also knew that Rob would never humiliate her again. She was sure that Ben cared, but even if he didn't. It didn't matter.

He'd already given her some hope for the future and right now, that was all she'd needed.

'Do you know what, Rob.' She looked up to the sky, felt a tiny drop of rain land on the tip of her nose and smiled at the irony. It reminded her of the chat she'd had with Ben and the advice he'd inadvertently given. 'I don't need you. But it's raining and right now, I'm going to go and dance in the rain.'

30

Pulling up outside her house, Kate felt her heart sink as she saw Rob's truck parked on her drive. It was a sight that made her wait outside. Where she sat and watched. She felt thankful that her mother had stayed with Eve and that right now, they'd be watching DVDs, wearing face masks and drinking wine. The idea of a movie night had sounded like fun, but Kate had opted to go home. She'd really wanted to get back to the cottage, take a bath and stretch out on her bed, but now she had no choice but to face Rob.

Angrily, she took in a deep breath, threw open the car door and stamped up to the house where she fully expected Rob to be packing. Or that he might just be sat waiting, ready to go. But as she entered the kitchen, she stopped in her tracks.

'Hey, baby. I've cooked us some food.' He spun towards the door, picked up the tea towel and casually threw it over his shoulder. Even in the soft, amber lighting she immediately saw the bruising that covered his face. Deep purple colouring surrounded his wrists, an obvious sign of being restrained and automatically she felt concern, wondered what he'd done to hurt himself so badly.

'We have a chicken pasta, garlic bread and roast courgettes, with garlic, tomato and parmesan.' He smiled, took a sip from a glass of wine and passed her the bottle. 'Here. It's cold. Just out of the fridge.'

'I'm not hungry.' She didn't know what else to say and with small, tentative steps, she inched around the island, kept it between them and stood, staring at him. He was cooking and sipping wine, like nothing had been said. What made the image even worse was that he never cooked, he never cleaned and he never normally drank. No matter how much she'd tried to tempt him.

'Come on, sit down. I have it all ready.' He gave her a smile, took two pasta bowls out of the cupboard, and placed them down on the table.

'I'm not hungry, Rob and I'm not sure if you remember this,' she said firmly, 'but, I told you to get out.'

Rob turned, and held a hand out towards her. 'Come on, baby, I'm trying to be nice. Now. Sit. Down. And. Eat.' Placing a dish of roast courgette in front of her, Kate felt her heart rate rise. She didn't dare speak. What she did want to do was reach for her bag and her phone that lay within it. Neither were close enough for her to grab. And right now, even if she could, she wouldn't know who to call. Serving dinner was hardly a criminal offence.

'Rob, I... I'm really not hungry. I'm off to take a bath.' She stood up, grabbed her bag and hurriedly headed for the stairs where she went into the bathroom and locked the door behind her, before picking up her phone, and texting Ben.

I asked Rob to leave. But he's still here. He's acting all strange. I've locked myself in the bathroom. x

Quickly looking around the room, Kate considered opening the window. She thought about climbing out and onto the roof tops, but the window was small, the drop much too high. In a panic, she began to run the water; she'd told Rob she was going in the bath and knew he'd be listening.

Sitting on the floor beside the bath, she watched her phone as she willed Ben to respond. But she knew a text couldn't save her and that ultimately if she wanted him gone, she had to face Rob. It was a thought she didn't have to consider for too long as just then she heard Rob's footsteps aggressively stamping up the stairs, and with an overwhelming sense of urgency, she picked up her work phone, and pressed in the panic code, just as Ben had taught her.

'Are you in the bath, Kate?' Rob questioned as the door handle was snapped up and down. 'Come on, Kate. Open the door.'

'Let me be, Rob. I just want to take a bath.' She swished the water, hoped he'd take the hint. 'Please Rob. You need to leave.'

'That's what you think, is it?' A loud noise erupted like a volcano. It was a sound that made Kate scream and the door burst open. 'You won't let it go, will you? You just won't let it go.' His frame filled the doorway and while crouching as close as she could to the floor, Kate went to get past him, but couldn't.

'Rob, I really want you to go.' She looked over his shoulder, saw the staircase and knew that her only escape was to get past him. 'Rob, I really don't want to fight.' She backed herself into the corner. 'I've phoned the police. They're on their way.' She called his bluff, saw the way his eyes dilated, deep, mistrusting and cavernous.

'Why would you do that?' He moved towards her. 'You love me. Don't you?' Again he took a step forward, reached out towards her. 'Come on, baby, don't make me beg?'

'Rob, you've never begged for anything in your life. Now, get out of my way.' She went to push past him, saw the look in his eye, felt fear course through every inch of her body.

'Oh no, baby. I can't let you leave.' Rob stared directly at her, with eyes devoid of emotion. He grabbed at her hands, began moving them up and down and then pressed his body against hers.

Feeling anxious, Kate tried to move away from him and angrily, she swung out with every ounce of strength she had, caught him squarely on his already bruised cheek. 'Get off me.'

Unexpectedly, he dropped her hands, and rested both of his hands firmly on his hips as he took in a deep breath. 'I know what it is.' He shrugged and stepped towards her. 'I'm doing it wrong, aren't I?' He laughed, a long, evil laugh before grabbing at her shirt and tearing it from her. 'You wanted to dance in the rain, didn't you?'

Panic rose within her. Rob was bigger and stronger than she was and effortlessly, he dragged her towards him. The next moment, she was in the bath and under the water. She couldn't breathe. Her lungs burned. Her hands grabbed frantically at his hair, at his face and then, the only thing she could see was the image of her brother's glazed, cold eyes staring back at her.

As panic threatened to overwhelm her, from nowhere, she heard a noise. A bang. A shout. A loud echo that surrounded her and then she was propelled out of the water. Rob's hands were gone, and as she tried to pull the air into her lungs, she began to cough and choke. It was only after a few moments that she saw Ben was standing in her bathroom.

'It's okay. He's gone.' Ben's arms were around her and she felt relief, followed by hysteria, as she felt her whole body go limp.

31

Feeling drowsy, and confused, Kate carefully opened her eyes at the sound of Ben's voice. She was in his bedroom. A room he'd kindly allowed her to use and which unlike her own tiny bedroom at the cottage, was nice and spacious. She could see a great expanse of carpet, the walls were white and the furniture minimalist. The bed was king-sized and she stretched out on it and stared out through the bi-folding doors at the miles of countryside that she saw lay before her.

'Hey, how are you feeling?' He moved to her side, gently brushed the hair away from her face that, for once, wasn't covered in make-up. His tenderness made tears spring to her eyes, and with a sudden clarity, her mind went back to the night before. Once again, she could see the fury in Rob's eyes, and felt the burning in her lungs as her body had wanted to breathe. There was a mixture of both gratitude and sadness; a million emotions blasting through her mind all at once, that were all stacked up with the knowledge that if Ben hadn't turned up at the exact moment he had, she'd be dead.

'I'm fine,' she blinked repeatedly, cleared her vision and lifted a hand to gently touch his face. He had a distinct swelling that surrounded both eyes and a cheek bone that looked red and inflamed. 'But you're not fine.' She smiled sympathetically, knew that Rob had attacked him too. 'And we could have probably both done without the five hours we spent at the hospital, last night,' she whispered as the colour rose to her cheeks. She hadn't liked being trolleyed into an ambulance with all the neighbours watching, and the barrage of questions the police had asked.

'What time is it?' She looked through the window, saw that the sun had risen high above the trees and guessed that it was no longer morning.

He gave her a smile. 'It's time you had something to eat. That's what time it is.' Ben said with a smile. 'And on the menu today is a bacon sandwich. Would you like it up here, or downstairs?' He walked back to the door, looked back over his shoulder. 'And there's a choice of tea or coffee?' he threw in for good measure.

Her stomach grumbled. 'Coffee would be great, and my stomach is saying a yes to the bacon sandwich. Thank you.' Her throat was sore, her arms and legs ached and as she stretched her arms above her head, she winced with the pain but smiled at the sight of her borrowed pyjamas. Ben's pyjamas hung loosely from her body and for a moment, she found amusement in the way she'd rolled the legs up. Her gaze landed on her small, hurriedly-packed bag that contained all the things she'd thought were a priority at the time and she felt the tears spring back into her eyes once again. How had her life come to this?

Trying to make the best of what she had with her, she washed her face and dressed as quickly as she could as the sound of Ben's voice drifted up the staircase as he hummed a tune to himself. She padded towards it, along the hallway and towards the smell of bacon.

'I just love your house,' she managed to say, as she entered the room. 'Thank you for, you know, bringing me here.'

Ben looked her up and down, pressed his lips tightly together and gave her a look of concern. 'Coffee's coming up and you are welcome. It's only a small place but I like it.' He paused, and turned the bacon. 'I sold the big house after... after Julia died. It felt far too empty.'

Kate nodded sympathetically. 'It must have been awful for you.'

The words made Kate think about her cottage. About the impact the attack would have and whether she'd ever feel safe in her house again.

Shaking her thoughts back to the present, Kate's eyes travelled around Ben's house. It was modern, masculine and it suited him. He looked at home behind the counter and she smiled as he twisted the knobs on his coffee machine, which looked far too technical.

'Is fresh coffee okay? I don't have any instant,' Ben suddenly said as he flashed her a smile. He stood by the stove, wearing tracksuit bottoms that hung loosely from his waist and a tight, white T-shirt that covered his chest. His arm muscles escaped the material and showed a chiselled shape that Kate admired. It was also the first time she'd seen him dressed in casual attire, and she had to admit, she really liked it.

'That'd be lovely. Thanks.' She inhaled deeply. 'What smells so good?'

He turned and stirred a pan. 'Home-made chicken noodle soup,' he announced proudly. 'Mum always used to make it for me as a kid. Her perfect antidote for any illness. I knew your throat must be sore and thought that if you couldn't eat a sandwich, the soup would have been easier to swallow.' He paused before walking across the kitchen and placing the coffee before her. 'And after the few days that you've just had, I thought you might need some.'

Kate sipped at the coffee, and slowly chewed at the bacon sandwich that Ben had prepared. He was right, her throat was sore, but she was hungry, and swallowed with care. 'I'm sure food tastes better when someone else makes it.' She began to laugh and swallowed again, then pushed the food to one side as the memory of Rob cooking in her kitchen sprang into her mind.

As though reading her mind, Ben stared at the worktop before speaking. 'I was worried about you last night. When I saw your text, I didn't stop to reply. I just jumped in the car. And then I heard the panic alarm and knew you were in trouble.' He raised an eyebrow, exhaled slowly. 'What if I'd got there just a few moments later?' He shook his head and then turned back towards the pan. It stood on a large cream Aga, which was set back in what looked like a brick chimney breast, but Kate knew that a chimney in a modern house was improbable. The kitchen was modern and pristine. Beams covered the ceiling and black granite worktops sparkled with a shine that stood out against the contemporary walnut cabinets. A mixture of old and new blended perfectly against the pure white walls.

'Looks like your mum taught you well,' she said as she picked at the bacon.

'She certainly did.' He smiled, stole a small piece of bacon from her plate, then happily munched it.

'What's she like, your mum?' Kate asked, genuinely interested. She knew his father and knew how much Ben was like him, but couldn't remember him ever mentioning his mother. Not before today.

Ben chuckled as he picked up a tea towel. 'Are you serious?'

'What did I say?' she offered, holding her hands outright as though waiting for an answer but once again Ben flashed her a smile and shook his head.

'Kate Duggan. You're unbelievably naive. I'm just going to throw some better clothes on and then I'll be back.' Leaving the room, he headed up the stairs and towards his bedroom. It was the room she'd occupied the night before, and with a rush of guilt, she wondered where he'd slept after she'd taken his bed.

Wandering from room to room. Kate admired the way that the kitchen made way to the dining area. A long oak table had been placed in front of a four-panelled concertina glass window. It took up a whole wall and gave way to the most perfect view over miles of lush, green countryside. The house might be small, but nothing had been done by half and Ben's personality showed in every detail.

A noise behind her made her jump. She spun around to see Ben leaning against the doorway; his wide, disarming smile lit up his face and took her by surprise. He wore a blue cotton shirt, with jeans that hugged him just a little too comfortably, making her eyes dwell for just a little too long on their contours.

'Okay, spill the beans. Why are you laughing at me and why do you think I'm naive?' she asked, going back to his earlier comment.

'Because Kate, Gloria is my mum. I can't believe you hadn't worked that out.' He chuckled again as Kate suddenly registered what he'd just said.

'Gloria?' she asked in disbelief. 'What – really? How come?'

'Well, my mother and father met. They fell in love and then I came along.' He ducked as a napkin narrowly missed his head, landing just short of the chicken soup. 'When you came to work for Parker and Son, did you just think it was me and Dad?' Ben walked over to where she stood.

'Of course, the name above the door indicates that, doesn't it?'

Again, Ben smiled. 'No, it doesn't. It says Parker and Son. Gloria was the original private detective, and then I was born. Hence, Gloria Parker and Son. My dad, he was an accountant and still is. He does all the accounts at the office, albeit Mum did teach him the tricks of the trade and eventually he became a really good detective too.'

Kate was both shocked and amused. It was true, she had presumed that the name was directed at William and Ben. William had been there on her first day. He'd spoken to her with authority and Gloria had appeared to be far too lovely to be the boss's wife. There had been no airs and graces, no attitude and definitely no acting like she owned the place.

'It... it kind of makes a lot of sense, about Gloria, now that you've said.'

Ben stepped forward and pulled her into his arms. 'I don't know what I'd have done, if he'd killed you.' His hand slowly lifted to the side of her face, the tension rose in her stomach and every part of her screamed to be held, yet deep within her, she was petrified of what would come next. Breathing in, she felt his breath on her face. His lips were just millimetres from hers and the musky aroma of his aftershave surrounded her senses.

'Ben, don't... don't feel sorry for me.' She swallowed hard and lifted her face towards his. 'I can take a lot, but not pity. Not from you.' Her voice quivered as she spoke, her gaze didn't leave his lips and then, as though he understood her dilemma, he lifted a finger and just as he had on the boat, he traced the scar.

'I don't pity you, Kate. I think you're beautiful.' Gently, he pressed his lips to hers. Shock waves raced through her body and sensing Kate's acceptance of his kiss, Ben's mouth began to move over hers, slowly but rhythmically.

But then, the kiss stopped. Ben stepped back and Kate could see the anguish tear through him as he raked his hands through his hair and took deep, deliberate breaths.

'What... What's wrong?' she asked tentatively, unsure she wanted to hear the answer.

Ben furrowed he brow. 'Nothing. Nothing's wrong. I just...' He closed his eyes, just for a moment. 'It's not the right time and I promised myself that I'd wait until it was. You, you don't need this, not after last night.' He paused, walked over to the soup and stirred it again. 'My timing sucks.' He laughed. 'I really wanted to court you, take you out, send you flowers. And I was waiting for the right time, until you were free, but then after last night, after I almost lost you.' He shook his head. 'It keeps going round in my mind. What if I'd got there just one minute later?'

Ben's revelation caught her off balance. She could see that he was struggling with his emotions, that the kiss had thrown him off balance too, which unnerved her. Closing her eyes, Kate knew that the moment between them had gone. That the kiss was over and desperately, she wanted to move on, to make the situation a lot less embarrassing for the both of them. 'Did the police call yet? Have they caught him?'

Ben gave her a look of concern and shook his head. 'I should have stopped him, but I was more concerned about getting to you out of the water, and if I'm honest, I was just pleased that he ran when he did.'

* * *

Climbing into the shower while Kate slept, Ben turned up the power as high as he could. The water was cold and pummelling, and he found himself holding his breath, as he allowed the water to fall on his face like the torrents of a waterfall.

He'd wanted Kate so much and with his eyes closed, he relived the kiss. It had had the promise of passion and even though it had aroused him in a way that he hadn't felt for years.

He still felt angry that it had happened at all, that he'd moved too quickly.

'Fool,' he whispered, clenching his fists. 'You did it all wrong.'

Trying to calm his arousal, he leaned against the tiles, and tapped his forehead with the flat of his hand. 'Why, why did you kiss her?' he asked himself, but already knew the answer. She was witty, and feisty, caring and vulnerable. She had so many qualities and insecurities, they were impossible to count. But that's what made her who she was and without any doubts, he wanted to fall into those big doe eyes and give her a world where she'd always be happy.

But with Rob still at large, Ben wondered if that would ever be possible.

32

Eve took in a long, deep breath and used every muscle she could to help her stand next to the kitchen unit. 'Come on girl, you can do this,' she said out loud as she used her hands and arms to take her weight. Being paralysed below the waist meant that the upper body had no option but to take the burden. But even though her legs were weak and trembled uncontrollably, Eve had built up enough strength to be able to hold herself upright.

She loved the days when there would be no interruptions, the days when she could work on her physiotherapy and the days when she could make progress without anyone knowing. Thankfully, her father had arrived early that morning and her mother had returned to York, which meant that Eve had the whole day to herself and with a determined effort, she intended to use it.

Looking down at her feet, Eve prayed for them to move. She concentrated as hard as she could and every millimetre that she moved was celebrated and even though she was exhausted by the smallest of movements, she kept going until she could do no more and then with an agonising thud, she landed back in her chair, and closed her eyes. It was only then that she allowed her mind to go over the call she'd taken from Ben.

It had been a moment when Eve's heart had almost stopped beating, and even though she was filled with fury, she had to be strong. For too long, she'd relied on Kate. She'd expected her to be there for her every time she'd phoned. What she hadn't ever taken into consideration was the fact that Kate might not always be there and with that thought in her mind, she looked up at the ceiling, closed her eyes tightly together, and prayed.

'God, if you give me back my ability to walk, I will be the best sister that Kate has ever wished for,' she muttered, 'I'll help her. I'll look after her and I'll sure as hell make certain that no one ever hurts her again.' She looked down at Max and ruffled his fur. 'Won't we, Max?' She patted her knee, encouraged Max to put his front paws up and onto her lap. She ran a hand across the dog's coat, laughed as he nuzzled in and then jumped up on the settee, ready to snooze.

'Oh, no you don't. Get off there,' she said, as Max looked up at her with big, sad eyes. 'Eric's coming later.' She quickly looked up at the clock and checked the time. Eric would be picking her up in just a few hours and with a determined smile she wheeled herself through to the bedroom and opened her wardrobe.

Feeling excited, she scoured the clothes. She just had to look good and without hesitation, she chose a pair of jeans and a skinny T-shirt that would hang from one shoulder. They were clothes she hadn't worn since before the accident, and cautiously she lifted them in front of her body, checked her reflection in the mirror.

'Would this be the outfit to turn his head?' Eve held the top up to Max, who'd followed her into the bedroom. He now lay on the bed, where he continued to snooze. She knew that Eric liked her and for once she needed him to look at her in a way that wasn't simply as a friend.

33

'Eve, calm down,' Kate whispered as she sat up in bed, and tried to look at the clock through eyes that were glazed and didn't want to open. 'What's happened?'

'Eric kissed me,' Eve sobbed, uncontrollably.

Kate switched on the bedside lamp, flopped back against the pillows. 'Okay, and that a bad thing because...?' She sighed, pulled back the duvet and slid out of bed.

'Because it was a real kiss, Kate. A real passionate one. Not just a peck and I really like him, Kate. But what if I'm not enough for him?' Eve continued to sob down the phone. 'One of the women at the book club.' She paused and Kate heard her blow her nose loudly into a handkerchief. 'She's slim, tall and has the most perfect figure and she keeps looking at Eric, giving him the eye and Kate? What if he likes her more than he likes me? He might take the better and easier option, don't you think? I mean, come on. He's not going to want to push me around in a chair forever, is he?'

'Eve, do you ever look in the mirror?' Kate hesitated and with her eyes half-closed, she imagined Eve sat there, staring at her reflection. 'Do you?'

'Of course I look in the mirror,' Eve whimpered her response and for a moment, Kate felt her heart strings stretch until they pulled tight. It was as though she and Eve were connected, heart to heart. A string that joined them together, which meant that every time Eve's heart lurched, so did Kate's.

Closing her eyes, Kate wished for teleportation so that she could land in Eve's house and for them to be curled up on Eve's bed. Just as they had so many times in the past. At least then she'd have been able to reassure her, help her and convince her that she was beautiful, that she had so much more than a wheelchair on offer and that Eric would be more than a fool not to see it.

'What do you see when you look in the mirror, Eve?' The question was direct and meant to provoke and Kate stared at the phone when she heard nothing but silence. Eve was thinking about her answer and Kate could almost guess what that answer would be. After all, every time she looked in a mirror herself, she knew what she saw. She saw the huge, puckered, red scar, that everyone noticed.

'I see a great big lump of metal on wheels, Kate,' she finally replied. 'I just see the bloody chair.'

'Well, that's the problem, Eve,' Kate answered. 'I never see the chair. When I look at you, I see a beautiful woman in the prime of her life, with so much to give. And do you know what, Eve? I'd say that Eric is a good man, and he sees exactly the same.'

Eve sniffed loudly. 'But—'

'There are no buts. Tell me what happened between you two?'

'It happened last night,' Eve acknowledged. 'He kissed me. Right after he brought me home from dinner.' She sobbed. 'Actually, that's not true. I think that I might have kissed him.'

Kate smiled at the way her sister had once kissed men for fun. Hadn't thought anything of it and with the phone firmly perched under her chin she began to think about Ben, about what it would be like to kiss him every day of the week. To see that sparkle light up his face and for her to be able to gaze into those dark eyes of his.

'Okay. Let's think rationally. Have you heard from Eric since the kiss?' Kate said as she walked down the stairs, and into the kitchen where she flicked on the kettle, before digging around in the cupboard, looking for coffee.

'He's been texting back and forth all night,' Eve replied.

'Eve,' she said with a sigh. 'So, what's the problem?' In the absence of coffee, Kate pulled open the fridge, spotted a carton of orange juice and poured some into a glass.

'I'm frightened, Kate. Everything got a bit heated and then suddenly, he got all nervous and he left. I'd wanted him to stay, but... what if he wants to have sex?'

'Eve, one kiss doesn't automatically equate to sex and it isn't like you've never done it, is it?' She laughed. 'I've lost count of how many times I used to walk in on you, or caught you at it in the back of our parents' car.'

'But Kate, everything's changed!' She stopped, began to take in huge gulps of air. 'And, I'm not sure how much I'll feel.'

Kate could hear the anguish in her sister's voice and tried to keep calm. 'Well,' she continued, 'it can't be so different, can it? And there are a lot of ways you could please each other...' She was suddenly aware that Ben was in the house and possibly listening and with a quick look over her shoulder, she looked into the lounge and saw where Ben's tall, broad frame that was much too big for the settee was sleeping. It was a sight that made Kate want to go back to his bed, to the place where his sheets still smelt of aftershave and in a perfect world, she wondered how easy it would be to convince him to join her.

'Eve, I'd come over, but I'm not sure I could face Mother, not at this time of the morning.'

'She isn't here.'

Kate had begun walking back to the bedroom, but stopped in her tracks. 'What the hell do you mean, she isn't there?' Kate panicked, her initial thought was that their mother could have gone back to the cottage and that Rob was still out there.

'Father came over yesterday. He took her home.'

Kate felt a sudden sense of relief. 'He came?' She smiled, closed her eyes, and thought of the bed that was stood just a few paces away. All she wanted to do was crawl back in and take Ben with her, but right now, Eve needed her.

Kate glanced into the lounge, she checked that Ben was still sleeping and satisfied that he was, she went up to the bedroom and quickly changed. 'Eve, I'll tell you what. Give me half an hour and put the kettle on. I'm dying for decent coffee.'

34

'What do you mean, the bloody shipment's gone?' Isobel screamed down her mobile. She walked from lounge to kitchen, out through the back door and entered the pool house, where Roberto ran on a treadmill.

'Half of the shipment. It's been impounded and Martin's been arrested,' Giancarlo whispered. 'But there's nothing I can do. Not from here.' His voice sounded distant, and crackly.

Isobel panicked. 'Where are you?' She held the phone tightly to her ear, heard him cough twice. It was a signal. One they'd used many times before. A way of indicating that someone was near, that, at least for a while, it wasn't safe to speak.

'I have to leave the country for a week or two,' Giancarlo finally continued. 'The police. They're onto me. It's me they will follow, so the further I am away from the rest of you, the better.'

'Giancarlo, don't you dare leave me here alone,' Isobel shouted. 'Will Martin talk? Are we in danger?'

'Don't be crazy. It's the last thing he'd ever do,' Giancarlo whispered. 'Roberto knows what to do. Customs are watching us, and we can't bring the shipment in through the docks. I've organised an alternative route. The captain of The Red Lady knows it's more dangerous, but both Luca and Roberto, they know what they're doing.'

Isobel knew that the Bellandinis had always stuck together; that at times of trouble they were like a pack of wolves and without exception they all did what Giancarlo ordered.

Again, there was a cough and another pause. 'Roberto will tell you everything. But you have to be prepared, my darling girl. I could be gone for a while.' His voice sounded calm, yet defeated. 'Just keep your head down. All will be over soon.'

'And Elena, is she to go with you?'

Giancarlo's silence spoke volumes. It was the only answer Isobel needed and with frustration building up inside her she kicked out at the equipment and watched as her bright pink yoga ball landed in the pool. 'So, you're taking Elena to safety, but not me.' She looked across at Roberto who ran on the treadmill at speed, oblivious to the call. But then, Roberto was oblivious to most things. He had no idea that she and Giancarlo had been together, or that she'd had a dalliance with Luca. Both were part of the same family. Each of them conquests. Like trophies she'd needed to win and had used them to make Giancarlo jealous. But now he was gone, and Isobel sobbed.

'Hey, *bello piccolo fiore*, do not cry for me,' he said. 'I'll be back before you know it. I've told you, there is a plan. If the shipment goes wrong, you need to do what Roberto says. You need to go with him to the safe house and you need to stay there and wait for me.'

His Italian words of 'little flower' rang in her ears as Isobel remembered the hushed plans often spoken between Giancarlo and Roberto. They'd looked at maps, discussed co-ordinates and had taken trips without explanation. It was obvious that an elaborate plan had been made. But none of the details had ever been shared with her and right now she wasn't sure she wanted to be a part of their plan at all.

35

After walking in through the front door of Parker and Son, Kate immediately noticed the different atmosphere. It was still only nine o'clock and even though Ben had said she should stay at home; the early morning wakeup call she'd had from Eve had been the push she needed to get herself up and out. And after spending the last two hours boosting Eve's self-confidence, she'd finally driven to work feeling better about the day ahead.

'Kate. What are you doing here?' Gloria questioned, as she walked across the room and lay a hand on the newly installed coffee machine that now stood behind reception. 'I don't know why Ben bought this thing. He has one at home, seems to think it will make my life easier.' She tutted at the machine. 'You want a cappuccino or would you prefer one of those latte ones?' she asked, while raising her eyebrows.

'Can we just have coffee?' Kate asked with a laugh, 'Or isn't it allowed?'

'Coffee it is. Now, you sit down and rest.' Gloria pointed to the settee with authority and Kate knew that Ben had already filled her in about the attack. 'Ben's in there, he's talking to William.' She pointed to the wall. Indicated that Ben was in the office next door. 'They're talking about the case, go and join them if you want to, I'll bring the coffee.'

* * *

'Ben, do you want to fill me in, because right now I don't understand.' Kate sat down in the tub chair that stood before William's desk, and looked between Ben and his father.

'Finally, I got that damned machine to work,' Gloria said as she entered the room and placed the tray down on the desk that held plates of carrot cake, chocolate cake and three steaming hot mugs of coffee. 'I'll be going back to my kettle before the end of the day, mark my words.' She laughed, looked affectionately at Ben, then patted his shoulder.

Kate felt her heartbeat calm as she sat back in the chair. It felt like such a long time since she'd first come to work here. Yet, it had only been just over a week and in that time, her life had changed considerably. She still couldn't believe that Rob of all people, was involved with drugs. He'd always been so strict about everything he'd put into his body. Even his daily calories were dictated by his exercise regime. But then, she wouldn't have thought him capable of trying to kill her either.

'It's time to turn the case over to the police. We're done.' Ben stared at his father, then threw a look at Kate. 'I won't put you at any more risk. It isn't worth it.'

'Oh, no. You're not losing the reward because of me – we're so close.'

William stood up. 'Kate, my dear, we have all the information we need. All we have to do now is pass it over and wait till the police take them down.' He looked at her, lips pursed. 'Ben's right. We won't put you in danger. Besides, do you remember that day in Whitby?' He placed his mug back down on the tray. 'Well, you were quite productive. You were spot on about The Red Lady. And what's more, those photographs you took gave us times, dates and co-ordinates. We know that the drugs are coming in by sea and it'll be The Red Lady that picks up the load.' He patted the evidence folder. 'But instead of coming into the docks, the drugs will be dropped over the wreck of the San Georgic. They'll be dropped in baskets, similar to lobster pots and from what we've heard, the pots will be collected by two expert divers and we're guessing that one of them will be Roberto Bellandini.'

'Who?' Kate was puzzled.

'Roberto Bellandini Kate. The man you know as Robert Bell is a twenty-eight-year-old drug dealer, related to one of the most notorious Italian families we've ever heard of.'

Kate threw her hands in the air. Was there anything else she didn't know about the man she'd lived with? 'As far as I'm aware, he has no idea how to scuba dive. He's quite fond of the shower, but not the sea. Trust me, I've had to clean the bathroom after him three times a day for the best part of a year.'

'He's actually an instructor, capable of teaching people from their first breaths, right through to teaching them how to become instructors themselves. He's quite an expert; been diving for years,' William replied, filling her in on another part of Rob's life that she'd known nothing about.

Standing up, Ben held out his hands to take hers. 'Kate. You're shaking; why don't you go home.'

She shrugged him off as the anger took over. 'Do you know what, Ben? I don't want to go home. I mean, where is my home right now? I can't keep staying at your house. Yet, after what happened at the cottage, I can't go there either.' She crossed her arms like a petulant child. 'I'm staying here, where I can see Rob put behind bars, along with Isobel, Luca and whoever else is running this stupid, bloody circus.'

* * *

Isobel paced up and down the living room, and felt the fear and anguish race through her as Roberto threw himself at the large, white corner settee and sat forward with his head hung low, and his hands clasped tightly together. 'If Giancarlo was arrested, which I suspect is true, we're all fucking doomed.'

'When... when did it happen?' Isobel couldn't sit down, couldn't settle and anxiously she picked up a packet of cigarettes and nervously pulled one out of the packet. Tapping it half-heartedly against the table, she searched for a lighter.

'Don't you dare light that. It's disgusting,' Rob shouted. 'And I hate the smell.' He stood up angrily and pushed opened a window.

'Roberto, you're a hypocrite. A drug dealing hypocrite.' She threw the cigarette into the fire and sulked.

'What, and Giancarlo wasn't?'

She leaned against the mantle, threw her gaze in his direction. 'Don't go there, Roberto.' Picking up a poker, she stabbed at the embers. 'Giancarlo is a good man.'

'Good man or not, he's going to prison.'

Picking up her phone, Isobel scrolled through the news, looking for any mention of Giancarlo's name. 'How did they get him?' she cried. 'If they send him to prison, he won't survive. He wouldn't fair well if he were surrounded by villains.'

Roberto laughed and shook his head. 'That's where you're wrong, you fool. He's one of them and they are just people like him. Drug dealing criminals.' He paused, then stood up. 'We just have to wait. Let's hope he was clean and that they can't pin anything on him.' He gave her a determined nod. 'After thirty-six hours they have to release him.' He walked to the door and with a swift pull of his hoody, he dropped it untidily on her settee. 'I need to clear my head. I'm going for a swim.'

'Swim?' she screamed. 'Giancarlo, is rotting in a foreign police station and all you can think of is going for a swim?'

Roberto moved quickly, his hand grabbing her by the throat. 'Isobel. Don't you ever challenge me about my family. Not ever again,' he hissed loudly, pressed his nose up against hers, then dropped her like a stone. 'I've told you. We have plans. And unless he squeals. He'll get out. Now, if you don't mind, I'm going to the pool to check the scuba gear, which we need if the plan is going to succeed.'

Angrily, Isobel massaged her neck. 'You ever touch me like that again, you bastard, you'll be breathing through a tube for the rest of your life.'

Roberto looked directly at her, and his eyes widened. 'Don't give me ideas, you might just regret it.'

36

Kate looked up at the new moon and studied it with interest. 'Why didn't they wait for a full moon?' she asked Eric, who was driving as slowly as he could. He'd already switched off the headlights and was currently navigating the lane with a small, battery powered torch.

'What?'

'The moon. You'd think they'd wait for a full moon. For it all to be much brighter,' Kate tipped her head to one side, leaned as far forward as she could and looked for pot holes.

Eric began to laugh. 'Not a chance,' he said. 'That's the last thing they'd do.' He pointed at the sky. 'The moon dictates the currents. When it's a full moon, the currents are much stronger, and the sea becomes a lot more treacherous.' Eric tapped nervously at the steering wheel. 'Now then, the story is, we're a courting couple.' He took the car out of gear, pulled on the handbrake. 'All we need to do is keep low. Use the blanket to cover us and hope that if anyone walks past, they'll be much too embarrassed to pay us any attention.'

Giggling at the thought. Kate kept a close eye on the clock and as instructed, they sat and waited until exactly eleven o'clock before climbing out of the car and with only the moon and stars to light their way, they crawled on their bellies, made their way to the edge of the cliff, where the abbey was standing eerily to their left and eighty feet below them stood the whole bay of Whitby.

'Where are the police?' Kate asked as she tried to peer through the darkness.

'I think they're on the quayside, hiding in one of the boats.' Eric pointed to a huge fishing boat. It stood in darkness with its winch lowered and its nets spread out on the deck. 'I think it's that one, but I can't be sure.' He then pointed to another boat, 'And that one...' he paused, and looked through his binoculars. 'I believe it's that one where Ben and the others are waiting.'

Turning her attention back to the sea. Kate kept her eyes on the small boat that had floated out through the harbour walls. 'And that...' She held her arm out, her finger pointed. 'Is that The Red Lady?'

'It is,' Eric confirmed. 'As soon as she pulls back into the dock, they'll all be arrested, including Rob.' He swallowed hard, tapped her forearm thoughtfully. 'Are you okay with all this, Kate. I mean. If you're not, just say so. I could take you back to the office, we really don't have to watch.'

Kate sighed. Eric had sounded sincere, and a lump had risen to her throat that wouldn't move. 'I think I'd feel better if we were down there,' she whispered, but Eric shook his head.

'It's quite a risk for us to watch from here. If the police knew Ben had allowed it, they wouldn't be best pleased,' Eric pointed to the harbour and to where he thought the police might be. Every one of them was waiting and hoping that by the end of the night, Roberto Bellandini would be put behind bars.

The name, Roberto Bellandini was still a name she couldn't relate to, even though he'd been a man who'd said he'd loved her.

He'd lived in her home and yet had been dealing drugs. It was a thought that made her stomach turn and her mind spin with a million questions she couldn't answer and for a moment, she wondered whether or not the police had had her on their radar and whether they'd had a plan to smash her doors down and search her home. And if they had, would she have been blamed? Arrested? Or even sent to prison? She could now put herself in the shoes of all those women she'd arrested in the past, the ones who'd protested their innocence and for a brief second she thought of all of Rob's friends who'd visited her house in the past. All the men she'd made coffee for, smiled at and talked to, who could have been his accomplices. And now, with her eyes firmly fixed on the sea, she watched The Red Lady. A boat that was getting smaller and smaller by the minute, travelling further away and the only symbol that now showed her, that Rob had ever existed.

37

Drifting on the tide, The Red Lady bobbed on the surface of the sea. The deck was in darkness, the engine cut and with Isobel sat by the wheel with just a small LED torch, she kept an eye on the captain. He'd been bound tightly, beaten, and pushed into a central low-sided trough that was currently void of its fish. With terrified eyes that stared through the moonlight, he pleaded with Isobel to set him free.

'I've done nothing wrong,' he pleaded. 'And, I have children. Five of them. They're all so small. You have to understand, they need their father.'

His voice had turned from a soft whimper to a screech and Isobel glared into the darkness where she could only just see the whites of his eyes staring back at her. 'Shut up or I'll get the boys to throw you overboard.'

'But I swear. I didn't do anything.'

'Roberto.' She rested a hand on Roberto's shoulder, watched the way he took the wheel from her and steered the boat. 'Do you really think he talked, because if he did…' She paused and winced as a wave splashed up and over the side. 'If he did, we're all going to prison.'

'It had to be him. No one else knew where Giancarlo was.' He began to lift the cylinders, move them from one side of the boat to the other. 'And now, we do things differently.' Roberto leaned in towards Isobel. 'Giancarlo included you in the new plan because for some reason, he wanted to save your ass,' he growled. 'And as for him, he'll pay for what he did.'

'What do you mean, he'll pay?' Isobel felt the dip of the boat with the constant movement of the waves. The smell of diesel filled the air and made her nauseous and she turned her face into the breeze where she caught sight of Luca, who was crouching down, whispering to the captain. 'And what the hell's going on between you two?'

Luca shrugged and walked back along the deck with his arms held to either side, as the boat dipped again on the waves. Nervously, he placed a gauge on his cylinder and checked the air. But Isobel knew he was up to something, and she didn't like it. 'You're imagining things.' He dropped the gauge back in his bag. 'Now...' he said, 'Let's get that engine started.'

Isobel bristled. 'We can't. Not yet. You know that.' She studied the water, watched the tide. 'We're still too close to the harbour.' She turned her back to Roberto, allowed him to zip up her dry suit. 'Luca's up to something,' she whispered. 'I think they're in it together.' She nodded to where Luca stood, weight belt in hand and then, with a look over her shoulder at the harbour wall, she clicked the engine into life and masked her words with the noise. 'There's something going on, I just don't know what.'

Quickly, Roberto stamped across the boat and thrust an arm outward, almost knocking Luca off his feet. 'What the hell's going on?' He looked between Luca and the captain, saw the terrified look that crossed both of their faces at once. 'Because if you two are in this together and if either of you snitched, I'll kill you both myself.'

Backing off, Luca began to pace nervously. 'Come on. Why the hell would I do that?' Once again, he looked at the captain. Their eyes connected.

'I don't know, Luca. You tell me.' Roberto took a step back. 'Because our family, they stick together. Right?' Patting him heavily on the shoulder, Roberto moved in close and with his face just millimetres from Luca's he forced a sneer.

'Roberto, I know the rules.' Luca nodded slowly and nervously looked over his shoulder at where the waves had begun to lap up and over the sides of the boat. The tide had turned, and the sea had become more unpredictable. 'Now. The dive.' He took a step to one side and picked up his cylinder. 'Can we get on with it, because all this talk is making me nervous.'

'Sure we can,' Roberto eventually answered. 'Just as soon as you've thrown the snitch into the sea.' His hand shot out and pointed to the captain. 'Which is him, just in case you're confused.'

With a look of dread crossing his face, Luca's hands went up defensively. 'Roberto... come on. Seriously. I... I... I don't want to kill anyone,' he shouted. 'He's just a papa. Like your papa, trying to make a living and feed his children.' Panic radiated from Luca's voice as he shook his head and moved backwards until he bounced against the side of the boat. 'I won't kill him.'

Moving quickly, Roberto launched his arm towards where Luca stood, his fist connecting with the side of his face and with an agonising yell, Luca fell backwards. 'It's either him, or you. One of you goes overboard.' He rubbed at his knuckles. 'So here's the deal, you throw him over now or we'll see how good you can swim.'

* * *

Isobel shook with anxiety. Her eyes went from one man to the other and for a moment, she wasn't sure what they'd do.

'Okay, okay...' Luca sobbed. 'Stop. I'll do it.' He grabbed hold of the captain, who while being dragged across the deck, screamed relentlessly.

'You can't do this!' He yelled. 'I didn't do anything wrong.' His feet lashed out and his body bucked. 'Please, you can have the boat. The money. Just...'

'Shut up.' Luca screamed and then with tears rolling down his face, he looked at Roberto. 'Please, don't make me do this.'

Sighing, Roberto strode towards him. Gave him a look of understanding, then with the strength of an ox, he picked the man up and without remorse, he tossed him over the side, like a piece of rubbish that no one wanted.

'I wasn't a part of that... not me, I didn't agree to murder.' Isobel's throat constricted. She began to gag repeatedly. Their drug dealing days had just turned to murder, a crime she hadn't been a part of, but one she'd be accused of abetting. 'Giancarlo...' she pointed to the sea. 'He didn't ask you to do that.'

'It had to be done.' Roberto's voice was suddenly gentle and calm. He was much too calm for a man who'd just murdered another, and Isobel moved slowly backwards out of his reach. She no longer knew who he was or what he was capable of. All she did know was that he'd killed naturally. Unlike Luca, who was now throwing up over the edge of the boat.

'I'm going back!' Isobel yelled. 'We're all going back.' She turned to the wheel, began to manoeuvre the boat. 'We could say he fell, that a wave washed him over.'

'Don't be stupid.' Within a second, Roberto had moved in front of her, and grabbed at the valve on the front of her dry suit which he used to yank her towards him. 'We're going nowhere. And you...

you need you to steer the damn boat in the direction I've chartered. Is that clear?'

With her heart pounding wildly, Isobel wanted to leave. Once again, she thought of the mirror, of how she'd looked at herself and of how she hadn't liked what she saw. Right now, she liked herself even less but knew that she had no choice but to do as she was told. Her main prerogative was to stay alive and with a determined effort, she turned the boat to follow the path that Roberto had charted for them. They were all in his hands now....

'We're nearly there. Are you ready?' She looked between Roberto and Luca. Waited for them to tighten their weight belts. 'Drop the anchor for me.' Anxiously, she pointed to the anchor and cut the engine.

'We can't. The anchor won't hold,' Roberto shouted back and then pointed to the water. 'Me and Luca, we will take care of the drugs. You need to hold this position and in twenty minutes, we'll be back on board.'

'What if...' She was going to go through the dive plan. Ask what would happen if they didn't come back, but stopped herself from speaking. Half of her didn't care if she saw either of them again, and with a sickening feeling taking over her stomach, she kept her eyes on the water. On the very spot where a man had just lost his life. And she'd done nothing to stop it.

'Okay,' Roberto shouted to Luca. 'Regulator in, air out of the jacket. Descend quickly. We'll locate the drugs at thirty meters.'

Through the darkness, Isobel gave both men a look. For a moment, she fixed her gaze on the silhouettes they made; the strong, masculine forms that stood out against a clear, cloudless sky. 'Okay. Are you ready for countdown?' She watched, waited for them both to secure their masks and for their hands to go up, the signal for okay given. 'You'll be over the wreck in, five, four, three, two, go.' She closed her eyes. Felt the relief flood through her as in unison, they both dropped backwards.

*   *   *

Twenty minutes later, Isobel began to pace back and forth on a deck that rose and fell with the tide. A group of large orange marker buoys had floated to the surface. It was a good sign that the lobster pots had been found and the drugs had been located but much to her frustration, they were just too far away to reach and with her own body rocking the boat, she willed it to move closer. For a split second, she considered starting the engine, grabbing the drugs and running. But with divers below, she couldn't. It would be far too dangerous and even though she currently hated them both, the last thing she needed was the wrath of Giancarlo when he found out that everything had gone wrong.

Checking her dive computer, she noted the time. The men should have been back by now and with the seconds now quickly turning into minutes, she couldn't decide what she should do.

No one had spoken of what to do if they didn't return. She constantly looked for the air bubbles that came from below and watched the marker buoys as they drifted closer to the boat. She leaned over and with an outstretched arm, she made a grab for the bag, then another. Each grasp eluded her until eventually she was balancing on her stomach, with her feet waving around in the air.

It was only then that she saw the bubbles. They grew larger and larger as they hit the surface. And with a feeling of relief she saw one of the divers ascend to the surface. A thankful smile crossed her face. She leaned forward and waited, until her relief was replaced by panic as a hand grabbed her around the neck, and she felt her body being dragged over the side and into the sea.

* * *

In the distance, Luca surfaced, inflated his jacket and pulled his mask angrily off his face. He stared at the water's surface, watched for air bubbles and prayed that Roberto hadn't watched his escape.

Surely by now he'd have realised he was gone. He knew that he wouldn't spend time on a search and would assume that he'd been lost at sea, and his body never found. Luca's plan would come to fruition.

The Red Lady bobbed up and down in the distance. The only sound he could hear was that of the waves thudding monotonously up against its side and he squinted in an attempt to make out where Isobel stood. And even though the bright orange lift bags still floated around on the surface, neither Isobel nor Roberto were anywhere to be seen.

With a final intake of breath, Luca descended and at a depth just below the surface he made his way towards the mainland and to the place where his friends were waiting. From now on, his life wasn't his own. He'd have no choice but to hide, to stay in the shadows and if he ever surfaced, he knew that Giancarlo would be waiting. He was ruthless, and family or not, Luca knew his days would be numbered and his only option was to disappear and whether he liked it or not, he had to leave the family behind him. But still – he was free.

38

Arriving back at the office, Eric and Kate both shuffled in through the door, made a run for the radiator and leaned against it.

'What the hell are you doing here? Don't you have a home to go to?' Kate asked Patrick, who was doing his best to operate the coffee machine and failing badly. 'Here, let me do it.' She pushed past him and after having watched Gloria earlier that day, she took charge of the machine and managed to press all the right buttons. 'There, is that what you wanted?' she asked, as she placed a frothy coffee on the table before him.

'Brilliant. I've been trying to get that damned thing to work for the past half-hour.' He lifted the coffee to his lips, took a short, sharp sip then blew at the surface. 'Ben rang. We all need to wait here. Until he gets back,' Patrick said quietly, then looked down at the floor.

Anxiously, Kate began to pace. Something was wrong. There was something she wasn't being told and her mind exploded with random thoughts. She went through every scenario, and every possible outcome, until wearily she flopped onto the settee, and closed her eyes with exhaustion.

* * *

The sound of the door opening and closing brought Kate back into a conscious state. She could hear Ben's muffled voice, garbled whispers, orders given and telephones answered. Then, she felt his presence.

'Kate, Kate, wake up.' He spoke calmly, stroked her cheek, waited for her eyes to flicker. 'Open your eyes, we need to talk.'

'What's wrong? What is it?' Her mind went from half asleep to wide awake in three seconds flat and quickly, she pushed herself up and yawned.

'It's Rob.' He shook his head. 'We don't know what happened. But it looks like they all got away. He, Luca and Isobel are somehow all missing.'

'Could they be dead?' Kate whispered the words. She could barely say them out loud and even though she hated Rob after what he'd done, the thought that he might have died, confused her. She had no idea how she should feel, how she should act and with her heart pounding uncontrollably in her chest, she lifted her legs up in front of her and hugged them as tightly as she could.

'The truth is,' Ben sighed. 'I don't know, but I doubt it.' He casually rested a hand against her knee, gave her a knowing smile. 'This is what I do know. The Red Lady was stationary for hours and in the end, intelligence took a boat out to it. When we got there, the boat was empty. A bit like the Mary Celeste. Everyone had literally disappeared and even the captain had fled the scene. The coastguard has sent underwater search teams in. But it all takes time.'

'What... I mean, do you...' She paused, took a breath. 'Do you think they knew we were watching?' Kate asked what everyone else was thinking, and they all looked towards Ben for an answer.

'I don't know, but whatever happened, they certainly had a

plan. They're probably still out there, and because of that I think you should come home with me.' He directed his words at Kate and then turned to Eric. 'And you need to go and stay with Eve. Don't leave her side, not until they're found, just in case.'

Eric picked up his coat and opened the door. 'Ring me if you hear anything.' He held his mobile up in the air and waved it around.

'What do I do, boss?' Patrick looked towards Ben for instruction.

'Patrick, I need you to go over to Isobel's. Take the small van. I need to know if any of them go back there.' He paused, pulled Kate into a hug. 'And I'm not letting you out of my sight. Not until they find him.'

* * *

Just a few hours later, Kate was following Ben through his house with the first rays of sunlight already making an attempt to creep in through the windows.

Since Rob had attacked her, Kate had stayed with Ben at his house. Yet for some reason, coming here today felt different, and with her heart pounding heavily in her chest, she took his hand and followed him down the hallway, up the stairs and onto the landing, where she automatically stopped and looked through the door at the bed.

'Ben... Maybe if I stay here much more often, then maybe I should you know, pop home and get some of my things?' She looked down thoughtfully. 'I'd love to go back to the cottage and grab some of my own stuff.'

Leaning against the window sill, Ben crossed his arms and pursed his lips. The sparkle she'd so often seen in his eyes had returned, along with the glimmer of a warm, but mischievous, smile. 'Or...' He leaned forward, pulled open his bedside drawer and slid a parcel across the bed and directly at her. 'I could give you these,' he said with a wink.

'What is it?' She looked down at the small cardboard box with its fancy design and pale pink satin bow. For a moment, she simply stared and couldn't bring herself to touch the gift, or to open it. With her breath held tight, she tried to remember when she'd last had a gift that had been only intended for her. Had it been months, over a year? The only person who ever bought her anything, was Eve.

'Open it,' Ben said eagerly.

'But...' Shakily, her fingers went to the bow and with her eyes dancing up to meet his, she gave it a tug. 'I didn't do anything to deserve a gift.' She took a step back, and peered anxiously at the box as though it might bite.

'Well, I was going to wait for a more appropriate time, but...' he lifted his eyebrows and rolled his eyes to the ceiling. 'Mum said that a girl couldn't sleep in a man's pyjamas forever,' he laughed. 'She gave me a bit of a lecture and said that I should get you a pair of your own.' He tipped his head to one side. 'And, I have to say, she was right.' He pulled open a drawer, central to his side unit. 'So, I cleared you some space.'

It was a moment of recognition. A way of showing how far their relationship had moved on and a clear indication of where it was going. Taking a step forward, Kate lifted the floral, satin pyjamas to her lips and kissed them. In saving her life, Ben had given her a second chance. A chance she intended to take and with a smile, she padded across the room and into the en suite. 'I'm going to put these on,' she shouted. But then leaned out of the door, and gave him a wink. 'And you...' she looked back at the bed. 'If you can't let me out of your sight, then you can't sleep downstairs.' She pointed to the bed, 'So, you'd better make yourself comfortable.'

39

Roberto rummaged around in the undergrowth. It was raining, more of a drizzle now than a downpour and for something to do, he'd taken himself out in the woods and had spent the last hour looking for anything he could burn. But he was failing miserably.

Up to now, he'd found a rotten, half-decayed branch, a handful of kindling and a broken pallet that had been tossed by the roadside. Not enough to keep the fire going all day though, but thankfully, not so much that he'd need to turn back yet. The last place he wanted to go right now was the hideout and the thought of being inside with Isobel for another minute longer than he had to, was driving him insane.

All she'd done for the past few days was moan. Her constant stream of criticism had fallen from her mouth in torrents and even though he was more than aware that the hideout wasn't a palace, it was a roof over their heads until Giancarlo told them what to do next.

Using the machete, Roberto cut through the undergrowth. But with his efforts close to fruitless, and his feet getting colder by the second, he walked back to the hideout, circumnavigated the building and checked for signs of disturbance. Once satisfied that no one was there, he pushed his way into the dismal, candlelit room, where he immediately saw the look of hope in Isobel's eyes.

'Is it dry? Can we burn it?' She lifted her eyebrows in question, and then gave him a look of disappointment as he dropped the items on the concrete floor.

He shook his head. 'Everything out there is soaked.' He pointed to a pile of wood that was stacked in a corner where rough plaster could be seen through what was left of the wallpaper. Running an eye across it as though he were counting the pieces, Roberto pressed his hand against the crude concrete wall of the property. It was cold, damp and he could almost feel the trees that were growing behind it. 'If I hadn't already collected all of this,' he said as he kicked at the wood, 'we'd have nothing to burn.'

'Which would be amazing if we were allowed to burn it,' she threw back sarcastically. 'I need to speak to Giancarlo, tell him how cold it is.'

Roberto simply shook his head. 'Do you think Giancarlo doesn't know how we're living? Do you think he didn't come here?' He paused, laughed. 'Well, he did. He knew we'd need a place to hide eventually and had always kept this place furnished, just in case it was needed.' He turned, looked down at the old pieces of carpet that had been thrown across the floor, the camp beds that had been stood on their ends and had now been moved as close to the fire as they could get. It was a far cry from the mansion Isobel had been used to. It was cold, but dry, and the few possessions that Roberto had managed to bring with them had just about made it bearable, at least for him. But a lack of electricity had made the days long and unpleasant and the nights had felt longer.

'Cook these.' He picked up a tin of beans, rolled them across the floor. 'Put another piece of wood on and warm them up, just...'

He waved a finger back and forth in the air. '...don't use too much. Once they're cooked, bank the embers right down.'

'But, I'm cold and it's getting dark. What harm would it do to make a fire.' Isobel sat on the edge of the hearth, close to the embers and with her hands held out over them in an attempt to get warmer, she gave him a look with hopeful eyes. It was a look that made him want to relent, to allow her to burn more of the wood. But he thought of the police, of how they'd be searching and he just had to hope that by now they were looking for bodies, and not for survivors.

Roberto shook his head. 'Not a chance. God knows how long we'll be holed up here. I've told you, the wood needs to last and we don't leave, not until Giancarlo tells us we can.'

'Giancarlo this, Giancarlo that. Well, if Giancarlo really did know how awful it was, he wouldn't make us stay.' Arrogantly, she picked up another piece of wood, and placed it on top of the embers before she opened the beans, and tipped them in an old metal pan. 'There's just a single slice of stale bread unless I make another loaf, which will take hours. You'll have to make do.' She pushed the slice onto a toasting fork, held it back from the flames.

Annoyed, Rob picked up a packet of bread mix and threw it in Isobel's direction. The rations were small but manageable, if only she'd cook them, and with an irritated grunt, he wondered how long even he could live with Isobel before his patience ran out.

* * *

'I thought Giancarlo would have come back for me sooner.' She picked up the packet of bread and tossed it back at Roberto's feet and. 'I didn't think he'd leave me here long enough to bake your damn bread.'

'What's that supposed to mean?'

'It means that Giancarlo wouldn't do this to me. He knows I have so many more attributes than cooking.' She watched as the information registered. 'You don't think I make him bread, do you? I'm precious to him Roberto. Why do you think he keeps me as part of the family?' Isobel carefully measured his response. Then laughed when he squirmed. 'I like men, not boys, and you... you were just a challenge, to annoy Giancarlo.'

'So you shagged my bloody uncle?' Roberto exploded. 'You dirty little...' His hand grabbed hers and forcefully, he pushed it towards the bright, stoked embers, where the flames had suddenly begun to lick the sides of the log.

'No, you don't.' She lifted the toasting fork with her other hand and held it up to point at his face, and with the prongs dangerously close to his eye, she moved it even closer. 'One more millimetre, and I'll shove this through your face. Now get your hands off me,' she said through gritted teeth. She was sure that Roberto would follow through with his threat and like on the boat, he'd show no remorse.

'I should burn you, you bitch.' He threw her away from him, laughed as she fell into the dirt and with an infuriated growl, he threw the back door open and slammed it behind him.

* * *

Roberto walked through the trees towards the cliffs. For the hundredth time that day he checked his phone. Saw that no one had contacted him and in the hope of getting a better signal he moved closer to the cliff, where he patiently watched it spring into life and with relief, he saw Giancarlo's name flash onto his screen.

'Giancarlo, thank God you called. What's happening?' Roberto sat down on the grass, closed his eyes and breathed in deeply. He felt sure that Giancarlo would send a boat to get him. A way of escape. And with an image of a sun-drenched beach, he tried to think through the options and the places they might go to.

'Well. What's happening? That's a good question.' Giancarlo snapped. 'Why don't you tell me?'

Roberto stopped and opened his eyes. He knew by the sound of his uncle's voice that something was wrong. 'Giancarlo, why are you angry? I've done everything you asked. I've even put up with Isobel and I swear that if you don't get us out of here soon, I'm going to bury her in the woods.'

Giancarlo laughed. A long, sadistic laugh. 'Well then, I'd say that everything turned out right and no more than you both deserved.'

'Deserved? What the hell are you talking about?' Roberto closed his eyes as the sudden realisation hit him; Giancarlo was not coming to help them.

'My boy. Didn't I always tell you not to cross me? Didn't I warn Isobel that she should stay faithful?'

Roberto pulled the phone away from his ear and stared at the handset. 'Giancarlo, I swear, I didn't know. You have to believe me.'

'Ahhhh, Roberto. That's where you're wrong. I don't have to do anything. You, my boy. You murdered Isobel's husband, and then you murdered your current girlfriend's bother, James Duggan, and from what I've heard, you murdered the captain of The Red Lady too. I can lay the blame for them all, right at your feet. And one way or another, you're going to prison.'

Roberto could feel his anger boiling. He stood up and walked towards the cliff edge and looked at the sea which threw itself angrily up against the rocks. Giancarlo had stitched them up and left them to rot. He closed his eyes and kicked out at cliff. He had no money and no drugs to sell. And the only thing he could do was go back to River Cottage. He had to get in and out without being seen, find his passport and then, he had to play the waiting game and sit it out until it was safe enough for him to leave the country.

40

'You're both here then,' Elizabeth Duggan said as Kate pushed Eve's wheelchair through the front door and into the substantial hallway of their parents' home.

'Yes, Mother, we're both here,' Eve replied, the sense of dread in her voice more than apparent and Kate felt sorry that she'd practically forced her sister into coming.

'I thought Ben was coming with you, dear.' Her mother looked past both her and Eve, as though expecting him to walk in behind them. 'I've heard so much about him. He just has to be nicer than the last one you had. And where's Max?'

Kate took in a deep breath, tried not to bite. 'We left Max with Eric. They like each other.' It had been two days since Rob had gone missing and for two whole days, she and Ben had spent every moment together. They'd eaten together, waited for news together and slept in the same bed. And on more than one occasion, Ben had gently kissed her, without any expectation of anything more. For all she knew, Rob was dead. But on the off chance he wasn't, and at Ben's insistence, Kate had stayed away from River Cottage.

'Katie, wake up, dear. Now, what are you wearing?' Elizabeth asked, as Kate looked down at the clothes she'd borrowed from Eve and automatically, she removed her pumps before dropping them into the wicker basket by the door and then helped Eve with her coat.

'We have roast chicken, new potatoes, cauliflower with a cheese sauce, broccoli and carrots. Is that okay, girls?' Elizabeth's voice rang out as though nothing had been said. It was as though during any given emergency it was their mother's job to cook the dinner and no one would stop her.

While she busied herself in the kitchen, Kate wished she'd been blessed with the kind of parent who would have been happy to see them. She thought back to their childhood when their mother had at least given them a hug and despondently Kate walked out of the kitchen and into the garden where the air was fresh and made her shiver. Taking a seat on the old wooden bench, Kate tried to think. Tonight was the first time she'd seen both of her parents together for months and it would be the perfect opportunity to speak to them both and to finally get their father to agree to the medical attention their mother clearly needed.

* * *

As though someone had set an alarm, the front door opened at exactly, six o'clock. It was Sunday, the day their father played golf and even though he hadn't been to work, Kate thought he looked older and more tired than she'd ever seen him look before.

Holding out his arms and so as not to be outdone, Kate watched as their mother immediately ran to him, kissed him on the cheek and then took his coat out of his hand. 'Give that to me, did you play well, dear?' she asked automatically, as she hung the coat up.

'Yes, dear,' came the customary answer. 'Now, let me take a

look at the girls.' He pressed his lips together, gave Eve a look of pity and as though waiting for her to run into his arms, he held them aloft, just as he'd always done when she was a child. Without hesitation Eve wheeled herself to him, and hugged him affectionately. But Kate stood back, waiting for the invitation that didn't come.

Sitting silently at the farmhouse table. Kate spent the whole time pushing vegetables aimlessly around her plate. Each piece of food was cut, moved, but wasn't eaten. Her throat was still sore and the thought of both chewing and swallowing still filled her with dread. There was no conversation. No chatter about work, or politics. Their father didn't mention his golf game or the traffic and with the increased the tension the room became surrounded by an unbearable silence.

Watching as her mother suddenly jumped up from her seat, wrung her hands on her apron and snatched the plate from before her, Kate flinched and closed her eyes as the content of the plate was noisily scraped into the bin and then rinsed before being placed neatly in the dishwasher.

Kate stood up from the table, kissed Eve on the cheek and took hold of her hand. There was a knowing look that passed between them, a silent promise that only twins could share. 'We have to do this.' She smiled, encouragingly.

Their eyes locked, and silently, but reluctantly, Eve gave her a nod.

* * *

'The accident,' Kate finally said, as she looked from her mother to her father and then to Eve. 'I want to talk to you about the accident.' She sighed, sucked her breath in slowly. She felt awkward but knew that unless this conversation was had, their father would continue to bury his head in the sand and their mother would never get the help she needed.

Turning to her father, Kate looked for his reaction. She'd hoped he'd make the conversation easy and lead the way. But their father was much too good at concealing his emotions, and being a barrister had given him the most practised poker face.

'What about the accident, dear?' His words were slow and clear and deliberate. 'I'm sure we've gone over this before,' he spoke dismissively and annoyingly, and flicked at an imaginary speck of dust on his shirtsleeve.

'Dad, Mum needs help.' Kate knelt down, stared into her mother's eyes. 'Mum.' She took hold of her hands and watched her recoil. 'You remember the accident, don't you? And you know that James is dead.' She waited for a reaction, and for an outburst that didn't come. Instead, her mother turned her nose in the air and stared into space.

'Kate, is there a point to all this?' their father snapped. 'You're going to upset your mother.' Agitated, he sat up straight.

'The last thing I'd have ever wanted was for James to die.' Kate continued. 'He was my big brother, and I loved him.' Once again, she took hold of her mother's hands but this time she didn't allow her to shrug them off. 'It wasn't my fault. I didn't drive the car that killed him and I... I can't live like this.' She paused and gulped for air. 'Mum, you're sick. You really need help and tonight, we came here to beg you to get it.' She turned to her father, looked him straight in the eye. 'You've got to have noticed that she thinks that James doesn't visit.' Again, she paused, allowed her eyes to lock with his. 'It isn't right and you... you can't keep blaming me either. Because I was hurt too and I need you, Eve needs you and...' She wiped her tears on the back of her hand. 'You used to love all of us the same. But since James died, you stare right through me. You don't even give me a hug when you walk in through the door but now, you can't even bear to look at me.'

'That's not true.' He looked to Eve for support, but then sighed with resignation.

'Rob tried to kill me... did you know that? He pushed me under water and I felt the life drain from me. There was a burning inside my lungs and....' Kate stifled a sob. 'And I could see James. His cold, lifeless eyes and for a moment, I envied him. I envied the fact that he didn't have to do this and I prayed that I'd die, too.'

'But you're not religious, dear.' Her mother suddenly spoke and immediately, Kate squeezed her hands, and stared into her mother's tear-filled eyes all the time looking for a tiny spark of recognition.

'No, Mum, I'm not religious.' Kate whispered as her mother suddenly looked at her husband with pain in her eyes.

'James... James is dead?' The words were simple, but were followed by a long, piercing scream.

* * *

Gerald settled his wife on the settee, while Eve held her hand and stroked her face. And then, for the first time in over a year, he looked directly at Kate. He looked at the scar and then at her tears. He knew he'd hurt her more than anyone else had ever hurt her and slowly, he edged his body to stand beside her. Fumbling with his hands, he reached out, slowly touched her cheek, wiped away her tears and then pulled her into a hug. With the grief of losing his son, he'd almost lost his daughter too and with every ounce of strength he had left in his body, he held her as tightly as he could. For just a few moments, she was his little girl. The same one that had often curled up on his knee, the one that had always needed him.

'Kate,' he whispered as his whole body crumpled and uncontrollable tears rolled down his face. 'I know how it looks, but I never meant to blame you.' He pulled away from her body, looked directly into her eyes. 'I blamed myself. I was supposed to keep you all safe and I didn't.'

Kate reached forward and pulled a tissue from the box. 'But you wouldn't look at me. You never kissed me goodbye or goodnight, not once, not after the accident and I thought you blamed me because James was gone and you'd loved him so much.'

Gerald Duggan shook his head. 'It... it wasn't like that at all.' He knew how it had looked, knew how she'd felt, but the truth was he'd been too terrified that he'd lose her too. 'It's true, he was the only boy, the eldest and you're right, I loved him, but not any more than you or Eve. I never loved any of my children more than the next. Surely... you have to know that.'

Kate stepped back, but still held onto his arms. 'So why? Why couldn't you look at me?'

Moving to sit on the settee, Gerald reached out and grabbed his wife's hand. 'Oh, Kate. I don't know... Maybe, both me and your mother were both just a little afraid to love either of you.' He paused and searched her eyes with his. 'I felt like I had to distance myself. From all of you. From your mother too. Which is why I go away a lot. It was the only way to stop the pain.' He swallowed hard, looked across the room and then back at her. 'Oh, I don't know, I must have thought it was self-protection, just in case either of you were taken from me too.'

41

Watching Ben pull up on the drive, Kate saw the way he slowed the car and looked up at the Duggan mansion. It was the first time he'd been, and nervously she threw open the door and with one hand smoothing down the short, black dress, she stood in the doorway and waited for him to climb out of the car.

'Kate, I'm so sorry it's late.' Ben cautiously stepped forward and with hands that were fidgeting with nerves, Kate lifted hers to his, held them tightly, and leaned towards him. 'I've waited all day to do this,' she heard him whisper before pulling her in close and breathing in deeply.

'I needed that too,' she replied. 'It's been quite a day,' smiling, she led him towards the house but stopped just short of the door. 'The doctor came and gave mother a sedative and both Daddy and Eve, they're taking turns to sit with her. Just in case she needs them.'

With a look over her shoulder, Kate sighed. She felt as though a huge weight had been lifted from her shoulders. The conversation with her parents had been heart-breaking, but necessary. She'd told them exactly how she'd felt and finally, she was satisfied that her family finally understood each other and that now they were in a better position to move their lives forward.

'I quite like that I get you all to myself,' Ben said with a genuine smile. His eyes sparkled with mischief, and carefully Kate lifted her mouth to his and took pleasure in the way he moved his mouth across hers. It was enough to send shock waves flying around in her body and without hesitation, she began to kiss him back, slowly but passionately. She now felt sure that Ben wanted to be with her.

'There's an annexe.' She glanced over her shoulder. Pointed to a second door that stood on the front of the house and pulled him roughly towards it. 'We won't be disturbed,' she whispered, 'not in there.' Pressing her mouth to his, Kate led him to the door and then walked backwards until they both landed heavily against the stairs and with a swift kick of her foot, she laughed as the door slammed to a close behind them.

'Jesus, Kate, I want you so much,' he whispered between kisses, 'I've always wanted you.' He pulled her tightly into the curvature of his body and for a moment, she simply took pleasure in the way his body was pressed against hers, and with an arousal that was fully apparent, Ben moved his hand beneath her dress, and passionately he skimmed her hips and thighs, while the other hand gently massaged her spine and sent currents of desire spiralling through her.

Instinctively, she arched towards him. Her dress was unzipped and dropped to the floor and then she gasped as Ben's arousal was pressed against her. His eyes locked with hers and without saying a word Kate gave him all the permission he needed and swiftly, he lifted her into his arms and with his mouth still on hers, he carried her into the bedroom.

Taking his time, Ben began to explore her and quickly she felt herself surrender to his touch. The pleasure was pure and explosive, but Kate wasn't satisfied, not until she'd given the pleasure back and slowly began to move her hands over him until she felt his body arch with wanting.

'Ben, make love to me. I mean... really make love to me.'

Kate stared longingly and lovingly at his naked body. The deep sparkle of his eyes shone back through the darkness, as his mouth immediately took over hers. Pushing deep inside her, their bodies moved rhythmically together as one. A shout of ecstasy left Kate's lips as, simultaneously, a crescendo of multiple explosions escalated through them both. Ben moaned with pleasure and finally Kate allowed the release to leave her body with a long, surrendering moan.

42

With Ben returning to the office, Kate dropped Eve off at home, then took a diversion to the supermarket. She had every intention of making Ben a meal and with care and attention, she took time to choose the ingredients. She even threw candles into the basket, in a determined effort to make it special.

Pulling up outside River Cottage, she sat and stared at the building she'd once loved. It had been her home for the past two years and her grandmother's home before that. So why did it suddenly look so distant, detached and unfamiliar?

Mrs Winters came out of her house next door, waved and walked off towards the shops. The postman pushed his bike up the road and Jimmy from the farm was out walking his spaniel, Dexter. Jenny from the corner bungalow walked by with her pram and everything appeared to be happening as it normally would. Yet somehow, nothing looked the same.

The thought of going in made her feel sick. Her heart boomed in her chest and she resented Rob for the way he'd made her feel. She'd loved this house for a lifetime and as she walked slowly to the back door, she jangled her keys and let herself in.

Stepping inside, Kate felt her world collapse. Her mind spun and she held onto the door for support. Her kitchen drawers were open, their contents scattered everywhere. Stools had been tipped on their side and everything in the recycling bin, the fridge and the washing basket were spread out all over the floor.

Falling to her knees, her whole body began to shake and nausea took over, making her heave.

'So, you're home,' Rob's voice came from nowhere. Kate looked up and saw him in the doorway and felt her body freeze with fear. 'I knew you'd come back eventually. I thought I'd wait, after all, no one was going to look for me here, were they?' His voice was calm, deep, and emotionless.

'What... what the hell are you doing here? Everyone thinks you're dead.' She looked around, searched for a weapon, for something to fall into her hand, something she could use to protect herself. But everything had been moved. Knife blocks were empty, pans had disappeared and all that was left was the carnage that he'd spread all over the floor and with her breath held tight, she looked at her bag and scrambled towards it. Then she felt the pain. First it was in her hair as he dragged her backwards and then at her throat as his fingers tightened. Fear hit her as the pressure grew tighter. Blood pounded through her veins. She couldn't speak. Couldn't scream. Couldn't breathe. The pain increased and her vision blurred.

'I'm gonna kill you,' his words were venomous and were spat through gritted teeth. The tip of his nose touched hers. His voice was poison and the look in his eyes was of hatred. And then, as quickly as he'd grabbed her, he let go.

Falling to the floor she gasped for breath. She made a frantic attempt to drag her body towards the door. Adrenaline rushed through her. She had to escape, but the pain came at her from every direction. Every second felt like a minute and her heartbeat boomed in her head, as Rob's monstrous figure loomed above her and the room was filled with nothing but his venomous laugh.

'P-p-please,' she begged, but Rob sneered in answer. His eyes were dark, evil and not those of the man she'd loved, and Kate closed her eyes, and prayed for someone to save her. Like a vision, she saw Ben's face flash before her, and she tried to smile. At least they'd had that one night of passion together. And as she tried to focus on Rob, on the animal he'd become, she prayed that if he was going to kill her, that he'd do it quickly.

43

Ben paced up and down the polished wood floor. He'd been home now for almost an hour, but Kate hadn't returned. He was anxious, picked up his mobile, and once again tried her phone. But a long continuous buzzing began to circulate his mind. His whole body felt as though he were balancing on a wire, waiting to fall, and suddenly, he knew that something was wrong.

Flicking through his phone. He checked his emails, text and messenger. Repeatedly, pressed each of the buttons, and held his breath for what seemed like the hundredth time, he paced around the house, up the stairs, and stared at the bed. All he could imagine was Kate lying in the bed, how beautiful she'd looked and how perfect she'd felt when he'd taken her in his arms. Their lovemaking had gone on for hours, but then they'd both curled up together and he'd watched her sleep with her hands clasped tightly together as though in prayer. Affectionately, he'd stroked her face, and kissed her jawline.

Staring at the phone, he tried to decide what he should do. All he knew was that Kate had gone shopping with Eve, and that at midday she'd called saying she'd be home by five and Kate was never late.

'Home...' Ben stopped in his tracks. Kate had said she'd meet him at home and to Kate, home was still River Cottage. Which was where she probably was, cooking the meal as she'd promised.

44

Isobel stood on the doorstep of the hideout. It was late afternoon and the fresh air smelt of the sea and the warmth of the sunshine felt good on her face.

Roberto had been gone now for the past two days and in that time, she'd made the hideout more homely and decided that being there alone was much nicer than being there with him.

Sitting down on the grass, she lay back, and allowed the sun to warm her face. It shone through her eyelids in shades of amber and even though Roberto would be furious if he caught her outside, she didn't care.

Instead, she lay and listened to the birdsong. She knew that the sea just had to be close and she enjoyed the constant cries the gulls made, and realised that they were noises she'd missed while being caged up inside.

Sitting up, Isobel picked at the flowers. She made a daisy chain and wrapped it around her wrist like a bracelet, just as she had as a small child and with her eyes half closed, she thought of all the bracelets she'd owned, all the gold, diamonds, rubies and sapphires. Of the clothes she'd had and of how she now wore clothes that would only fit men. All of them were far too big and then, she glanced back down at the home-made bracelet. It was pretty and it made her smile in the knowledge that it was the one and only piece of jewellery that she now possessed. Everything else was back at the house and she... she had no way of getting back to it.

Sighing, she wondered how long it would be before Giancarlo arrived or, after what Roberto had said, if he'd ever arrive at all. The thought of sitting it out and waiting for him was crushing her inside. Especially now that Roberto had disappeared and she had no way of knowing if they'd left her to die out here in the wilderness with the food running out. Or perhaps they had all been imprisoned and at any moment, the police would pounce?

Turning her back on the hideout, she anxiously walked along the edge of the trees. She stared into the woods. They were thick and deep, but not impenetrable. The further she walked, the louder the sea sounded and finally the trees gave way to a small narrow track, where the grass was flat, and the cornflowers, buttercups and poppies looked as though they had been crushed.

Was this the way that she and Roberto had walked?

Nervously, she took a final look back before stepping onto the path, and walking through what was left of the trees. It all looked different in daylight and from here she could see the cliff tops, the beach and the sea. What she couldn't see were the steps they'd climbed or at which part of the cliff they'd climbed them.

Admiring the view, she felt the anger rise up inside her. Roberto had left her alone and it had been his job to chop the wood. He'd been the one who'd got to walk in the trees, but then without warning, he hadn't come back. Not for days. 'You stay in and keep the door locked,' had been his final barked instruction. But the beach was there and more than anything in the world, she wanted to walk along it.

45

'Eric, I need your help,' Ben yelled down the phone. 'I've called the police. Kate's house is a mess, ransacked.' He paused, with pain flooding his heart. 'Kate's missing and I think Rob's been here.' He moved from room to room, searching for clues. 'Call Patrick, tell him to go over to Eve's, she needs to know what's happening and we need to know she's safe. Get Patrick to take her back to the office. She'll be safer there with you.'

Eric gulped. 'Oh my God. I tried to call Eve a few moments ago. She didn't answer.' His voice began to shake. 'Right, Ben, tell me what to do.'

'Follow procedure. Start with CCTV. Look at the roads going in and out of Caldwick. Also, login and try and get a signal on Kate's work phone.' Ben stepped over the kitchen carnage and walked into the living room where Rob's passport had been discarded.

Ben took a deep breath as he saw the police car park outside. 'The police are here. Look at every vehicle leaving Caldwick and phone me back the minute you find anything. If Rob is back, and it looks like he is, I need to know where he's taken Kate and as fast as possible.'

* * *

Ben's words struck deep, making Eric gasp for breath. He grabbed hold of the desk and felt his fingernails sink into the wood. His whole body felt as though it had been punched and he doubled over as though in pain, took deep, measured breaths and took the time he needed to compose his thoughts. Rob was dangerous. He could easily overpower Kate, and as for Eve, he knew deep down that she wouldn't stand a chance.

Please, God. Let Eve be safe, let them both be safe. Eric had never really believed in God, but at that moment he prayed and then with his eyes open wide, he stared at his screen and began to follow Ben's orders.

His phone rang again.

'Yes, Ben. I'm on it.' Eric took in a deep breath and stared at the computer screen. 'I've tried to find Kate through her phone. I'm not sure it's switched on.'

'It has to be on,' Ben shouted. 'And if it isn't, then switch it on remotely. The only way that the phone will become inert is if it's been burnt or frozen. Other than that, I want a way of tracking it.'

Eric searched the screen, and hoped. Every investigator who worked for Ben had a phone that was connected to a linked system. If they were on, a light would show up on the screen and Eric willed Kate's indicator to bleep. To give him one light. It was all he needed to pick up her coordinates.

'Eric, what do you have?' Ben growled.

'We have a coordinate, but damn it,' he cursed, 'it's at River Cottage.'

'Fuck!' Ben shouted and the sound of rummaging filtered into the phone. 'Eric. I've got it. Her bag, it's here and her phone's inside.'

With a sinking feeling taking over his mind, Eric closed his eyes. Without the phone their hope of finding both Kate and Eve was remote and with his eyes focusing on the screen, he suddenly sprang into action. 'Ben, how about I try and tap into Eve's phone?' he suddenly asked. 'If they're together, it will help us. Right.' Pushing his glasses back up his nose, Eric keyed Eve's number into the system and then jumped in his seat as the door to his office flew open and Luca Bellandini stood in the entrance.

46

Kate's whole body shuddered with the cold and she struggled to open her eyes. Everything around her was blurred and her hand reached out to feel a rough corrugated metal floor and the sound of an engine made her quickly realise that she was in a vehicle, and travelling at speed.

Where am I?

She tried to sit up but couldn't. Her whole body ached and every part of her felt bruised, her muscles throbbed and her head pounded. She tried to open her eyes, but the slightest amount of light sent shooting pains to the back of her eyes and with a deep, disturbing sob that came from inside, the trepidation rose inside her.

Again, she tried to open her eyes, but struggled. The piercing pain continued, but her need for survival took over and she peered around her, through the tiniest of slits. Kate tried to rub her eyes, but her hands were bound together and awkwardly she pulled herself up, to stare at the area around her.

'Oh, Kate, you're alive.' Eve's sob came from somewhere close by and suddenly the pain in her eyes didn't matter. She opened them wide and immediately saw her sister curled up on the floor beside her. Eve's hands and legs were bound too, and with a tear-stained face, her eyes were pleading for help.

'Eve,' Kate whimpered. 'Eve, are you okay?' The last thing she wanted was for Rob to know they were both awake and while taking short, shallow breaths, she watched for the gentle nod of Eve's head. 'That's good.' She nodded, tried to wriggle her hands free of the ties.

'I... I thought he'd killed you,' she said, before bursting into tears and within a second, Kate had automatically manoeuvred her body towards that of her twin. They always felt better when they were close enough to touch. 'The power of two', they'd always called it in the knowledge that together they could easily become invincible. Of course, they'd thought they were super heroes when they were younger, but this was real, and a terrified sob reached Kate's throat and burst out through her mouth. Swallowing hard, she held onto Eve's hands, knew she had to be the strong one, for her sister's sake. But deep down, she knew Rob, knew what he was capable of and knew that if he was happy to hurt her, then he wouldn't think twice about hurting Eve.

47

As the van came to a sudden halt, Kate heard Rob jump out. The side door opened, and she saw how quickly the sky had begun to turn dark. She had to work out where she was before that happened.

'Get out,' Rob barked as he reached forward to grab Eve by the arm, dragged her across the van floor and picked her up. Throwing her around like a rag doll, she heard Eve scream and felt her own anxiety soar.

'Rob, for God's sake, leave Eve alone. She's never done anything to you' Kate shouted, 'Please, I'm begging you.' Kate tried to pull at his arm, but with her hands still restrained, it didn't take much effort for him to push her away.

Letting go of Eve, he laughed as she dropped back to the van floor. 'You're begging me, are you?' he jeered. 'I remember begging you for another chance. I remember trying to be nice. I cooked you dinner and what was it you said to me?' He paused and thought. 'I think "go to hell" could have been your words, Kate. So I did go to hell and I brought both of you "to hell" with me.' A sadistic laugh came from within him and as though he were picking up weights, he grabbed at Eve, picked her up and carried her towards an old concrete shack. He looked around, checked the front and back, then kicked open the door and walked inside. 'Now, get in.'

Quickly, Kate did as she was told, dragged herself out of the van and followed both Rob and Eve into the old, derelict shack. It was crude, with whitewashed walls and an open fire, that was barely lit. It was a building that made her shiver with fear as she watched Rob drop Eve cruelly onto a camp bed, before grabbing at a handful of kindling and throwing it into the dying embers of the fire.

'Bitch, where the hell is she?' He stamped furiously around the room and opened the back door. 'Isobel, get your backside back here now!' he shouted, and stared into the woods as he watched and waited. Then, as though he didn't know what else to do, he slammed the door again angrily.

'What... what's Isobel doing here?' Kate couldn't resist but ask the question and carefully, she watched for Rob's reaction. 'Has she left you? Or maybe she was arrested and she's talking to the police and any minute now, they'll be here to arrest you.' Kate saw the anger in Rob's eyes and took a step back. She sat down beside Eve and had every intention of protecting her, if Rob came near her. He was pacing, anxiously and Kate didn't like it.

'Don't move,' Rob suddenly shouted, 'or I swear, I'll kill you both. And don't think you have time to run. I'll be less than two minutes and you wouldn't get far, not with the cripple.'

Within a few seconds, he'd left the shack and with the van starting up and the smell of diesel filling the room, Kate knew that he'd gone. Creeping to the door, she peered out and watched as his van disappeared into the distance. Everywhere around her was woodland, a remote area where nothing could be heard, except – Kate tried to concentrate – except the sea?

'Eve, listen to me. We have to run and we have to run now.' She heard the words fall out of her mouth and then looked down at her sister's legs. 'I'm going to help you.'

Eve began to sob. 'Kate. You go. He'll be back any moment, and he shouted for that woman. She'll be somewhere close. She'll see us and you know we won't get far.' She pressed her hands into Kate's. 'Now, please, you go. Go and get help for both of us.'

Kate looked into her sister's terrified eyes and knew beyond doubt that leaving her was the last thing she could or would ever do. 'No way, Eve. We're the power of two, right?' She shook her head and ran to the door. She could see the woods, and with them a million and one hiding places and with a deep breath, she turned to Eve.

'I have a plan.' She began pulling at the tape that bound her wrists. She looked around and saw a toasting fork and grabbed at it, and passed it to Eve. 'Hold it steady, I'm going to use the prongs to stab the tape.'

* * *

Kate ran through the darkness. Her heart pounded and her legs hurt, not to mention her feet that still wore the high heeled boots she'd had on for her shopping trip, but she kept on running as far away from the place where she'd left Eve, just a few minutes before, lying on her belly, and cowering helplessly beneath a bush.

It had taken them a while, but Kate had managed to hook her hands under Eve's arms and drag her backwards into the woods and quickly, they'd chosen a place for Eve to hide, just off the main track. 'Stay here, and don't move.' Kate had said to her, 'You'll be safe, so long as he doesn't see you.'

It had been a risk, but even if Rob came back and ran down the track, the chance that he'd veer that far from the path in the dark while searching was slim and hopefully he wouldn't even consider the idea that Kate might leave Eve alone. But after a tearful goodbye, both she and Eve had agreed that she'd be faster alone. That she had to leave and get some help.

With the darkness dropping fast, Kate stumbled. Her toes hurt and her ankle twisted, but she couldn't stop running. But then she stopped as though she'd hit the brakes.

'No... no... no... this is not happening.' She spotted the cliff, made her way along its edge, and looked as far as she could see. But all that lay ahead of her was a sheer drop, the boulders and rock pools below, cutting off her escape. With a deep sigh, she looked back at the trees and tried to work out how she'd got it so terribly wrong? With the feeling that she'd have no choice but to go back, she wondered how easily she could find Eve again and whether the two of them could hide in the bushes till the morning.

'Really thought you were clever, didn't you?' Came Rob's unmistakable voice from within the trees. It was a sound that made Kate tremble, and she spun around in the darkness searching the tree line where he emerged, looking both smug and determined.

'Rob, you're there. I... I was looking for you,' she lied, while searching the grounds around him, looking for a way to escape.

He stopped in his tracks. Scratched his chin and held his hands out aloft. 'And why on earth would you do that?' He shook his head. 'I think you made it very clear that you wanted me in hell.'

'Because...' She had to think quickly. '...Rob, I love you. I thought we could talk, and you know, sort things out,' she rambled. 'We had a good life together once. A home. Surely, that has to count for something, doesn't it?'

He walked closer to her and stared directly into her eyes with a look that reminded her of the day he'd attacked her. The day he'd dragged her into the bath. The day she'd thought he would kill her.

'A good life – is that what you think?' He looked over the edge of the cliff. 'Long way down, Kate, isn't it?' He laughed a long, sadistic laugh. One that echoed around the trees. 'And no one can hear you scream, you do know that, don't you?'

Kate tried not to look behind her. She didn't want to see how far the fall would be or how jagged the rocks would be below. 'Look, no one has to get hurt, Rob. No one knows you are here. All you have to do is let me go. We... we could go together. We could start again and make a life somewhere new.'

'Do you think I'm that stupid?' he growled. 'I'm never going to let you go. Don't you understand that?' Once again, he laughed. A loud and evil, malevolent sound that made Kate's entire body shudder and her skin crawl.

Rob's hands went across his face and with a loud, piercing scream he raked them violently through his hair. 'It's all your fault, you see. I was ordered to get close to you. Made to follow you. Instructed to be around you. I didn't want to be with you, but Giancarlo made me.' He continued to hold his head in his hands, and spun around on the spot. 'It's all your fault, everything is your fault,' he spoke as if in a daze, then lifted his face to stare at the sea over her shoulder.

Tears ran down Kate's face. 'What... Why... Why me?'

He physically shook before her. 'I had to infiltrate the homes of the rich. I had to sell them the drugs and you, well your grandmother was well loved in the area and you were the daughter of a barrister. Everyone trusted you. They trusted your family.'

Kate's world fell from beneath her feet, and she dropped to her knees. 'So you only loved me because of who my family are?'

Rob nodded. 'I had no choice. I had to do the drug runs and sell them or lose my family. I couldn't have one without the other. Yet here I am, my family are gone, and I've been abandoned.' He shook his head fiercely, walked towards her, knelt down and grabbed her by the shoulders, looking pleadingly into her eyes. 'You have to believe me? I didn't want to sell drugs... you know how

I hate them. But I had no choice and I ended up just like my family: importing, selling, killing.'

She carefully lifted a hand and risked touching his face. She was prepared to try anything to save both her and her sister and if that meant seducing him right here, right now, in the darkness on the cliff top, she would. 'Please, Rob. We can sort this out, I'm sure we can and maybe you *were* instructed to get close, but most of it was real, wasn't it?' Her mind spiralled out of control as the words fell blindly from her lips.

For a moment Rob's eyes searched hers and with a need almost too painful to endure he lifted his face towards hers and brushed her lips with his. Then, as though his life depended on him never letting go, he grasped hold of her and clung on tight.

'Everything's such a mess, Kate.' He sobbed, his face nuzzled into her shoulder. 'Giancarlo's left the country; he's abandoned me, and I don't know what to do without him.' Pulling back his face, his eyes pleaded with hers. 'I'm in so much trouble. I know I've done wrong, but I can't go to prison. I'd never survive.' He nestled his face into her neck again. 'No one was supposed to die. The car you were in, it should have just left the road, but it was covered in mud and oil, and the car – it skidded too much. The water in the stream was higher than I'd thought and I did what I could. I saved both you and Eve, but I couldn't get to your brother, not in time. I tried, I swear to God, I tried, but I couldn't save him too.'

Kate held onto the man that she'd once loved, as her breath caught in her throat and felt her world break into a million pieces. She couldn't believe what Rob was saying and like a violent explosion, her mind went back to the accident. First to the car and how it had swerved and rolled into the water. Then she'd been on the grass with Eve at her side... but Rob... she had no memory of him being there. But he had been. He'd caused the accident. He'd killed her brother and he'd caused Eve's disabilities and it had all been his fault, not hers. Her breathing suddenly became shallow and with every nerve in her body, she wanted justice for both James and for Eve. With his back to the cliff, she considered pushing Rob and watching him fall, but a noise caught her attention and she saw that Rob's demeanour had altered too. 'Who's there?' he shouted, before pushing Kate away and walking towards the edge of the woods.

'Rob, just leave it, it'll just be an animal or something. Please, we need to talk.' Kate's eyes searched the woods, fearing that Eve had ventured out of her hiding place and that somehow, she'd managed to drag herself through the trees.

'Ohhh, so that's where your sister is hiding, is it?' He began pulling at the bushes and staring into the darkness. 'Now then, what am I going to do with you both?' he shouted, but then took a step back as Isobel emerged from within the trees.

'Yes, Roberto. What are you going to do with them?'

'W-w-where the hell have you been? I've been looking for you. I told you to stay at the sh-shack,' Rob stuttered, obviously shocked by her sudden appearance. He pushed her out of the way and stomped back to where Kate was still by the cliff side, and still on her knees.

'For God's sake, Roberto,' Isobel yelled at him. 'You've done some bloody stupid things in your life, but bringing her here has to beat them all. What the hell will Giancarlo say?'

'Don't you dare bring my family into this. My family love me... Do you hear that? They love me, not you!' he screamed, and his voice echoed back through the trees.

Kate's anger boiled. It was because of his so-called family that her brother was dead, that she was scarred and her sister was paralysed. Yet still, all he cared about was what his family might think. 'Your family don't care, Rob. You just said it yourself. Giancarlo has abandoned you. He's left you both here to rot.' She could see him grinding his teeth, he couldn't argue with the truth and continued to pace up and down the cliff edge.

'Is that true. Has he deserted us?' Isobel screamed. 'Because if I've lost everything, for nothing, for you, I swear, I'll—'

'You'll do what, Isobel. I'll tell you what you'll do, you'll do nothing.' Rob stopped and stared at the sea.

Kate watched his movements. She knew he'd stopped watching her and she took the opportunity to stand up, and with her breath held as tightly as she could, she waited for him to get close.

With an angry look he marched towards Kate and grabbed at her throat. 'And you, Kate, you think you are so strong and clever but you're not. After all, it would be so easy for someone to trip, and to fall from up here, wouldn't it?'

Kate screamed. 'Rob, pl-please...' she cried out as he physically moved her by the throat and as the heel of her boot caught against the undergrowth, she felt her feet slip beneath her. Her whole body crashed to the floor and she landed heavily on her back with Rob's body now pressing down on hers. She couldn't breathe, couldn't see and felt his hand squeezing her throat even harder.

'One more squeeze, Kate, and you'll suffocate.' he laughed. 'Or shall I give your neck just one little push and snap it like a twig?'

She stared at him. Her eyes felt like saucers, but she refused to close them. Refused to give him the satisfaction that he'd won. 'Then, kill me,' she managed to whisper, with her eyes still staring into his.

'Rob... Stop... I've told you before, I won't be party to murder,' Isobel screamed, and Kate saw her launch herself at his back. 'You have to stop; you're going to kill her.'

Kate was aware of the thuds that vibrated through Rob's body and into hers, and that Isobel was striking him hard from behind, and for a split second, she wondered why Isobel would help her, or why she'd care. But with Rob still holding her neck her world suddenly turned dark. She began drifting in and out of consciousness and as her eyes flickered, she heard a long, animalistic scream as Rob swung out and Isobel stumbled. Falling backwards. Isobel lay by the cliff edge and Kate held her breath, as Rob walked towards her, ready to kick her over the drop to the rocks below.

It was an act Kate couldn't allow, and with no thought for herself she threw herself towards the woman she'd once hated. She screamed and even though she was terrified, she kicked out as frantically as she could.

'Oh, Kate, you always were stupid,' Rob said calmly.

Once again hysteria filled her body. Rob grabbed her by the hair and she felt herself being dragged into the air. Her feet had physically left the ground and all she could see were the dark voids of Rob's eyes. 'Do you know what, Kate? I didn't love you. Not ever. Why would I?' It was the final insult and Kate launched herself at him. 'And that sister of yours, you wait till I find her, she won't be able to fight back like you can, and I'm going to toss her off the cliff like a rag doll,' he snarled.

'Oh, yes she can,' Eve's voice screamed as she held a boulder high above her head and launched it in Rob's direction.

With a thud, Rob twisted in pain. His hands let go of Kate and she scurried across the ground to where Eve stood. With loathing in her eyes, she turned and watched as Rob's legs gave way, his footing was lost and in what felt like a split second, he'd fallen backwards and over the cliff, screaming as he fell.

Running to the edge. Kate could see the way he clung to the rocks below, the fear and the terror that went through his eyes and even after all he'd done, she couldn't allow him to fall. Her instinct was to save him, to grab his hand, but as she held her hand out in his direction, he shook his head defiantly.

'Rob, come on; take my hand. You're strong. I know you can

pull yourself up from there.' Once again, she grabbed at his hand, but coldly, he shrugged her off.

'I'm sorry, I'm so sorry... for everything.' They were the last words she heard, as the rock gave way and Rob hurtled backwards, towards the sea.

Falling to her knees, Kate immediately vomited. Then she turned slowly and stared in shock at Eve, who was still stood before her, pale, and wobbly, but standing. Unaided.

Eve dropped to the floor and they both looked to the trees where a noise could be heard. Within seconds, they were surrounded. Ben, Eric and Luca Bellandini had all emerged and ran towards them.

Finally, they were safe.

48

Kate waited for the car to stop, before climbing out and proudly unfastening her four-week old son from his car seat and passing him to Ben. 'There you go, go to Daddy.'

Hugging the baby close to his chest, Ben held an arm out towards her, pulled her into his body and circled her with love and as though it had been planned, they both turned in unison and looked up at the church.

'I can't believe we're about to christen him, Kate, here in Bedale,' Ben whispered as he dropped a kiss lightly against her lips. 'And I can't believe that it's a whole year since you wound your window down and called me a moron!' He pointed to the very spot where Kate had pulled up, and the very place where they'd first met.

'Well, for what it's worth, you're the nicest moron I ever met.'

* * *

The sound of 'All Things Bright and Beautiful' echoed throughout the church, making both Gloria and Elizabeth smile. Their mothers had become close, much to the disapproval of both William and Gerald, who both counted the cost after every shopping trip they took, but who also benefitted from the hours they both now spent on the golf course. Eve and Eric sat together, hand in hand, and Kate smiled, knowing that the next time they entered this church would be in the summer, for their wedding.

The singing stopped and the vicar walked from the front of the church to the back, where he lifted a jug of holy water and poured it into the font.

'Could I have the parents, grandparents and the godparents please?' he asked.

It was a moment for Ben and Kate to step forward, but also for Gloria, William, Elizabeth and Gerald. And as Eric pushed Eve into position, Kate smiled with pride as Eve stood up and slowly walked the last few steps to take her place at the font.

The vicar then held out his arms. 'May I?' He took the baby from Ben and with a smile, he walked around the font, then paused and turned to Kate. 'We name this child?'

Kate locked eyes with Ben, who nodded. She looked up and then individually at each member of her family, before turning back to the vicar. 'With my parents' permission, I'd like to name him James Benjamin Parker, in honour of the brother that I lost.'

Cries of delight filled the church and baby James was held over the font, where holy water was slowly dribbled over his tiny head.

* * *

Kate's world was now complete, but as she stepped out of the church, the rain began to fall and full of parental concern, and with James in her arms, she quickly headed towards the car.

'Kate, wait.' Ben's words followed her and with a soft shake of his head, he held his arms out for their son.

'But he's getting wet.' She smiled with concern, but did as Ben asked and then laughed as he took James in his arms and began spinning him around in the rain. 'What are you doing?' she asked as both of their parents began to join in, along with Eric, who spun Eve's wheelchair around and around.

'Come on.' Ben held a hand out to her, 'We once made a promise that whenever we could, we'd dance in the rain.'

Kate thought of all the nightmares she'd lived through. The accident, of how her brother had been killed, Eve paralysed and the scar on her face; of how Isobel had risked her own life to save hers, but who was now behind bars for her involvement in the drug deals and of how Rob had fallen to his death.

'Kate, come on, trust me,' Ben shouted and held a hand out towards her making it more than obvious that Ben was doing all he could to turn her worst nightmare into one of her happiest days. A day where her whole family were together, and they all danced in the rain.

ACKNOWLEDGEMENTS

I began writing this book shortly after being involved in a life-changing car accident, or should I say, two accidents? That's right, I didn't just manage to get hit by one car from behind, at speed. I was hit twice within forty minutes.

During the first accident, my car had come to a stand-still on the motorway and while constantly checking my rear-view mirror, I could see a van aiming towards me. Its driver was busily chatting to his passenger, laughing and joking and by the time he saw my car, I could literally see the whites of his eyes. He hit his brakes, all too late.

After spending a good half an hour at the side of the road, I decided to try and get my car off the motorway. I drove carefully and slowly and got to the top of the slip road where I had to wait for another car to move off. I then felt another huge bump and looked up to see that a bright yellow mini had run straight into the back of my car. I was left with life-changing injuries. Both of my shoulders were damaged, and I could barely move my arms above my waist for around six years.

It was following my accident that I came up with this story. I tried to work out how life-changing accidents affected different people, whether or not the accident would affect other people, other family members and how, on a daily basis, people got on with their lives afterwards.

I'd therefore like to thank my husband Haydn for looking after me during those six years. My friends and family members, Kathy

Kilner and Jayne Stacey, for reading my work and giving me their very honest feedback. And special thanks to Jane Lovering, without whom this book would have never happened. Her critique service is amazing and without a doubt she kept me going on the days when I'd have quite easily quit.

Finally, I'd like to thank my publisher, Boldwood Books and my editor, Emily Ruston. They bring the sparkle and shine to the books, create the most amazing covers and ensure that my books get the very best marketing that I could wish for.

ABOUT THE AUTHOR

L. H. Stacey lives in a small rural hamlet in Yorkshire, with her 'hero at home husband' Haydn, and her puppy 'Barney'. In 2015 her debut novel won a prestigious publishing contract.

Sign up to L. H. Stacey's mailing list for news, competitions and updates on future books.

Visit Lynda's website: http://www.lyndastacey.co.uk/

Follow Lynda on social media:

- facebook.com/LHStaceyauthor
- x.com/Lyndastacey
- instagram.com/lynda.stacey
- bookbub.com/authors/lynda-stacey

ALSO BY L. H. STACEY

The Sisters Next Door

The Serial Killer's Girl

The Weekend

The Fake Date

The House Guest

The Safe House

The Accident

THE *Murder* LIST

THE MURDER LIST IS A NEWSLETTER DEDICATED TO SPINE-CHILLING FICTION AND GRIPPING PAGE-TURNERS!

SIGN UP TO MAKE SURE YOU'RE ON OUR HIT LIST FOR EXCLUSIVE DEALS, AUTHOR CONTENT, AND COMPETITIONS.

SIGN UP TO OUR NEWSLETTER

BIT.LY/THEMURDERLISTNEWS

Boldwood

Boldwood Books is an award-winning fiction publishing company seeking out the best stories from around the world.

Find out more at www.boldwoodbooks.com

Join our reader community for brilliant books, competitions and offers!

Follow us
@BoldwoodBooks
@TheBoldBookClub

Sign up to our weekly deals newsletter

https://bit.ly/BoldwoodBNewsletter